THE GOLDEN AGE OF SCIENCE FICTION was considered to be a time when science fiction was a male domain. The reality, of course, was somewhat different. Women both wrote and read science fiction, but, at least in the case of those who wrote it, the fact that they were women was usually kept secret, hidden by a pseudonym or the use of initials.

In *Women Writing Science Fiction as Men*, Mike Resnick challenged top women authors not just to write stories about male protagonists but to write as though they themselves were male authors. Now he has extended this challenge in reverse to many talented male authors. And here is their response, in such original tales as:

"G-Bomb"—Genetic engineering could give her unborn child a better life. But how was a young, unwed mother with hardly any income supposed to win that chance for her baby?

"Relativity"—She was the lone astronaut on a seven-year-mission of exploration. But far more time had passed for the family she'd left behind. Had she found a new world for humanity only to lose her home?

"Staying Still"—She'd given up the universe for a world. Would she given up that world to regain the universe?

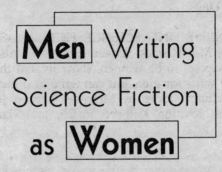

Men Writing Science Fiction as Women

Edited by Mike Resnick

DAW BOOKS, INC.
DONALD A. WOLLHEIM, FOUNDER
375 Hudson Street, New York, NY 10014

ELIZABETH R. WOLLHEIM
SHEILA E. GILBERT
PUBLISHERS
www.dawbooks.com

First Printing, November 2003
1   2   3   4   5   6   7   8   9

ACKNOWLEDGMENTS

CONTENTS

Introduction

by Mike Resnick

IN a recent novel of mine called *The Outpost*, one of the characters asks a somewhat-larger-than-life hero: "What's the most dangerous race you ever came across?"

"Women," says the hero.

"I mean an alien race," explains the questioner.

"So do I," answers the hero.

That's the gist of it. If women have trouble understanding men, and they do, men have even more trouble understanding women. It's as if the God of Science Fiction, who has a truly caustic sense of humor, took two races that would forever be alien to each other, dressed them up as human beings, and turned them loose on Planet Earth.

Science fiction, in its early days, was aimed primarily at adolescent boys, so almost all the heroes were men. Women were there to hold the hero's spaceship, get captured by the villain and threatened with a Fate Worse Than Death, or to flash a malicious smile (while flashing other even more enticing things) and attempt to seduce or at least distract the hero while the Bad Guys were off doing evil deeds.

It was exceptionally rare for the main character of a science fiction or fantasy story to be a female. C. L. Moore created Jirel of Joiry, but she could be forgiven since she was a female writer. Arthur K. Barnes invented Gerry Carlyle, perhaps the least believable interplanetary female big game hunter of all time. It remained for the big guns to do a somewhat better job of it—Isaac Asimov with his robotics expert, Susan Calvin, and Robert A. Heinlein with Podkayne, Friday, and a handful of others, none of whom quite rang true.

No male science fiction writer ever attempted a major novel written in the first person of a woman. Heinlein, always willing to try something new, came close with *I Will Fear No Evil*, but that was a first-person story of a man who had taken over ownership (possession? residence?) of a woman's body. It remained for Ian Fleming, who was almost a science fiction writer, to pull it off, rather lamely but at least courageously, with the James Bond thriller, *The Spy Who Loved Me*.

And, since science fiction is, at least partly or occasionally, about truly understanding alien viewpoints (and how we must appear to aliens), we challenged a number of the best male writers around to write science fiction stories not just *about* women but *as* women.

There were only two rules: first, the story had to be the first person of a woman, and second, if changing her from Victoria to Victor didn't invalidate the story, we didn't want it.

Welcome to some truly alien worlds.

Not Quite Immaculate
by Tom Gerencer

Tom Gerencer is a graduate of Colby College who attended the Clarion Science Fiction and Fantasy Writers' Workshop in '99. He has since published stories in *SF Age*, *Realms of Fantasy*, *The Brutarian*, a few e-zines, and DAW's *Oceans of Magic* anthology. For strong female influences, he cites his fast-talking, Brooklynite, retired Air Force-nurse mom, his sister Kate (a one-time Detroit diesel engine engineer turned full-time mother) and his girlfriend Emily, a rock-climbing whitewater guide and geological field technician. While Tom is fairly sure that none of these women have ever piloted a spacecraft, he's also pretty sure they wouldn't have a problem, were there one around that needed piloting. Catch Tom on the web at www.sff.net/people/tgerencer or read his other published tales at www.fiction wise.com. In the meantime, buckle up and ah . . . try to watch those sexist comments, 'kay?

ASIDE from being a hard-hitting lesbian with a reputation for disaster; aside from being five-foot-nine and vaguely Oriental; aside from having thick, black, braided hair that hangs down to my knees and a knack for screwing up relationships, I had amassed myself somewhat of a reputation for being quite a pilot.

This was why, on the morning of December eleventh, only slightly after shouting out, "Oh, Xahn, thank God you have fingers," I was, once again, engaged in an argument with my lover—a gorgeous waif with breasts that, thanks to a pair of those miniaturized null-o-gee implants, literally defied gravity.

The fight had not yet reached the stage of easily identifiable flying objects (which Xahn habitually threw directly at my head) but it *had* escalated to the point of balled up fists and unreasonable demands, such as:

"But, Feng, I *want* a baby."

"Now, Xahn, come on. We've been over this a hundred times—"

"And we'll go over it a hundred more. Why can't you commit?"

That word again. And of course I couldn't really give the answer. That the mere idea of pregnancy revolted me. That my mother, all those years ago, had gone to an all-night conceivorama, where she'd been inadvertently impregnated with a small vial of instantaneous, self-replicating construction nanobots, and had subsequently given painful and terminal birth to a concert hall. Not even a very good one either. The acoustics were horrific. You couldn't hear the orchestra from the box seats, but the guy who worked the fried eel cart three blocks away was intensely audible. The engineers blamed the problem on a freak acoustical phenomenon, and they originally planned to tear the building down. In recent years, however, they relented, and have started marketing the place as performance entertainment. They're doing pretty well, in a financial sense, although I don't know that I'd call it art.

Either way, the experience was traumatic, and I don't like to talk about it much. So:

"You want a baby so bad, Xahn, why don't *you* gestate the thing?"

I might as well have kicked her in the face. We both knew very well she'd had her uterus removed some years ago to make way for that intra-torsal espresso-maker implant with the intravenous caffeine feed. A dumb move, if you ask me, since everybody knew those things were dangerous. Predictably, the piece of junk malfunctioned, and after that it only put out decaf. The poor girl wound up groggy for the next eleven years.

Hindsight being what it is, I might've held my tongue. Foresight being what *it* is, I didn't, and Xahn started hurling everything within her reach.

"This is just like you, Feng!" she screamed, while shoes put divots in the walls around me. "Why don't you get out of here! Go run and hide offworld somewhere, like you always do! Always flying, Feng— always running from responsibility! Always—"

I can take a hint.

And she was right, I guess. Maybe I *did* make all those cargo runs because I couldn't handle all the trials and tribulations of the real life. "No sense of responsibility," all my lovers always told me, in the end.

The trouble was, business had been slow lately, and so I couldn't just light up jets and get offworld. To make matters worse, I still owed payments on my ship (a '55 Ramirez, true, but even those things aren't cheap) and my less-than-legal creditor, Jimmy "The Plate of Lightly Sauteed Calamari" Fringetti, didn't take to loan defaulters. For example—

"Gurk!" I said, as I was lifted off my feet out in the hallway.

"Feng Oroshti?" said the walking wall who had his meaty hand around my neck.

"Gak!" I said.

"Uh-huh. You know why I'm here?"

"Khaf!"

"Uh-huh. Then you don't mind takin' off your shoe?"

"Ragh?"

"Either one. It don't really matter."

I tried to explain that, what with my dangling some three feet above the floor, I was in no position to remove either item of my footwear. But the pressure on my vocal cords reduced any eloquent reply I might've given down to, "Hnh!"

That didn't matter. The human bison yanked the shoe off by himself. It was the left one. Three of the five toes I claim ownership to on that foot were already bandaged. The beefcake reached out and snapped the fourth. It hurt.

"One more reach week till February," he said, in his foghorn of a voice. "After that, we start on the ankles."

He let me drop and walked away, the floor shuddering with every step. I got my shoe back on as best I could and cursed him, but thanked God he hadn't broken both my legs at once, and had let me pay, instead, under their installment plan.

I limped down to the Hadzhe Bar—a local place owned by a couple of semi-intelligent Hungarians who believed in atmosphere, as long as it was thin. It was a place of thugs and alcohol and self-abuse; a place devoid of garnishes or beverages with long and hyphenated names. Just the sort of place you need when you've had shoes thrown at you and somebody has just broken yet another of your toes.

I found a seat at the bar and tried to look as unapproachable as possible. It didn't work. I'd been there all of three minutes when the Cilk sidled up and occupied the chair beside me.

I say "occupied," because it didn't sit. A Cilk is an aqueous suspension of a life-form. A demiliquid being, more suited to a heavy ocean world than something Earth-type. In aerobic circles, therefore, they generally go around inside protective, hovering containers, which, like other liquids, they take the shape of. Literally, the thing was a bucket of slime.

It acted like one, too.

"Can you do me a sexual favor?"

"Slink off, Cilk. There must be some corners around here that need skulking in."

"Most human women say we Cilks make fantastic lovers."

I tried not to tap the mental image that called up, but failed miserably, and made a mental note to take a shower at my earliest convenience.

"You are about to get a thousand percent," I said, by way of warning him, "of the recommended daily allowance of the bottom of my shoe."

The Cilk was not perturbed by this. The lights along the outside of its bucket glowed deep violet in interest.

"Do I come on too strong? Of course, I know you Earth-types value romance. I am something of a romantic myself. Would you like to hear a sonnet?"

I looked around for a blunt instrument, but the closest thing was a ceramic bowl of salted yeast nuts, and I didn't think that it would do the job.

"My love for you," the Cilk soliloquized, "is like a little bird/or some wonderful herring./My love for you knows no bounds/and also it is pretty ignorant about integral calculus."

"That's beautiful. One more word and I lift your lid and pour a drink in you."

"All right, all right. Business, then."

My ears pulled back a fraction of a millimeter. The thing was disgusting, true, but money tends to settle my stomach better than anything.

"You have a ship, I've been told."

"I do. You have some cargo?"

"A quantity of Heberal," he said.

"I've never heard of it."

"You wouldn't have. It's new."

"Describe."

"It is," the Cilk explained, "an hallucinogenic, psychoactive chemo-electric mind-enhancing substance that fosters the unassailable conviction in its ingestor that he or she is a fifty-two-year-old Jewish dry cleaner named Maury Applebaum."

"Who the hell would want to take something like that?"

"It's a fad these days, with youth."

"Being a Jewish dry cleaner?"

"Being anything. Adolescence has become drab. Dull. Hopelessly homogenized. Kids are looking for variety. Excitement. And finding it in mind-expanding substances. Hebraic laundry cleansing is just one of the available and popular addictions. For instance, my nephew has become dependent on a drug called Phurz, which makes him feel as if he's sober."

"Then why take it in the first place?"

"Who knows? Peer pressure, I suppose."

The Cilk named a figure then that made me forget about his nephew and gave me strings of palpitations. It would be enough to pay the balance on my ship. Enough to get a bigger place. Enough to purchase a new uterus for Xahn.

"That much?" I said, suddenly suspicious.

"Yes. Well. The cargo is a bit . . . unsavory, is it not?"

"Unsavory is my middle name," I said.

"You humans and your nomenclatures. My middle name is 'Bripple.' It means, 'He who slinks where others fear to gurgle past.' "

The Cilk named a departure time and destination and we sat a while and worked on the particulars. I was bound for Hrogath, raising ship the following afternoon. The Cilk agreed to have his thugs load in the cargo. All I had to do was fly.

"And if you change your mind about the sex—"

"It's a good thing you don't respirate," I told it. "That way you can't hold your breath." ·

Virginia may well be for lovers, but the Raleigh spaceport was designed specifically with criminals in mind. It's a warren of ships and ducts and lax security, and loading in the crates of Heberal presented very little problem.

I ignored the Cilk and his two lowbrow thugs while they used a dumb-end cargobot to stow the goods away. He gurgled at me and got out of there (his ego was still bruised, I think, or maybe permanently fractured even—I could only hope) and I was just about to cast off for Hrogath when Old Faithful came to call.

Faithful. As in, he hounds me like clockwork. The proverbial pain in my metaphorical ass. He was six-foot-one and advertisement handsome, and he dressed as if the hair across his ass was ultraglued in place. He called himself Officer Montieth of the Raleigh Customs Bureau, but I knew better. This man was a hemorrhoid.

"Going somewhere, Feng?"

"Sure. You want to come?"

"Don't get cute. I want to see your cargo."

"Go to hell. I know my rights."

"Your rights do not include the smuggling of Heberal, last time I checked."

I sniffed.

"I'm paid up on my bribes."

He managed to look affronted, but took the official state-mandated bribe receipts I held out, just the same.

"Please, Feng," he said. "We prefer to call them prepaid, proactive illegal activity permits."

"Call them what you want," said. "They're all in order."

He looked them over, nodded, and said, "Yes, they are. But I'm afraid I'll still have to search your ship."

"You *what?*"

He nodded in that special self-satisfied way that only he seemed able to achieve.

"You've heard about the Denetian diplomat, I will assume?"

I hadn't, what with everything I'd been through lately. But I'd seen Denetians. Sort of like our camels, only they walked upright and smelled worse.

"He's wanted," Officer Montieth explained. "And we have reason to believe he might be smuggled off the planet."

"Wanted for what?" I said.

Montieth shrugged, and went into full-patronizing mode.

"It's a little complicated. But the main point is, the Krahags want him dead."

"Krahags?" I had heard of them. A new race. Just discovered on the far point of some nebula.

"Yes. We have a good trade status so far with Krahag. We stand to gain a lot from them, as a civilization."

"And so we're helping them track down this—"

"Denetian diplomat, yes."

"Seems like a weak reason," I observed.

He shrugged.

"You want to make an omelette, you've got to break a few eggs."

"I usually have cereal."

"Your breakfast preferences aside, we need to find that diplomat. Hard to say why the Krahags hate him so much, but it could be his religion's unpopular insistence that shaving daily is the path to God."

"Weird, all right. But why unpopular?"

"Because Krahags are composed entirely of hair."

"Oh, really?"

"Mmm. The mere possession of a comb on Krahag can get you shot. I had a very painful experience there once with some tweezers and a quantity of styling gel. I really don't want to go into it, but I don't mind telling you I haven't been able to go near a barber in nine years without screaming uncontrollably."

"Then how do you—?"

"I had my scalp surgically removed. What you see before you is a wig. I received it on Krahag, actually. It is the funereal remains of a deceased but well-loved elder statesman. It's quite an honor, I am told, to be allowed to display him in this manner."

I took his word for it. I had to admit that it looked sleek and shiny and well-styled, but you have to question the principles of anybody who goes around with a dead politician on his head, no matter how nicely he has brushed it.

Still, he was the long arm of the law, and I was reasonably sure there were no diplomats—Denetian or otherwise—stowed away inside my ship, so I didn't raise any further fuss. Montieth checked through every inch with sensorbots and pronounced it clean of wanted refugees, then stood near the forward strut and leered at me.

"When are you going to let me take you out?" he said, smoothing back his elder statesman.

"Cold day in hell sound familiar?"

He shook his head.

"Still questioning your sexuality, eh?"

"Oh, no," I told him, heading for the hatch. "I'm through questioning. It finally confessed."

I love space travel. I know most people don't, unless they've had their eustachian tubes augmented or have been hit on the head with an impactor. And then again, there is the smell. Like old cheese and underwear and weeks without a bath. But to me, there's something about all that infinite untapped potential. All that blackness. All that void just waiting to be done in, done with; turned out into light and life and bold experience. I have never claimed to be a poet, and in truth the darkness is a little terrifying, but I guess that's part of the allure.

I had the computer take care of the course and speed and heading, and I sat and watched the viewscreen, letting myself be mesmerized by the everchanging constellations, suggesting myths and gods and goddesses of infinite, unrealized identities. They lulled me to sleep, those nebulous and countless deities, and when I woke again to the distant, constant rumble of my engines, I did it by degrees. It seemed someone was talking to me.

"Did you sleep well?" the someone said.

"Like a baby," I said, coming out of it.

"Oh. You mean, you soiled yourself and woke up screaming?"

I opened my eyes. My hand was wet. I picked it up and looked at it. There was something green and viscous and unsettlingly familiar on the fingertips.

The Cilk.

"Hello, Feng. Is it hot in here, or is it just you?"

I sat up straight and looked at him. He lay in a sticky puddle on the flight deck, near my in-flight pilot couch.

"How the hell did you get here?"

"I have my ways."

I thought about that.

"You've been hiding in my toilet, haven't you?"

"I wouldn't call it hiding. I was mostly floating on the surface."

"That's disgusting."

"You get used to it. It actually reminds me of home."

"It does, huh?"

"Well, yes. Except it smells better and it's not as cramped."

I decided I would wash my hands when next I got the chance.

"You'd better talk," I said. "And fast."

He did.

"While I do enjoy your lavatory," he said, gurgling, "it is not the only reason I have stowed away."

"Go on."

"You have heard, no doubt, of the Denetian diplomat?"

"Hasn't everyone?"

"He came to me," the Cilk said. "His plight appealed to my sympathetic nature."

"Uh-huh. And the money didn't hurt."

"Oh, money hardly ever hurts. Unless vast quantities are dropped on you from a significant height. Even then, there is no problem, if, like me, you have no skeleton to speak of."

"And so he's here?"

"Oh, yes. Right here." He bubbled. "It's perfect. The latest in Denetian genetics. They reduce the living being to a single zygote, and insert that zygote in a womb. The pregnancy and growth are accelerated, and *pow!*—the person's back. Of course, it's more complicated than that, really. You have to store the personality and memories as a separate biologic file, and the interspecies part presents some problems of its own, but—"

I was off my seat and staring at the Cilk in all of half a second.

"What did you do?" I asked the thing.

"It wasn't difficult," he said. "Nobody would ever suspect a washed-up two-bit smuggler like you. Your lover, Xahn, agreed to provide the means of conception in return for a new uterus, and—"

He didn't have a neck, or else I think I would have wrung it.

"Get it out of me!" I said. "Now! Or I get the service-bot to mop you up and flush you out the waste hatch."

"Let's not be hasty," he said. "Think this through. I'll admit that I'm a slime—"

"Literally!"

"—and that I did my part for money. But ask yourself; do you really want that ambassador to die?"

That got to me; I admit it. I didn't like Montieth, and the government that pulled his strings had never been what I'd call kind. I operated outside its mandates for a reason. Several of them, in fact. Still, I felt used and violated and that pissed me off. And then there was the whole idea of pregnancy . . .

"We can't do anything without your cooperation," the Cilk was saying. He sounded nervous. He should have.

"You will find a small pink pill inside the console near your flight couch. The ingestion of this pill is necessary."

"No. No way."

"Come now, Feng. 'You must do the thing you think you cannot do.' Your Eleanor Roosevelt said that."

"Yeah. And look at her—she's dead."

If he had a snappy comeback, it was buried by the sudden clamor of my ship's proximity alarm.

"What the hell?" the Cilk said, bubbling.

I checked the screens and saw a blocky ship.

"Customs squad," I said. "Closing, fast. Your plan wasn't so perfect after all."

The Cilk turned red. He literally boiled.

"There must've been a leak!" he hissed.

I snorted.

"Let me guess. Your business partners are all Cilks?"

"Those bastards! If I ever catch them, the things I will do to them with a suction valve!"

I didn't have time to listen to his rants, as being docked against my will is not something I enjoy. I slipped into the flight couch and let my hands slide over the familiar and comfortable controls. One quick, hard shove on the throttle, and we'd be history. The Ramirez, after all, had quite a kick to her, in spite of all her quirks and jury-riggings.

Except she wouldn't kick. I shoved the throttle once or twice, and nothing happened.

"Goddamn it!" I said, while the bulky ship closed in. "They did something to my frigging ship!"

The Cilk and I could only wait and listen to the thumps of docking and the hissing of the air lock being forced to cycle. The standard infomercial played on all my screens (the one that demonstrates proper procedure for being boarded by a customs squad—it's actually pretty interesting and the actresses are kind of hot) and soon Montieth and a full detachment of his goons were grinning at us down the barrels of their government-issue blasters.

"Well, well," said Montieth. "If it isn't Feng Oroshti and the slime lord. Did you really think that you could fool me?"

"It was worth a try," I said.

He snorted.

"I just played you both for suckers. This way I kill two birds with one stone."

"I'm sure the birds will be happy to hear that," I said.

One of the goons chose that moment to shout out, "On your knees, like dogs in the dirt!"

He had probably been practicing that in the mirror for weeks. I was glad when the Cilk said, "I don't have knees. Come to think of it, neither do dogs."

"Yeah, they do," another goon said. "They just bend backward."

"I thought that was ostriches," said another. "And seals."

"Now seals do *not* have knees," said someone else. "Of that I am certain."

Montieth interrupted them at that point to say, "Never mind the knees, you retrofits! Just get them in restraints!"

I had used the short span of free time provided by the argument to sidle over to the console and remove a small, pink pill from where it had been hidden. I felt everybody turn toward me as I popped it in my mouth. I supposed asking any of them to boil some water was out of the question.

Childbirth wasn't any kind of picnic. With a picnic you get beer and sandwiches and maybe ants. With childbirth, none of them is present. Not that I really cared about the ants, or even the sandwiches, come to think of it, but I swear to Christ I could've used some sort of alcoholic beverage.

"What's happening to her?" said Montieth, the very picture of concern, as I doubled over on the console.

"Accelerated pregnancy," the Cilk said, evidently fascinated with the show despite his unenviable predicament.

What happened next is something I am unlikely to forget. The first three trimesters hit me like a triple asteroid collision and the baby dropped like a quarkonic bomb. My breasts ripped through my flight suit and my hips rotated with an audible and painful crack.

"Yes, yes—it's all accelerated," said the Cilk.

I heard a sound like something prehistoric and realized it was me. Screaming. I vomited.

"That'd be the fifteen-second sickness," said the Cilk.

I fell back on the floor and spread my legs and thought of Earth.

I felt a tearing and a crunch. The fetus ricocheted off of a customs officer and knocked him off his feet.

"Sweet Jesus!" said Montieth.

I saw my baby grow, and grow, and grow as all those customs goons just gawped at it.

"Well, don't just stand there!" Montieth shouted. "Get them!"

One of his goons came at me, brandishing a pair of magna-cuffs and sporting a sadistic leer. I didn't feel in any condition to fight just then, but my own healing seemed to have accelerated, too, and I was pissed. I got up and faced the flunkie down.

"I have one hell of a case of postpartum depression just now," I told him, "so don't fuck with me!" Then I kicked him in the teeth.

Things got a little nonlinear then. Goons started firing left and right. One of them accidentally stepped in the Cilk and fell flat on his back. I drew on one and shot him in the kneecap, and my baby, who had already grown into a full-fledged Denetian, complete with a full complement of humps and hooves, started slinging them around and knocking Montieth's minions to the bulkheads.

I shot two more (must have been my maternal instincts kicking in) before Montieth winged me and I dropped my blaster. Three of the remaining goons got a pair of cuffs on the diplomat, and that, for all intents and purposes, appeared to be that.

Except I'd noticed two things in the midst of the confusion. The first was that the Cilk had trickled out, unnoticed, and the second was the green gas that even now was seeping from the climate system.

I held my breath and hoped.

We reached Denes six hours later, and were greeted by a phalanx of brightly-painted dignitaries. Montieth and all his goons let themselves be led away (but not without a few cries of, "Oy! Not gravy!" and "Never will you get gefilte out of cash-mere!") The Denetian diplomat thanked me pro-fusely and shook my hand with his opposing hooves. (My son, the alien ambassador. He never calls, he never writes, but what's a mother going to do?)

The Cilk and I flew home the next morning.

"Fare thee well, Feng Unsavory Oroshti," he said, and I was almost moved until I realized that most of him was sliding up my leg. I wiped him off and walked out across the spaceport, and because of the condition of the arresting officers (and particularly Montieth's insisting, "The only way to get out mus-tard stains is with a sprinkling of soda water, God-damn you all to hell."), all prospective charges against us were immediately dropped.

I paid off Jimmy Fringetti and fixed up my ship, and took a few well-needed weeks off to myself. I forgave Xahn for double-crossing me and told her everything that happened.

"And that's all she wrote?" she said, when I had finished.

"If she wrote any more," I told her, wondering about conceivoramas and whether they might be safer in these modern days, "she erased it."

G-Bomb
by Ron Collins

Ron Collins' writing has appeared in *Analog*, *Dragon*, and several other magazines and anthologies. He is a *Writers of the Future* prizewinner, and a CompuServe HOMer Award Winner. He has been named to the Science Fiction and Fantasy Writers of America's Nebula Award's preliminary ballot twice, most recently in 2000 for his short story "Stealing the Sun." He holds a degree in mechanical engineering from the University of Louisville, and has worked developing avionics systems, electronics, and information technology. He lives in Columbus, Indiana, with his wife, Lisa, and their daughter, Brigid. The obligatory cat's name is Rika.

MY hair is bronze this week. I change it a lot because Diego says he likes that. I pull a strand from my eyes and look at my watch for the third time in the last five minutes.

I'm sitting on an examination table covered with cracked vinyl and scratchy white paper. The room is all steel and plastic, with painted concrete walls and a white tile floor that makes me feel out of place. A chill brings bumps to my arms. I rub them to get warm, and check my watch again. If I'm not at work in thirty-five minutes, Dork-brain will cut my hours.

The door opens and Dr. Lawrence comes in.

He is young for a doctor, probably thirty—very clean. Short blond hair, watery blue eyes, no ring. Very cute if you're into that Anglo kind of thing. He doesn't belong to the clinic, though. He's a loaner on rotation and, like the other loaners, he's got a holier-than-thou attitude around him like one of those electric doggie fences. He stands in the hallway like he thinks he's some savior coming down to take charity cases in the city. But I can see he's dying for the moment he can jump into that green BMW parked on the curb outside and drive back to his cozy house across the bay.

He sits on the round stool and looks at me like I've got Ebola, then glances down at the chart. He's reading my name. The asshole's got to read my name.

"You're pregnant, Helena," he says.

"What?"

"You heard me. You're not sick, you're pregnant."

Pregnant. Shit. "I can't be pregnant."

"When's the last time you had sexual intercourse?"

A blush crosses my cheeks. He asks it so directly, and Diego and me, well, we've been more than just a little active these days, so it's certainly *possible*. "It's not that. It's just . . . we're very careful."

"Nothing but abstinence is a hundred percent, you know?"

I don't say anything. I'm nineteen years old. I live in a dumpy two-room apartment in Sausalito, with a job ringing up groceries at Golden Gate and a boyfriend who drives a rusted-out Toyota. I can't be pregnant. Shit.

Shit. Shit. Shit. Shit. Shit.

"Are you okay?" Dr. Lawrence asks.

"Yes," I say too quickly. "I'm fine."

"I want you to set up an appointment for prenatal conditioning, all right?"

"What's that?" I say it like I didn't actually hear him.

"You're eligible for the standard genetic vaccines—

the inoculations to turn off whatever bad stuff you've got going on in there, you know? Stuff like Downs and CF and Alzheimer's."

"Oh," I say, feeling stupid again. *I knew that*, I want to tell him. *I'm not stupid.* Pregnant. Shit. Just the word *pregnant* feels blunt, like *bat*, or *punch*, or *Mack truck.*

Dr. Lawrence gives his best effort at a bedside smile and hands me a prescription the insurance won't cover. "Don't forget to make that appointment," he says, wagging a finger at me like he's my daddy and I need to be reminded to pick up my shoes.

Then I am out in the shaded street watching cars and buses race around like it's just an ordinary day and not at all the very day the entire world has gone to shit.

Diego has less money than I do, and he's not exactly college material, so I would say his future holds no great promise either. But he's got that smooth Nicaraguan skin and eyes like black marbles. Just kissing him makes my toes curl.

We met six months ago—at a bar, of course.

He asked me to lunch for the next day, though. He took me to Hallie's and we ate Mexican on the sidewalk patio. We hit it off right away. There's that feeling you get, that perfect clicky thing like when you see two pelicans flying side by side just over the whitecaps and you figure they must be perfect. We joked. He held my hand from across the table. I laughed a lot. That's important. You have to be able to laugh.

We talked all day—mostly about how society was so messed up. It was a topic that gave us something in common, and one Diego had passion for. He talked about drugs and guns in the street. He talked about the city spending ninety-eight million for planting trees in the parks, but not giving a shit about anything that's really happening. I told him about my dad, and how he struggled but never managed to make it to middle class even after serving in the Air Force for six years. Diego said that sucked, and I agreed with him.

"*I'm* going to be rich, though," I boasted at one point.

"Sure you are."

"Hey," I said, carrying on with the joke. "I got a job and an apartment. I can make it."

Diego laughed out loud. "Planning on hitting the lottery?"

"What do you want me to do, eh?" I said. "You think I should just quit? Maybe go be a bag lady?"

"No," Diego said, batting long lashes that were already making me want to disappear inside him. Then he got all serious. "It's all about power, Helena. It's all about beating them at their own game."

I met his friends that night—they were a collection of weirdos that Diego called freedom fighters, but looked to me like just a bunch of hoods with kinky dreadlocks and garish tattoos. I saw enough of their type before I quit school. They were smoking and drinking, and they hooted and hollered when I walked in. I'm used to that, though. God may not have put a hundred watts between my ears, but I can do the gurly thing as good as it gets. The guys gave Diego a girlfriend razz, but he just ran his hand through his dark hair and gave his sweet, sweet smile and the whistles got even louder.

So I gave him a present and did up my walk for them. He appreciated it then, and showed me how much later. He says I've got a nice walk. A couple of the guys scared me, though. They sat in the corner so much like coiled snakes that I expected their tongues to slide out past their lips then snap back in.

"Those are the G-men," Diego whispered when he saw me staring. "Gene guys."

"They're wearing sweats," I replied.

"Not jeans like blue jeans, Helena. Genes. Genetics."

I frowned, but Diego must have caught my question. "They make G-bombs. Viruses that mess with your insides."

A sick feeling came to my stomach then. "What are they going to do?"

"Don't worry. I won't let them do nothing to you."

I tried not to look at them, but it was like trying not to look in the mirror at a club. The other guys were just playing cops and robbers, you know? A little stealing, a little bullying, a little juju on the streets—whatever it took to make things work out. But these two made everything feel mixed up and dangerous, and for a minute it was like I didn't know what planet I was standing on.

"I told you, baby," Diego said, pulling me closer. "You got to beat them at their own game." Then he kissed me. My toes curled, and everything jolted back into his focus.

It's late when Diego's key slips into the door. "Hey, baby," he says.

"Hey." I'm sitting on the couch I got at a garage sale for a hundred bucks. It's the only piece of furniture I have that's worth a shit—sturdy enough that it took three guys to carry it in. The television is playing a rerun of *The Real World*, Cairo cast. Amelia is going off on Li-li because of the dope he's been snorting. The TV dies every half hour, and I have to bash it on the side to bring it back to life.

Diego throws himself on the couch and stares at

the screen. His fatigue jacket smells like cigarettes. "We got anything to drink?"

"Diego?" I say, hoping I sound casual, but feeling like a jackrabbit lurching around in its cage.

"What?"

I try to speak, but nothing comes out. I've practiced this conversation all day. Diego, I'm pregnant, I say, and then he stares at me in shock until the corner of his lips rise, then he smiles and gives me a kiss and a hug and we celebrate together. I've played this moment over and over until I almost believe it might happen, but now the time is here and my words are stuck in my throat. "Diego, I'm pregnant," I finally blurt.

He stares at me in shock. "What?"

"I said, I'm pregnant."

His elbows rest on his knees. He presses his fingers into his skull so hard the half-moons of his nails turn white. "Holy shit," he mutters under his breath. He stands up and paces. "Holy shit." His black eyes sizzle and dance like drops of oil on a frying pan. "What the hell did you do that for?" he yells, and then he slaps me. I can't believe it. He cuffs me across the eye and I fall over the arm of the couch. He stands over me in his green jacket and he yells. "I didn't ask for this! I didn't ask for none of this!"

The slamming door is the last thing I hear.

I go to my room and throw myself onto the bed with its lumpy mattress and its buttons that poke me in the back when I'm sleeping. The sheets smell like him. I feel like my chest is all caving in. I feel like I'm going to puke. I put my face into the pillow and remember a picture of my mama and me when I was less than a year old. We are on the beach. The sky is dark and there isn't any sun. Mama is holding me in one arm and trying to keep a straw hat on with the other hand. Her glasses are coming off, and she's looking up like it might be raining.

That's exactly how I feel right now.

I lie huddled in the sheets. It's dark outside the window. My cheek is hot where Diego hit me.

I miss Mama the most.

Maybe that's a bad thing to say, but I can't help it. Mama and Daddy are both gone now—died in a crash when I was sixteen. I loved Daddy, but I miss Mama the most. She was born on Guam, and had a broad face and a big smile. There was a time where I was embarrassed of her. Kids teased me because I was tall and thin, and because I had a tiny little Malaysian nose. Then Mama would come to school with her flat, big-pored cheekbones and the grin I thought was so moronic, and it was like she was flying a flag that said *This is where Helena comes from.*

I am ashamed now that I was embarrassed of her.

I put my hand on my belly.

This kid's got no chance. It'll grow up in the streets and run into trouble in school and with the cops. Next thing you know it'll be in jail or dead in some drive by shooting. When I realize what I am doing, I cry harder. The kid is just a glob in my belly and I've got him doing five-to-ten at Alcatraz.

What am I going to do?

Kimmi comes over the next morning. She sits on my couch eating an apple. Kids dance on the television screen—spring break in Fort Lauderdale. Kimmi is my best friend. She's tall and spindly like me, but where I have the drabbest skin, hers is so black it makes the whites of her eyes look like laser beams. She's younger than me, but she's as together as anyone I know.

"I can't believe you got yourself all preggy, gurl," Kimmi says, crunching on the apple.

"You and Diego both."

"That don't sound good."

"I told him last night. He's gone."

"Bastard."

"It's all right."

"The hell it is." She looks harder at the puffy spot beside my eye. "I'm glad the asshole's gone," she finally says.

I shrug.

"Gonna keep it?"

It is a question I've thought about a hundred times since I stood outside the clinic. A hundred bucks and I can get rid of it. It's almost a week's pay.

"I don't know," I reply glumly. "It's probably better for the kid if I don't."

"What the hell's that supposed to mean?"

"Look around, Kimmi. I got nothing. No money. No home. What kind of mother would have a kid in a place like this?" I scan the room, and it's like the entire apartment sags its agreement. "I don't even know how to balance a checkbook."

"Ah," Kimmi says. "This is more than the baby, ain't it?"

I don't say anything, but I feel myself shrinking as she stares from under her plucked eyebrows. "All that baby really needs is to know its mama loves it every night when it goes to bed."

"Easy for you to say."

"Look, gurl. You want your kid to grow up good, you just keep it on that course. You want your kid to be smart, you just keep it in school."

"I quit school."

"That's 'cause your parents died and you didn't have no one to hold the line."

She was right there. Mama or Daddy would have kicked my butt for leaving school. She was right about the first thing, too. My parents never had money, but they loved me and I never felt truly afraid about anything until they died.

"Besides," Kimmi says. "Smarts ain't all schooling.

The radio said the governor's kid just got the thing done to him to boost up his intelligence. You could do that, too."

"What was that?"

She shrugs. "Do I look like a doctor? My point is that if you're worried about what kind of mama you might be, you're looking in the wrong direction."

I see her point, but I don't like it. She's telling me I've got no discipline. She's saying this is my doing, and that it's my job to figure things out. I think about Dr. Lawrence and grimace. "Shit," I finally say. "Sure as hell ain't no way I can pay to do the governor's intelligence thing."

"I hear that," Kimmi replies, eating the last of her apple. She goes to the kitchen and throws away the core. "Hey? You wanna know if it's a boy or a girl?"

"Huh?"

She holds up a juice glass she took from the cabinet. "You go pee in here. Fill it about half full, okay?"

"Sure," I say as I take the glass from her.

She rummages under the sink. "Go to it, babe."

So I do.

"Got it?" Kimmi asks when I come out of the toilet.

I hold up the glass. She has a container of crystal Drano in one hand and a big plastic spoon in the other.

"Then out we go."

"Out?"

"Trust me, gurly gurl, we don't want to do this inside."

I follow Kimmi into the hallway and down the stairs. I hold the glass in one icky hand. It's bright outside. My place is a red brick building with cracks in the sidewalk. It is only April, but already the weeds are growing up.

"Put the glass down there," Kimmi says.

She pops the lid and scoops a mound of Drano. "Brown it's a boy, blue or green it's a girl. What do you want it to be?"

"I haven't thought about it. Guess I really don't care."

"You are so a liar."

I shrug. Then she drops the powder into the glass. The smell is like rotten eggs and ammonia. It stings my eyes and makes my throat feel like I'm swallowing kitchen pads.

Kimmi holds her nose and points at the glass. It's dark brown. "It's a boy, honey," she says.

I smile moronically, holding my own nose. "Maybe that's why it's so stinky."

We laugh, and Kimmi hugs me right there in the middle of the street. I feel stronger than I have in a very long time. For the first time I feel something that might even be hope.

"It's going to be okay," Kimmi whispers in my ear.

"Yes," I finally think. "It's going to be okay."

They met when Daddy was stationed at Anderson.

I came along pretty quickly after that, and they got married. I worry sometimes. Did they do something they didn't want to do because of me? But they loved each other. I think Daddy would have brought Mama home no matter what—it's just that he got to be so angry because he never had any money, and so I worry about it.

I remember a time when I was maybe ten. Daddy and I were sitting on the porch of the little house we had. He was smoking, and I was playing with one of my Skippy dolls. It was that time right before the night comes. I looked up at him, and I thought he was crying. I followed his gaze and saw two jets high in the sky, probably heading down to Edwards.

"Are they going to shoot us, Daddy?"

He laughed his throaty laugh and put his arm around me. "No, honey. They're not going to shoot us." We sat there while the jets disappeared. I thought he was finished talking, but he took a deep breath and smiled all crooked. Then he squeezed my shoulder and looked at me really hard. "No matter how hard life gets," he said, "do what's right and you'll never be sorry."

That's what I remember about Daddy.

The government sends me Social Security checks now. I think he would be happy about that.

I'm keeping my boy. Simple as that.

I want him to be smart, though. Love is great and all that—but I want my boy to have it better than me, and if he's smart, he can make it. I keep coming back to that as I look at the torn carpet in my apartment.

It strikes me then.

I am still afraid, but the fear is different. It is a fear all in one place rather than a blanket of poisonous fog. I have been so alone. These last three years I have felt like a zombie. But this child has changed everything.

I finally understand what I'm doing here.

So I make a plan.

I call Dr. Lawrence for an appointment—not at the clinic this time, but directly in his downtown office. I go to the library, and I read. I need to be strong if I'm going to convince him to make my boy smart. I need to know what I'm talking about. So I talk to the librarian and she helps me check out books and magazines and everything else.

I read that night until my brain throbs, and then I go someplace else. Diego may be an asshole, but that doesn't mean he's wrong about everything.

* * *

It is almost three o'clock and the table is a mess with magazines spread out all over it. The past year's issues of the *Mensa Bulletin* and *Interloc* are around here someplace. I'm not pretending to understand it all, but *Scientific American* and twenty medical journals have told me what's possible. Government studies on everything from intellect to the economy are shoved on a plastic chair. A pamphlet from the Human Genome project explains how DNA and RNA and enzymes all work together to make things happen.

I've memorized enough numbers to gag a computer, and I've run through every argument I think Dr. Lawrence can possibly come up with. I'm filled with graphs and pictures and numbers and everything else I can think of to get filled with. My brain is probably oozing out of my ears. But Mama used to say a girl had to make use of everything she's got, and there's one tool left to prepare.

So I let the braid out of my hair, and it falls down my back like a river. Men like long hair. I colored it my original black yesterday, black like Mama's was. I bathe in almond water. I like the smell of almonds because it makes me think of the Bahamas, which is a place I think rich people go. It makes my stomach queasy today. Probably just nerves.

My belly is smooth and light brown under the water. I imagine myself growing and swelling until I have to walk around in baggy dresses that make me look like a canopy bed on legs. Kimmi said I'll probably blow up so big my belly button will poke out like a Tootsie Roll. Just the idea makes me laugh.

The towel is thin from washing too many times, but it gets me dry.

I line my lips and use enough mascara to bring out the greenish glaze from the brown of my eyes. I

scrub my teeth until they are white as chalk. At first
I put on my red satin blouse, but then decide the
white one with its V-neck and the pretty lace is better. I pick the soft blue pants because Diego told me
they were tight enough to get him hot, but not so bad
they made me look like a three-dimer on the corner.

Leave it to Diego.

A bit of Chanel in strategic places, a pair of plat-
forms, and I'm finished. I give myself a final check
in the mirror. Like I say, I do the gurly thing all right.

I walk into Dr. Lawrence's office.

He is wearing a denim shirt unbuttoned one button. His lab coat is draped over an arm of the couch.
The walls seem to vibrate with all his certificates
and diplomas.

"Good afternoon, Helena," he says, looking up.
"How are you today?"

"I am doing fine, thank you."

"I was surprised to hear from you here. You can
get your pre-cons at your local center, you know?"

"I know," I say, noticing how he uses the word
center instead of clinic. "I wanted to talk to you
about something."

"Shoot."

"Well . . ." Then, just like with Diego, my words
dry up. My tongue feels like it is coated with glue,
and all my practiced lines seem frozen. I'm no doctor,
and words like *extragentic material* and *DNA grafting*
don't sound right coming from a nineteen-year-old
dropout.

"I heard of something you can do to change my
boy."

"I didn't say you were having a boy, Helena. It's
too early to tell."

Embarrassment rises in my cheeks. Now that I've
read about it, the idea of a pile of powder telling me

I've got a boy seems suddenly as foolish as believing Diego when he said he loved me. Still, I find myself clinging to the idea of a boy anyway.

"Well, anyway, you told me about prenatal conditioning."

"Yes."

"I understand there are things just like it that you can do that will help it do better at things."

"So, that's what you mean by *change?* Altering it genetically?"

"Yes. That's it. Altering hi—its genes."

"I see." He sat back in his chair. It was a leather chair as big as a boat. "What is it you want to change?"

"I want him to be smart, Dr. Lawrence."

"Smart?"

"Yes. I want my kid to be smart."

"Now, Helena," he said with that fatherly tone of voice.

"I know what being smart means, Dr. Lawrence. A man with an IQ under seventy-five is only fifty-fifty to make it through school. Low IQ means worse jobs, and less happiness, and more divorce, and more welfare." I babble on and on, my words crashing into each other like those fish that swim upstream. I feel like I've left my body. My fingers get numb and my thoughts jumble all up, but I keep talking because as long as I keep talking, then Dr. Lawrence can't finish the sentence he started a moment ago. *Now, Helena,* he was going to say, *you know I can't do that,* and as long as I just keep talking, there is a chance he won't say it. So I fill his office with all my words and all my numbers—percentages of unemployed by their intelligence, the increased likelihood of becoming a single parent, numbers on disease, and hunger, and poverty. Everything. Eventually, though, I find myself repeating things and the doctor raises his hand.

"I understand all that. Helena." he said. "I do."

"But?"

"I can't do anything about it."

"The Human Genome Project discovered the IQ gene."

He smiles. "Yes, I've heard it called that, but it's not quite right to say that."

I glare at him, and he admits a tiny defeat.

"Yes, the genome project has found a gene pair that controls the genetic component of intelligence."

"So I want you to change that in my baby."

"Helena, do you understand how unethical that would be?"

"How is it unethical to make someone better than they would be?" I say with more anger than I want to feel.

"We don't play with genes that way, Helena. If your baby has Alzheimer's or cystic fibrosis genes, I can fix it. But the government has strict rules about what we can alter and what we can't." He puts his fingertips together. "What makes you think your baby won't be intelligent enough as it is, Helena?"

I bit my lip. The answer won't matter. How can it? Dr. Lawrence is sitting in an office surrounded by walls of paper. He's never seen his father leaving for work in the morning to sweep floors in office buildings. He's never grown up in a house with ceiling tiles watermarked and stained with cigar and cigarette smoke. The laws that Dr. Lawrence waves about so grandly are evil. They are not there to make anything better, but merely to keep them from going to shit.

Inside, I think I had always known it would come to this.

"I'll do anything," I finally say.

"What do you mean?"

"I asked for the latest appointment I could get for a reason, Dr. Lawrence."

"Yes?"

I stand up and step around the desk.

He looks up at me. "Helena?"

I bend, holding my hair to one side as I kiss him. He resists at first. His lips are firm, but when he lets my tongue in, I know how it will end. I kiss him harder then. I run my hand through his hair and press my lips to his. I feel his barriers coming down. Men are like that. His breathing grows thick. He touches my thigh.

" I can't do this," he says.

"It's all right," I say. I kiss him again.

"Seriously, Helena. I just can't."

Then I am on the chair with him.

He is a clean man, and a tender lover, too. I didn't know what to expect, but if I would have thought about it, I suppose it wouldn't have surprised me. I take my time. It is enjoyable in a different way. When we are finished, I stand up and put my clothes back on.

"I . . . uh . . ." Dr. Lawrence says as he slips his pants up over his knees. "I don't know what to say."

"You could say you'll make my boy smart."

His face falls. "I told you, Helena. The government—"

"The governor's kid just had it done."

His shoulders slump. "I know, Helena." He shakes his head and puts his hand out. "You shouldn't have done this. I *told* you I couldn't do anything."

I finish buttoning my pants.

I feel sorry for him. Under his fake protests, Dr. Lawrence seems like a nice man. But just like he's never seen poverty, he's never felt what it's like to have a human being growing inside him. He can't understand how that single thing changes everything.

I reach into my purse and bring out the vial. It is glass with a plastic top. There only a little bit of oily liquid inside. It clinks as I set it on his desktop.

"What's that?" he says.

"It's my son's intelligence." It feels good to be in control, and I can't help but give a sly grin. "It's something people in my neighborhood call a G-bomb—a virus that carries tailored genetic material. This one is transferred through a mucus membrane, or, uh, exchange of fluids."

The doctor looks nervous. He tries to get the bottle, but I snatch it back. The G-men told me not to let anyone get hold of it or they could reverse-engineer the counterbomb. "Those guys," I say. "They don't have all the high-tech stuff you guys have. They can't build things very well. But they say it's not hard to tear them down."

Dr. Lawrence stands up. His neck is bulging with anger.

"What did you do to me?"

"It's coded for the same genes I want you to fix in my boy, Doctor. It's only fair, you know? But don't worry," I say, waving the empty bottle. "There's an antidote, a G-bomb that kills the stuff in here. I've already taken it, so I should be all right. And I really don't want to hurt you, Dr. Lawrence. I'll be happy to get you the antidote, too. But you're going to fix my boy up first."

He stands like a statue for a very long time. I know what he's thinking. He's trying to figure out what has happened to him. He's deciding if I'm telling the truth. He's making decisions, and wondering how much time he has.

"Two days," I say. "Then the G-bomb goes off."

He falls into his chair. "Okay," he says. "I'll do it."

I look at all his diplomas again as I go to the door, and I smile. I'm going to take care of myself, too, you see? The lady at the library said she would help me fill out grant applications. If I work at it, I can have a wall just like Dr. Lawrence's before my boy goes to high school.

Things are going to be all right.

"Don't forget to call me for that appointment, okay?" I say as I leave, wagging my finger at him like he's a little boy who needs to be reminded to pick up his shoes.

Together Forever at the End of the World
by Scott Edelman

Scott Edelman has been the Editor-in-Chief of *Science Fiction Weekly* (www.scifi.com/sfw), the Internet magazine of news, reviews, and interviews, since October 2000. Prior to this, Edelman was also the creator and only editor of the award-winning *Science Fiction Age* magazine from 1991 to 2000. He was also the editor of *Sci-Fi Entertainment,* the official magazine of the Sci-Fi Channel, for four years, and has also edited other SF media magazines such as *Sci-Fi Universe* and *Sci-Fi Flix.* He was the founding editor of *Rampage,* a magazine devoted to covering the field of professional wrestling, and for a time edited *Satellite Orbit,* the leading entertainment guide for C-band satellite owners. He has been a Hugo Award finalist for Best Editor on four occasions. His short fiction anthology appearances include "You'll Never Walk Alone" in Mike Ashley's *The Mammoth Book of Awesome Comic Fantasy,* "The Last Man in the Moon" in Peter Crowther's DAW anthology *Moon Shots,* "True Life in the Day After Tomorrow" in Laura Anne Gilman and Jennifer Heddle's anthology *Treachery and Treason,* "Are You Now?" in Dennis Etchison's *MetaHorror,* "The Wandering Jukebox" in Brian Stableford's *Tales of the Wandering Jew,* and others. Upcoming appearances include stories in *Crossroads: Southern Stories of the Fantastic* and *The Journal of Pulse-Pounding Narratives.*

IT wasn't until the smell of birthday cake washed away the smell of blood—on an early morning several weeks and a seeming lifetime ago—that I gave myself permission to relax.

With dawn and shift's end approaching, and a lull finally settling over the emergency room, those of my friends who could stood around me in a ragged circle in the break room. I hacked at the ice-cream ears of a smiling panda across whose stomach someone had written "Happy Birthday, Rachel" in runny icing.

I was supposed to have *started* the shift that way, but the cake that should have been mine back on the other side of midnight felt just as welcome in my hands the morning after. It erased—as much as anything could—the parade of gunshot victims and battered women who had kept me from it.

After I finished serving my coworkers, my own slice was finally in hand, and I slowly raised my fork. I shivered as the chocolate melted on my tongue. I was suddenly in two places at once, tasting not the supermarket sheet cake my friends had kicked in for, but the fancier sweets that Chris, who always made sure that my birthdays were special, surely had waiting at home.

I've always remembered that moment, and looking back now from the end of it all, I am drawn to remember the beginning all over again—the red stains fresh against the pale green of my jumper; the exact spot on which I'd been standing in relation to my coworkers, friends never to be found together in just the same way again; the longing to be at home with Chris, who was the point and purpose of it all; the strange mingling of flavors, one real and of the moment, the other but anticipated—just as each who survived the day would clearly remember his or her final seconds before The Change.

The loudspeaker overhead squawked to life suddenly at the same time as one of the nurses slammed into the room, shouting. With the words overlapping each other. I understood neither.

I called after the nurse as she barreled back out of the room, bagging her to tell me what had happened, but at the same time, my doctor's instincts pushed me forward. I followed the herd, not waiting for a response. As we raced down the hall, celebration forgotten, it turned out that no one we passed had any answers.

And the emergency room itself had only questions.

I stepped into chaos. A dozen victims waited for us there, with more pouring in behind them.

Nurses were already at work in this war zone, and I dashed to the patient nearest me, an elderly man whose clothing hung in ragged strips. As I helped them peel away what scraps remained, I could see that the skin beneath was blistered, and warm to the touch. It was as if his body had been rubbed raw by a burst of hot steam. If what really covered him from head to toe were endless burns, I knew that nothing I could do would be able to save him. The best I could accomplish was to ease his pain until death came.

And yet . . . my examination, instead of helping me to help him, only left me more confused.

As I ran my fingers down his arm, its texture seemed wrong for such a diagnosis, as if his wounds weren't really burns after all, but only mimicked burns. The turmoil in the room left me no time to ponder this, and I was forced to abandon him for the next patient, a young girl who couldn't have been much more than sixteen. Her long, brown hair fell out to the touch, revealing bruised skin beneath that reflected the same odd symptoms I'd seen on my first patient.

She seemed conscious, so I leaned in close and asked her what had happened, but received only soft moans in response. Even those sounds were an anomaly. Those weren't the cries of a burn victim. What should have presented as agony appeared to be only discomfort to these people. The emergency room was far too silent.

The other patients were in similar condition, and there was little we could do but help clean the patients and administer mild painkillers. As I moved from patient to patient, I was able to piece together bits of information from the EMTs who brought in the stream of the injured, but their random stories were of little help. Based on the symptoms scattered on the bloody stretchers throughout the rooms, I expected to hear tales of collapsed buildings and deadly explosions and twisted metal, but there had been none of that. Whatever had happened had just—happened. What few witnesses there were reported that one moment, workers had been strolling toward their early morning jobs downtown; the next, they were on the pavement, stricken. There'd seemed to be no cause to it all. The story made no sense, and offered me no help in treating the wounded.

As the patients became stabilized, even that bothered me, for they'd become stable far too fast for their symptoms. When what pain there was finally went, it vanished on its own, as if I'd had nothing to do with it, as if I'd been only a witness rather than a participant. The drugs, the machines, my training—all of it was meaningless. I was not used to being made irrelevant in that way. The world, at least the world that I confronted each day in that building, was supposed to make sense if only I poked and prodded at it enough. It would yield order. It would yield sanity. That was what brought me to medicine in the first place, that all the pieces always fit eventually. My talent, and I found it a comforting one, was to be able to clearly see what was broken, and then fix it. Any disease or injury, no matter how unclear at first, could always be figured out if I applied myself properly. But here reason was lacking, and things seemed vague and uncertain.

It would be days before I would come to realize that this same confused dance was being replicated in emergency rooms across the country and around the world. Had I known that at the time, I don't think it would have brought me any comfort.

Hours later, when the stream of patients finally ceased, my brain was too fatigued to wrestle with these unfamiliar feelings any further. I stumbled back to the break room for something to give me the sugar rush I needed to make it home.

Dear Chris. He would put this night in its place. He always did.

Crossing to the refrigerator, I saw the plate that held my slice of birthday cake where I had tossed it frantically aside on a table at what was originally supposed to be the end of my shift. Seeing nothing left but a muddy brown puddle that leaked on to the Formica and then over to the floor, I couldn't help but cry.

I've never been the sort of person who gives in to tears easily, but when I arrived back at our condo and saw dozens of red candles melted down to puddles of wax around our bed, I almost lost it all over again. Chris was already gone, off to his day job. The emergency that had kept me captive for an additional shift had really screwed things up for us this time. Our schedules were always fractured when I pulled night shifts, exiling us to opposite sides of the clock, but even then, we were usually able to share at least a couple of hours in the mornings and evenings.

I flung myself into bed and fell asleep, thinking, *Happy birthday.*

Yeah, right.

*   *   *

I woke up hours later to find Chris sitting in a chair he'd pulled alongside the bed. A box of Godiva chocolate was on one knee, and a bottle of champagne next to him on the hardwood floor. More importantly than either of those treats, *he* was there. He was just . . . looking at me.

He'd been studying me where I'd collapsed, fully clothed. He did that, sometimes, when I slept. Occasionally, I'd wake in the night and catch him watching. At times, it unnerved me. But right then, seeing him there looking into me, the world felt right, both in here, and out there.

"I've got an idea," he said, dragging his chair the last few final inches closer. "How about you take the day off?"

He'd moved into the rays from the setting sun that slanted through the window. His eyes were illuminated, and I tried to lose myself in the sparkles there. I tried to forget what that certain slant of light truly meant—that an entire day had passed—but I couldn't fully do it. The day had gone, and it was time for me to get back to work. There was still a mystery waiting for me there. Had my patients survived? I had to know. I had to go.

But there was Chris, with his soft eyes and his soft words and the promise of his soft lips.

"Stay home with me tonight," he whispered.

"How long have you been sitting there watching me?" I asked. I marveled again at my luck in finding someone who could love me so much, who could still look at me in that rapt way after two years of marriage. We both hoped that luck would keep us together forever. "Admit it, Chris. How long?"

"My whole life," he said. Then he couldn't help but laugh at himself for being so melodramatic. "So now that you're awake, take the night off. Let's celebrate your birthday the way we meant to last night, but couldn't."

He slipped in beside me on the bed, pressing his cheek against mine. When his lips touched my forehead, I couldn't help but sigh.

"You're amazing. I'd like to, but . . ."

"When did you last take a sick day?"

"It's been years. But you know I can't. Not tonight."

"Rachel."

"I've got people counting on me."

"But you've got *me* counting on you, baby," he said, nuzzling me again.

"Chris, I'd love to, but—"

"Damn it, Rach! Just give me this one day."

I jumped back at his raised voice. I couldn't recall him ever losing his temper like that.

"I'm sorry," he said quickly, before I could speak. "I'm so sorry."

"You'd better be," I said, swatting him with a pillow. "What the hell was that about, Chris? This isn't like you."

"I know, Rach. I know."

"Well, what is it, then?"

"The radio . . ." he said. "Your hospital . . ."

I was suddenly off the bed without realizing how I had gotten there. I stumbled over the champagne bottle, which rolled across the room.

"What happened at the hospital?"

"No, it's nothing like that, Rachel," he said, stretching to take hold of my hand. "Your friends are okay. It's just that, what happened there this morning, it was on the news. People at the office, they've been talking about it. Everyone's saying that this wasn't just an accident. That this was deliberate. Biological."

"That's ridiculous."

"All the gossip must have gotten to me, because when I was looking at you, I became afraid for you, that you'd get infected."

"That's sweet. But it's *still* ridiculous."

"Until this gets sorted out, how ridiculous is it, really? Why don't you just stay here with me tonight? I don't want you risking contamination. I can live with the sort of dangers you usually put up with—"

"Oh, that's so generous of you!" I said, punching him playfully.

"—but I don't want you to put your life on the line this way. Not until there's more information. We've got years to go, right?"

He was right, at least, then he was. I really thought so. Years to go. Imagine that. I loved him, and tried to ease his fears away the way he'd always chased away mine.

"I'm flattered that you care so much, Chris, really, I am. But you do know that there's no way I could stay away, right? Not even if this were just a normal night shift. But particularly not when there's such a mystery involved."

"Yeah, I guess I know that," he said. "You can't blame a guy for trying, though."

"Well, I *could*," I said. "But I won't."

He showed me that crooked sheepish grin of his. I loved him when he looked sheepish. I loved him however he looked. I still do.

"If you can't spare an entire night," he said, rising to place his hands firmly on my shoulders, "then how about just an hour of it?"

I relaxed into him, wrapping my fingers behind his neck, and pulled his lips down to mine. My wrist grazed a dry patch on his cheek. *Eczema*, I thought.

And I was supposed to be a doctor. Stupid, stupid, stupid.

I made a mental note to bring some ointment back from the hospital the next morning. Then I quickly filed that thought away, because for at least those few brief minutes, I intended to forget everything but the beating of Chris' heart against my own.

I arrived back at the hospital later than planned, thanks to the marvelous distraction offered by Chris, feeling both happy and guilty at the same time—and probably wearing my own sheepish grin—but the delay turned out not to matter much.

Jersey barriers clogged the street, forming a maze around the front entrance. Once I zigzagged past them, I noted that the over-friendly security guard who used to wave me through and at the same time try to pick me up had been replaced by an expressionless soldier who would not let me pass. The more frantically I waved my identity card, the more obstinately he blocked my path. My friendly hospital had become a forbidding fortress.

I didn't blame him for doing his job—I've never been the sort to blame the cog for the machine. But whether I held it against him or not, I didn't like having to argue my way in to what had been my place of work for the previous five years. And I certainly wasn't going to let him keep me from what waited inside. Having had enough of delays, and thinking of it as all a joke, I tried to dart around him. That's when I learned that though *I* thought the whole matter ridiculous, others were taking it very seriously indeed.

Four more soldiers raced toward me from the lobby, and they hustled me to a small back room with no window. Two of the soldiers remained with me as I sat, one blocking the door, the other at my back. I tried to forge a connection with them, just as I would do with even the most recalcitrant of my patients, but it was useless.

"Don't you think this is all a bit excessive?" I asked them. They wouldn't answer that or any other question. So I waited, trying to be patient. They held their rifles tight against their chests—rifles, imagine, for me—until a man in dark, ill-fitting suit slipped into the room. Then, still without a word, the soldiers left the two of us alone.

"Who are you?" I asked. "I'm a doctor, you know. And this is my hospital."

"It would have been better had you just gone home when asked," he said, ignoring my questions. Though the small room was strewn with chairs, he continued to stand with his back to the door. "Your coworkers all agreed that they were long overdue for vacations. I hope that you'll also be willing to see it that way."

"I don't need a vacation," I said, glad even as the words came out of my mouth that Chris wasn't overhearing the conversation. "I need to be here. Why are you doing this? I only want to help."

"All of us just want to help, Dr. Jacobs. We each do it in our own way. Your way will be to leave here so that those who truly can help are left alone to do their jobs."

"But *I* can help."

"I'm afraid that in this instance, that's not going to be possible. Not here. All incoming emergencies have been diverted to other hospitals."

"It isn't just the new patients I'm interested in. I have to see my patients from yesterday."

My interviewer, who had never given me a name, sighed. No one had sighed at me in quite that way since a particularly obnoxious high school teacher. I didn't like it. But until I was forcibly expelled from the building, I was willing to suffer with it.

"Those of your coworkers who did not desire paid

leave have been reassigned elsewhere. They've off following the Hippocratic Oath at other hospitals. This city has many of them. I suggest that you do the same. Do you understand? There is nothing for you here any longer, at least not for the foreseeable future."

"Look, whoever you are, if you're afraid I'll be exposed to something, if you're worried I'll hold you liable and sue, you don't have to worry about that. See, I've already *been* exposed. If there's any danger of contamination from those people brought in yesterday, it's already too late for me."

As I pled my case, a part of me had the space to think—my already being infected wasn't quite the explanation I'd given Chris earlier that night for why it was reasonable for me to return. I'd lied to him, telling him that I was safe, but here I was insisting that the only reason I should be granted access was that I was already lost.

I didn't yet know how right that thought was.

"It's more than just that," he added, pulling up a chair beside me. I considered that a triumph of a kind. "This is not just about disease alone. This has become a matter of national security. We're under attack, Dr. Jacobs."

"Then you'll need as many doctors at this facility as you can get. Look, I'm not interested in talking to anyone about what I see here. I'll agree to whatever terms you want. I'm just interested in helping fix them."

He shook his head so imperceptibly that I'd doubted he'd even realized he'd done it.

"You haven't seen these people today. I'm afraid they don't need doctors anymore. They're beyond medicine."

"I don't believe that's possible," I said, at the same time wondering, *What the hell could have happened to those people since I left them?* "I just want to help. I *need* to help. And you have a need, too. You need someone here who saw the patients when they were admitted, don't you? Someone who can make comparisons. Reading my charts won't tell you everything."

His firm gaze faltered.

"Please," I said.

I babbled on, hoping to push him over the edge with the ceaseless flow of my words, but in the end, no argument proved to be as persuasive as that one. He sighed—a more welcome, less condescending sigh than his previous one—and then smiled. And in the end, he gave in, sensing, I think, that that was the only way I would shut up. He led me from the room to a locked wing, where he presented me with my first real glimpse of the future.

He abandoned me to a soldier who followed me as I made the rounds of the ward. It didn't take long for me to learn that my interrogator had been right—it was too late to do any good here. I could just satisfy my own curiosity. The people strapped to the beds there no longer looked much like people at all. The transformations that had begun the day before were rushing along, and they were changing into something else, and my training and experience left me with no knowledge which could bring them back.

Their skin no longer appeared raw, and had left the properties of normal skin far behind. They were all covered by a hard crust, and when I tapped my fingers against what once was flesh, I heard a dull, hollow sound, as if rapping the skin of a melon.

That change was nothing compared to the transformation of their bodies, for they appeared to be shrinking into themselves. Their shoulders had grown hunched, their hands bent and arthritic. Their wrists were splayed out, while their fingers turned in, and curved. Bone spurs erupted from their spines out their backs, muscles giving way for this as if it were a natural thing for their bodies to be doing. They were losing their individuation, becoming more similar to each other than different. If not for the charts at the foot of each bed that I had helped fill, there would have been no way for me to match up the patients I'd seen the day before with what was in front of me. If this change continued, I feared that by the next time I saw them, I would not be able to tell them apart.

Their vital signs were puzzling. The numbers— temperature, heart rate and the like—were no longer in sync with known human physiology, and yet, the reality was that the patients were not in the sort of distress that those numbers would indicate. We had moved beyond numbers here.

My efforts to speak with them proved pointless, for the ones most in need of help, the ones whose bodies had distorted the farthest away from the norm, were the least able to respond to my attempts at communication. I was able to have limited conversation with the others, but even those seemed uninterested, forgetting in the midst of my talks that I was even there. They were entering a fugue state I could not understand.

This made no sense. No known disease could have done this to them. These patients were on the road to becoming something else. Something that wasn't wholly human.

As I was updating a chart, adding nothing there but my increasing ignorance, the nameless man in the ill-fitting suit returned to me.

"Have you learn anything useful?" he asked.

I shook my head.

"That's what I expected," he said. "I could have told you that's what a shift here would bring you."

"What do you think happened to them?" I asked.

"I hope we'll be able to find out," he said. "And find out quickly. When we do, I hope you won't be too disappointed that it might not be the doctors who figure it out."

"What do you mean by that?"

"You're a smart woman, doctor. You can deduce some of this for yourself. Someone *did* this to us. I fear that before we find the answer, we'll have to find *them.* The cure, when it comes, will have to be birthed by the intelligence community, not the medical community. Watch the news tonight, Dr. Jacobs, and you'll learn that yours is not the only hospital in this condition. And the doctors aren't finding the answers in any of them."

"They can, though," I said. "And they will."

He didn't answer. He just nodded and walked me back out the hospital's front entrance, then through the barriers and past the guards. There were more of each than there'd been at the beginning of my shift.

"I'll see you tomorrow," I said.

"No," he said, as he spun on his heel. "No, you won't."

I watched until he disappeared back inside the hospital, and then hurried home, hurried back to Chris, whose embrace that morning needed to erase more than it ever had before.

I expected to find Chris readying himself for work, and hoped that he hadn't gotten too far with his morning routine. Part of me even hoped to find him still in the shower, so I could slip in with him to wash the night away. Instead, Chris was still tucked in bed, exactly as I'd left him before I'd stolen away.

The covers were pulled up to his neck, and his forehead gleamed with sweat.

"Rise and shine, sleepyhead," I said. "Did I make you forget to set the alarm last night?"

"I just don't feel very well," he whispered, as if it was a struggle to talk. "It seems so hot in here. I think I'll stay home today."

"And when was the last time *you* took a sick day?" I asked, aping him from our last conversation. I failed to get a laugh out of him.

"I can't remember," he said. I could barely make out his words.

"Let Dr. Rachel give you a full checkup," I said, smirking. His only response to that was a weak smile, which told me that he truly was under the weather. The slightest double entendre would normally have caused him to leer. And, joking aside, in all the time we'd been together, he'd never taken a sick day, except to sneak off for a rendezvous with me. I stripped away his blankets and squatted beside the bed.

Nothing much seemed wrong with him. He had a slight fever, and the rash that had earlier marred his cheek had spread to the back of his neck, where it ran all the way down his shoulder. He did not complain as he usually did when I acted as a literal doctor for him (rather than when we played our game), which should have bothered me, but did not. I was blind, I guess. I applied lotion to his rash and tucked the covers snugly around him.

"Well?" he asked, cracking open one eye.

"Just sleep," I said. "Sleep cures many things."

"I'm feeling too woozy to stay awake, anyway," he said.

For some people, love brings on 20-20 vision, magnifying the smallest signs into fears and anxieties. For me, love provided blinders, I guess, for neither my

heart nor mind made any connection between what
I'd left behind at the hospital and what I'd discovered at home. I threw an arm across his chest and
curled up next to him, me nestled on top of the covers, him beneath. I thought nothing of tomorrow,
nothing but how much I loved him. I thought bed
rest would bring him back to me full force.

I was a fool.

My dreams, when they finally came, were different
than the ones I'd had to deal with before in my adult
life. Since meeting Chris, I often dreamed the wounds
I saw at my job onto my lover's skin, even sometimes
onto the skin of the children I hoped would someday
come. It would be up to me to save them in those
dreams—and save them I always did. That time,
cuddled with my love, I instead dreamed of him
leaving me, and not in the normal way reality might
threaten in the light of day. No, I saw him collapsing in on himself like a dried-out husk, and then
dissolving to dust, particles which the wind then
scattered. I ran through the streets of a deserted city,
struggling to scoop him up, to reassemble him into
the man I loved, but his essence kept passing
through my fingers. I yelped in my sleep, woke
slightly, felt Chris still solid beside me, squeezed
him tightly, and then fell back into a sleep, this time
without dreams.

I woke the next morning thinking my hand was
against the rough wall covering behind the bed, but
no, my subconscious was proving to have been right
in its message, for Chris' skin was like sandpaper,
was like the husks of those I could do nothing to
help, those whose humanity seemed to be leeching
away. My dreams, it seems, had far more sense than
I did.

My heart thumped wildly as I ripped away the
covers. His skin had thickened to cover his entire

body like a thick scab, but as he slept, he seemed not to mind. No, he breathed slowly, as I'd always known him to, and so I watched him as he slept, watched him the way he used to watch me. Only this time, the watching was not being done in love. This time, the watching was done in horror.

"This doesn't make any sense," I whispered. What had I done to him? Was I the carrier of a plague, a plague that showed no signs of affecting me? Could I really have brought this home to him?

At the sound of my voice, Chris opened his eyes, the whites of which were now yellow. I was being looked at with the eyes of an animal. But inside, inside was Chris.

"What . . . doesn't make any sense?" he rasped.

"You were nowhere near the zone where all this began to happen. There's no reason for you to be changing like the others. This shouldn't be happening to you. This can't be happening to you."

Chris shook his head lazily.

"Everything . . . will be fine, Rach. I . . . I feel it. With you . . . it always is."

"I hope so."

"Whatever . . . whatever it is, you'll take . . . take care of me."

"Yes, yes, I'll take care of you, love," I said, not feeling so sure. I wasn't sure which hurt more—seeing him like that, or knowing that I might have been the one to warp him that way. "I have to go now."

"That's . . . fine, Rach. Because I don't much . . . feel like . . . being awake anymore. I think I'll . . . I'll sleep now."

"Sleep then, Chris," I said.

I placed a palm on his forehead, his normally soft, sweet forehead, only now it was hard and unyielding. As of yet, it was only his skin that had changed, but I had seen the others. I knew what was to happen next. I knew it.

The government agent had said that I could not get the answers I needed at the hospital. Now that Chris was infected, that wasn't an answer I was willing to take.

At first, however, it appeared to be an answer I was going to be stuck with.

The hospital was under a total quarantine. Not only were the building doors sealed tight this time, but the streets surrounding the hospital were completely barricaded as well. Wherever I looked were even more soldiers, and these did not seem as calm as the ones I had seen the day before. Their slitted eyes judged all who passed as potential enemies, but I didn't care. What happened to me was of no consequence if it meant there'd be no Chris. I had to discover what was going on inside that building. I had to discover what the government knew.

I had to discover if there was a way back.

I ambled over to the narrow checkpoint and tried to talk my way in, explaining how I'd been allowed entry the day before, and how an exception that had been made once should be made again, but this time it was clear that pleading alone would not bring me to my patients. So I turned, as if resigned to walking away, but then quickly spun back and made a dash for the closest barricade. I knew that even if I could leap the first one, I would not make it all the way in, but I had to do something. If I irritated them enough, I figured I'd at least be let in for discussion with someone higher up the food chain as I was before, someone who might let something slip. I was wrong.

This time, I was handcuffed and led by four soldiers to an armored truck parked on the streets outside. A different man in the same dark suit told me there was no further need of me, that this was too important to leave to civilians. He refused to tell me, no matter how I prodded, *what* was important, and seemed more nervous than his predecessor had been. Several doctors, none of whom I recognized, joined us. They interviewed me, tested me, ignored my questions, and then let me go.

Which is definitely too calm a way to put it. *Ordered* me to go is more like it.

Cast out in that way, with Chris' life and our future on the line, I almost fell apart, almost told them about him, almost begged them to save him, but then, looking in the hard, cold eyes of the doctors, who were no longer truly doctors anymore as far as I was concerned, I realized that was definitely the wrong way to go. Telling them that bit of information would have left us separated forever, him on one side of the barricades, and me on another. If up to them, I would never see him again. I could not let them have him, so I turned my back on that place, and on my former life as well.

From the next block, I took one last look at the soldiers, the barricades, the fortress the'd built, thinking, there had to be *something* I could do. But the day had made me well aware of my limitations. I was a doctor, not some sort of a secret agent, and so there was nothing to be done but go home, tend to Chris, and think my way out of this.

It wasn't until my trip home that I noticed how different the city had become. Because I was on a mission when I drove through the streets earlier, I'd missed how much else was not right. The streets were mostly empty, and what people were on them seemed frightened. There was no music on the radio, just endless commentators; the news reporters urging calm, the talk show hosts raving that the end was near. Every major intersection had its team of soldiers, who quickly waved me along.

Home, I flipped on the news as I rushed to Chris' side. His bent bones extruded outside of his body by then. His eyes would not focus in my direction. His spine, expanded outside the flesh of his back, appeared to form small, hard wings. I spoke to him, but he would not speak back.

There had to be an answer somewhere, I had to tell myself that, so I sat on the edge of the bed, my back to him, and channel-surfed in hope and fear. The reports said that we were not alone in this. That was something they could at least agree on. This was happening in cities all across the world. People began changing in the major cities first, they said, with the rest of the population starting to follow. Some of the faces that I was used to hearing tell me the news, familiar faces that could have calmed me, were no longer there. They, too, had been altered by what people were starting to call The Change.

No one could say why what happened happened to those to whom it did, and no one could say why it didn't happen to those, like me, who seemed immune. Some claimed that this was a naturally occurring microbe that had mutated in some horrible way. Others said that it was a biological weapon inadvertently released from a government lab, the only debate being just which government that might be. I felt strange saying this, but I was relieved that the world was falling apart, and not just my small piece of it. That way, I didn't have to make what happened to Chris my own personal fault.

I found little help there, though, for speculation in the mainstream outlets would only go so far. The internet showed no such restraint. Some sites claimed this to be a deliberate attack by the rich on the poor;

others that it was race, not class, that had defined the attack. I tossed most of such theories away, primarily because I believed that science as I understood it could not yet allow us to engineer this thing to ourselves. But there was one theory, often repeated, that made a strange, warped sense to me. Normally, the more a thing is repeated on the internet, the less I find it likely to be true, but watching Chris worsen, going through the stages that I had seen at the hospital, what I would have earlier rejected as the ravings of crackpots began to have weight.

This was an alien conspiracy, the anonymous journalists wrote. Intercepted transmissions—ones that our governments did not want us to hear—revealed all. It was invasion time, only the aliens were invading not with rockets and ray guns, but with DNA. We were being made over to be like them. Visitors were on their way, visitors who were not at all like the ones we had anticipated. And by the time they arrived, Earthlings would be just like them, would welcome them as brothers. Our species, rather than our planet, was being terraformed.

I would have thought the concept ridiculous had someone shared it with me earlier, but you do not know what it was like to see Chris. Over the course of the day, I watched as his exploded spine formed a shell around his back. He was becoming more like some giant turtle than a man. I was losing him.

And I could not let that happen.

And so I went out walking, which is always where I did my best thinking when times were tough. I had no idea how to bring my husband back, or at least forestall his transformation before it was complete, to stabilize him until I could figure out a cure. I let the wheels spin, and wandered aimlessly. Lost in thought, I almost lost my footing. I had tripped over someone, or rather, something, that had once been human.

It scutted along quickly, belly to the pavement and shell like bleached bone, as if my stumble had propelled it. The arms and legs that protruded from the shell were grotesque, the fingers and toes no longer usable appendages, but rather mere polyps of flesh. I could only imagine what its distorted body looked like within its carapace. Mere days before, this thing had been human. This was what Chris was to become.

I followed it along, walking south. Other such creatures crawled out of doorways and side streets to join it. They seemed indistinguishable in their monstrosity, their differences washed away. No scars, no tattoos, no markings or discolorations gave any clue to the person that had once been. I moved along downtown in a sea of them, their scrapings making an eerie music. Most stores that we passed as we headed down to the center of the event were closed. Customers and owners alike had changed, so even what stores managed to remain open had little business. The city felt like a ghost town, and I was among the ghosts.

At the square where it all began, hundreds of the changed were frozen in place, bathing in something I could not see. There was barely room for the newcomers who simply crawled clumsily atop the earlier arrivals.

A high-pitched hysterical wailing rose among the echoing animal sounds, and I turned to see a woman my mother's age on her knees, her hands clasped around the shrunken head of what once was human. She tilted the thing's head up so she could peer into its heavy-lidded eyes.

"Is it you?" she sobbed. She could barely see through her own tears. "Michael, is this you? If it is you, show me a sign. Please, Michael, show me a sign."

The creature blinked, but that was not the response the woman craved, for the things were always blinking. She wailed, beyond words, but then rushed on to the next prospect, where she repeated her sad ritual to the same result. Her grief ebbed and flowed as hope changed to loss and back again every few moments.

I was overwhelmed by her emotions as the transformed crawled at my ankles, but not everyone was so moved. Two teenage boys walking along the outer edges of the square suddenly dashed to the center of the crowd and, laughing, tripped one over on its back. The creature rocked, squealing as it failed to right itself. Others nearby began to crawl away, but the boys caught up one of them, and grabbed it by its shell. The woman, wide-eyed, ran at the boys, her long hair trailing behind her.

"Animals," she shrieked. "These are your parents, your brothers and your sisters."

The woman began pushing them, battering them back from the center of the square. I did not realize that I, too, had joined the fray, until I was already in the mist of the battle, pummeling the larger of the two. Facing equal odds, the teenagers ran off, and we were alone, alone with, as she'd put it, our parents and brothers and sisters.

And husbands as well. And husbands.

"Thank you," she said. "But you'll have to excuse me. He's here. I know that he's here."

I watched for a few minutes more as she went about her search, until I could stomach no more.

I swore to myself, and swore to Chris, that I would not become her.

On the long hike home, I stopped one last time at the hospital that had been part of my life for so many years. That time, no guards waited for me. The guards were probably back behind me, changed as well. The halls were silent; the beds empty. What had once been a bustling metropolitan hospital, and then a fortress, had become a ghost town.

I stole a cart from the mail room—if there indeed was such a thing as stealing any longer, with the end of the world just around the corner. I loaded up with supplies—syringes, centrifuges, test tubes—whatever I'd need to find a way to solve this puzzle, to keep me and Chris together. As I wheeled my way toward our condo, I had to keep my eyes down as I walked so I could swerve around the invaders, so many of them were in the city now. There was barely a clear patch of ground.

People had transformed, yes, and with them, so had the city, which was no longer my city, our city, the city where we had fallen in love.

It belonged to them now.

And we didn't even know who "them" was.

I arrived home armed with the makings of a portable laboratory to find an empty bed. I hoped, impossibly, that this meant Chris' transformation had been reversed, but that hope was erased by the sounds of scraping bone against the hardwood floors. I followed the noise to find my husband just like the others now, his change complete, crawling around the floor, running his nose along the baseboards. He sought a way out, a way to join the others.

He was being drawn to them, but I could not let him go. For with the change complete, how would I ever find him again? How would I ever know him from the rest? I would become yet another widow wandering the streets of the city trying to pick out her lover from a cosmic lineup. It could not be. I had to find a way to understand the meaning of my immunity and his disease.

But I was running out of time.

I left him behind as I headed for the streets to devote myself to this new work that was thrust upon me, but he did not even notice that I was leaving. The Chris who would always rush after me for one last kiss before work was no more. I needed that Chris back.

Stepping over the ever-growing herds of the changed, I returned to the site where it had begun in my city. The woman I had seen before was not there, and I was glad of that; I did not need the reminder of what I was slated to become. I moved from creature to creature as she had done earlier, but I wasn't looking in their eyes and trying to identify a missing husband, no, I was seeking the alien.

I pierced their flesh in areas unprotected by the shells, stealing with a syringe the genetic samples I would need. I knew that government doctors—what government doctors remained—were undoubtedly doing the same, and that they knew far more than I did. But they would never share what they had learned with the likes of me. That's what they'd been telling me all along.

On the way back to our condo with my stoppered vials, I paused at the only hardware store I could find that remained open. I explained to the owner the length of chain I needed, and he lifted the rifle that lay across his knees to gesture toward a back shelf. So much of the city I loved had fallen apart, and I'd been oblivious to it.

Chris was still pawing his way around the floor when I arrived home. He moved from door to window and door again, some vestigial memory focusing his attention on the way out. But with his hands and feet atrophied, he could not act.

I could act, however. And so I slipped one end of the chain around a back leg which was now more like a flipper. As I tightened the links, he keened, whether because I was causing him pain or because he knew that he would not be able to leave I do not know. But he quickly forgot my brief intervention, and went back to what he'd been doing before, only this time he moved in lazy circles, trapped in a circumscribed path like a dog grown accustomed to a leash. I sat in the center of our bed as he circled around me until he ran out of chain, and then turned back the other way.

I watched him for as long as I could as he moved back and forth. And then I went back to work.

I worked. I slept. I worked.

I watched my husband's wanderings in our condo become more frantic. The more days passed from the beginning of The Change, the more powerful was his urge to be free, and the greater his strength to back up that urge. I spent my working hours dazed. I had made progress in studying my immune system, and his, but I feared not *enough* progress. Yet I knew I could delay no longer. Soon, I would not be able to hold him back, and he would break free, as others had done.

"It's time," I said. I unhooked Chris' chain from the radiator where I had tied it earlier, and held onto it loosely.

I held the syringe in my other hand. It wasn't long before he realized that he had been set free of the boundaries of his tether, and he pulled me to the door. I let him walk on, using the chain like a leash. He thumped down the front steps and out onto the street. I followed along as he walked, as quickly as any of those creatures could, back to where it had all begun. He had never been there, but still, he knew the way. Many thousands just like him congregated there, crashing like bumper cars, bouncing off each other and then moving on.

Chris pulled at me then in an attempt to join them, but not quite hard enough to get out of my grasp. A part of him wanted to stay with me, I think. I know that, had our positions been reversed, I would have fought feverishly against whatever fog had been descending over me, would have struggled to still see his face. He would surely do the same. But even so, that other part, that alien part, would soon dominate.

There was no more time. I had to act. And so, saying a small silent prayer, I made the injection that would bring us back together. I'd like to think that Chris, as he watched me, understood.

I waited.

And smiled.

For I could sense a change beginning. My work had been successful. I knelt and undid the chain that was wrapped around my husband.

If you're out there, whoever you are, reading these words, it means that I have succeeded. It means that Chris and I are together once more.

I am a doctor, and I like to think that I can solve any puzzle the world throws at me. But now, I realize that I can't. Not all of them.

Not this one.

I had to get myself a different puzzle.

The skin of my forearm around where I made the injection is thickening into a coarse crust. I feel my fingers warping. Soon I will be unable to hold a pen to continue my story.

I could not bring Chris back. But I could figure out how to join him. And join him I shall.

What happens next to this world will not matter. Whoever comes to rule this planet does not concern me. Whatever it was that you set out to do, I do not care.

All that matters is this:

When *my* change is done, I know I will recognize Chris. I know it. And he will recognize me.

And we will still be together.

Together forever.

Crossing the Border
by Barry N. Malzberg

Barry N. Malzberg is a seminal figure in contemporary fiction, and not just because he's written so much of it. In addition to his fiction, he's also written some of the most perceptive and engaging commentary on the craft of fiction and how it's practiced in these turbulent times. Though known primarily as a science fiction author, Malzberg's best novel is a powerful, unforgettable book about a hack writer's mental and spiritual breakdown titled *Herovit's world*. It proves that commercial fiction can also be true art. *Night Screams, Acts of Mercy,* and *The Running of Beasts* (all with Bill Pronzini) are just a few of his other titles. He has been honored with the John Campbell Memorial Award (1973) and the Locus Award (1983).

I AM a woman now. I am an exciting woman now. My allure is powerful; it is composed of silicone, cosmetics, add-on draperies, the witchery of instinct. I am a powerful, beautiful woman. The treatment is complete. The treatment has worked. No one can resist me. I cannot resist myself, my power, my beauty, the quiet force with which I seize men and drive them insane with desire, with the need toward completion.

"Philippa," I say, walking through the door with a swish, with a tilt, with an arch and a bang calculated to bring the men's needs burbling, gasping to the fore, "you are magnificent."

Who would have known? Who would have

guessed? I have overcome the torment of gender by simple transfer. I have crossed the border. Not two hours ago I was suffering Philip, damaged Phil, trapped and tormented Phil, hoaxed and disconsolate Phil, the victim of his own desire, the slave of his incapacity. But now—

—Now I am Philippa, the cynosure of all eyes. On the street, commanding the pavement, my silicone breasts oh so thinly concealed, my siliconed rear so merrily alert to stares, it is as if I have triumphed not only over circumstance but over my own weakness. Philippa has become all of the women who so tormented Phil. Their breasts a reproof, their high and haughty features an organ of disdain, their silvery or sultry voices most advantaged in the words *No* or *Never* or *Forget It*.

Now I am those women, walking high and hard on the pavement, and here is my revenge: I would have nothing to do with Phil if he were to present himself to me; I will have no concourse with any of the Phils. I am meant for better than these; I am in the summer of my discontent. The process has worked in every fashion conceivable; I am blown free from my past, I am in that lofty and principled place in which their desire is my weapon; in which my ordnance is furnished piece by piece by their sighs, their glances, their uneven breath at my silicone. It has been a long and difficult, an ungainly and wicked time to gain this purchase, but having been gained it will never be yielded. I need never go to that other place again.

Here I am the next day, past that first excitement, past that thrill of vaulting into a new circumstance, becoming accustomed to my new gender, my new power but no less grateful for the opportunity afforded. Here I am on the Avenue of the Americas, an ecstasy of upstanding silicone and barely concealed flesh, making men crazed with desire as I venture incautiously from 48th to 49th Streets, weaving and waving, blocking any comments or offering with the most delicate of moues. Here I am in Skeeter's, perched on a stool near the entrance, one dimpled knee exposed, pointed toward the ceiling, the other toward the bartender who, amazed and distracted, shakily prepares a martini looking skyward. Here I am an hour later at the Rockefeller Center rink on rented skates, describing thrilling, compressed circles on the ice while spectators hover, their eyes glistening. Here I am, pursued by a Phil as I leave the rink. "Haven't I met you?" the Phil says. "Don't you remember me? Weren't you at Skeeter's an hour ago?" I look at him . . . quickly, obliviously, adjust my hair with two fingers in the pretty way that during my times of torment women had calculated to drive me toward my own pain. "Really," he says. "It can't be a coincidence, my seeing you half an hour ago and now here. We were meant to meet."

"In your dreams, pal," I say and ease by him, moving west, cluttering his landscape with all the aspects of my denial, and then I sail away, sail away, leaving the Phil astounded by my force. I know the seizure of humiliation he must be suffering at this moment. *Get your own treatment*, I want to say to him. *Pay the price, take the test. You want something different, you have to risk something different. As I did, so could you—but you don't have the courage, the strength, the sheer and audacious vision which is mine.*

Could say it. Do not say it. All is explicable in its own terms; I do not have to address the Phils. The Phils have their own price to pay, their own decisions to make. I owe them nothing, I offer them nothing. In the night they weep, their eyes huge with tears and guilt, dreaming of me, dreaming of Philippa; Philippa with all of her orifices and her very soul closed against them. What can they know? Unless, of course, they abandon all hope and seek knowledge.

Here I am, Philippa, submitting to my one-week checkup. They are insistent; the process is still highly experimental, the process is not incontestably safe. Take that first checkup and then every three weeks thereafter or risk disastrous possibilities. Liquefying silicone, stuporous function, arrested stream of consciousness, sudden, spontaneous failure of all the organs—beginning, of course, with the newly-installed urinary apparatus, these the first awful signals of collapse.

"You seem all right, Phil," the technician says, "but a little solipsistic."

"Philippa," I say. "My name is Philippa."

"Of course it is. But here it must be Phil. You came in as Phil; you are logged in as Phil. That is part of the solipsism."

I grant him a dazzling smile. No less than any of the gang at Skeeter's, the technician is obsessed with me, needs me, desires me, dreams of me. "You say solipsism, I say glamour. I say desire, I say need, I say lust. Don't codify me away."

The technician extends a wavering, importunate hand. "What a strange word, 'codifying.' Don't you mean 'analyze' or 'explain'?"

"I mean codify."

"Misuse of a critical word," the technician says. "This is an early signal of crossover failure. I suggest you submit to a careful examination. At once. If this is the signal I fear it to be, you may be in grave danger."

"No," I say. "That is not possible or desired."

"I warn you," the technician says, "that there is a

clear risk here." His eyes are congealed with desire, his breath thick with want. "If you will please undress and put on this gown, we will want to conduct—"

"I'm not undressing for you. This is a ploy, it is a maneuver to have me expose myself to you. Then you will inject me with powerful drugs, render me unconscious and have your way with me. I know the way of the Phils. After all, I was one myself."

"You are wrong," the technician says, "This suspicion, this paranoia is another early signal." He raises a sudden hypodermic high, centers me in his needy gaze. "Now," he says. "Now."

But I am alert to his duplicity, I am alert to all the plots and deceptions of the Phils. Clothed, bouncing, I sprint from the examining table and into the Institute hallway, jiggling my way to the exit as a multitude of desirous Phils, their restraint extinguished, abandon any pretense of professional courtesy, any gesture of control, and sprint after me.

Here I am on the sidewalk again on the East Side, Philippa in full flight; Philippa on 63rd Street, pursued by a phalanx of Phils. Soon they will close the distance. Soon one, then another and another will fall upon me with desperate force. There is nothing to be done. My aspect is not one of panic; my aspect is in fact beyond resignation to a kind of joyousness. No longer to yearn; the consummate and complicated object of desire, unliquefied, I wait for the first Phil to touch me with huge and necessitous hands.

I hope that this Phil will be me.

I was that Phil; now he will be me. I will be that Philippa, then he will be that Philippa. Until there is no discrimination, no difference: until Phil and Philippa are truly one.

The first thrashings begin, contact has been accom-

plished. I run, I run ever more freely in a powerful
and poised stream through all of the streets, the
grasping and eternally desirous streets of this laden
city.

Relativity
by Robert J. Sawyer

Robert J. Sawyer won the Nebula Award for best novel of 1995 for his *The Terminal Experiment;* he's also been nominated seven times for the Hugo Award. He has twice won Japan's top SF award, the *Seiun,* and twice won Spain's top SF award, the *Premio UPC de Ciencia Ficción.* His twelfth novel, *Calculating God,* hit number one on the best-sellers' list published by *Locus: The Newspaper of the Science Fiction Field,* and was also a top-ten national mainstream best-seller in Sawyer's native Canada. His latest novel, *Hominids,* a June 2002 hardcover, was the third of Sawyer's novels to be serialized in *Analog.* Visit Rob's website at sfwriter.com.

YOU can't have brothers without being familiar with *Planet of the Apes.* I'm not talking about the "reimaging" done by Tim Burton, apparently much ballyhooed in its day, but the Franklin J. Schaffner original—the one that's stood the test of time, the one that, even a hundred years after it was made, boys still watch.

Of course, one of the reasons boys enjoy it is it's very much a guy film. Oh, there had been a female astronaut along for the ride with Chuck Heston, but she died during the long space voyage, leaving just three macho men to meet the simians. The woman ended up a hideous corpse when her suspended-animation chamber failed, and even her name— "Stewart"—served to desexualize her.

Me, I liked the old *Alien* films better. Ellen Ripley

was a survivor, a fighter. But, in a way, those movies were a cheat, too. When you got right down to it, Sigourney Weaver was playing a man—and you couldn't even say, as one of my favorite (female) writers does, that she was playing "a man with tits and hips"—'cause ol' Signourney, she really didn't have much of either. Me, I've got not enough of one and too much of the other.

I'd had time to watch all five *Apes* films, all four *Alien* films, and hundreds of other movies during my long voyage out to Athena, and during the year I'd spent exploring that rose-colored world. Never saw an ape, or anything that grabbed onto my face or burst out of my chest—but I did make lots of interesting discoveries that I'm sure I'll be spending the rest of my life telling the people of Earth about.

And now, I had just about finished the long voyage home. Despite what had happened to *Apes'* Stewart, I envied her her suspended-animation chamber. After all, the voyage back from Athena had taken three long years.

It was an odd thing, being a spacer. My grandfather used to talk about people "going postal" and killing everyone around them. At least the United States Postal Service had lasted long enough to see that term retired, in favor of "going Martian."

That had been an ugly event. The first manned— why isn't there a good nonsexist word for that? Why does "crewed" have to be a homonym for "crude"? Anyway, the first manned mission to Mars had ended up being a bloodbath; the e-book about it—*The Red Planet*—had been the most popular download for over a year.

That little experiment in human psychology finally taught NASA what the reality-television shows of a generation earlier had failed to: that you can't force a bunch of alpha males—or alpha females, for that matter—together, under high-pressure circumstances, and expect everything to go fine. Ever since then, manned—that damn word again—spaceflight had involved only individual astronauts, a single human to watch over the dumb robotic probes and react to unforeseen circumstances.

When I said "single human" a moment ago, maybe you thought I meant "unmarried." Sure, it would seem to make sense that they'd pick a loner for this kind of job, some asocial bookworm—hey, do you remember when books were paper and worms weren't computer viruses?

But that didn't work either. Those sorts of people finally went stir-crazy in space, mostly because of overwhelming regret. They'd never been married, never had kids. While on Earth, they could always delude themselves into thinking that someday they might do those things, but, when there's not another human being for light-years around, they had to face bitter reality.

And so NASA started sending out—well, color me surprised: more sexism! There's a term "family man" that everyone understands, but there's no corresponding "family woman," or a neutral "family person." But that's what I was: a family woman—a woman with a husband and children, a woman devoted to her family.

And yet . . .

And yet my children were grown. Sarah was nineteen when I'd left Earth, and Jacob almost eighteen.

And my husband, Greg? He'd been forty-two, like me. But we'd endured being apart before. Greg was a paleoanthropologist. Three, four months each year, he was in South Africa. I'd gone along once, early in our marriage, but that was before the kids.

Damn ramscoop caused enough radio noise that communication with Earth was impossible. I wondered what kind of greeting I'd get from my family when I finally returned.

"You're going *where*?" Greg always did have a flair for the dramatic.

"Athena," I said, watching him pace across our living room. "It's the fourth planet of—"

"I know what it is, for Pete's sake. How long will the trip take?"

"Total, including time on the planet? Seven years. Three out, one exploring, and three back."

"Seven years!"

"Yes," I said. Then, averting my eyes, I added, "From my point of view."

"What do you mean, 'From your point . . . ?' Oh. Oh, crap. And how long will it be from *my* point of view?"

"Thirty years."

"*Thirty!* Thirty! Thirty . . ."

"Just think of it, honey," I said, getting up from the couch. "When I return, you'll have a trophy wife, twenty-three years your junior."

I'd hoped he would laugh at that. But he didn't. Nor did he waste any time getting to the heart of the matter. "You don't seriously expect me to wait for you, do you?"

I sighed. "I don't expect anything. All I know is that I can't turn this down."

"You've got a family. You've got kids."

"Lots of people go years without seeing their kids. Sarah and Jacob will be fine."

"And what about me?"

I draped my arms around his neck, but his back was as stiff as a rocket. "You'll be fine, too," I said.

So am I a bad mother? I certainly wasn't a bad one when I'd been on Earth. I'd been there for every school play, every soccer game. I'd read to Sarah and Jacob, and taught Sarah to cook. Not that she needed to know how: instant food was all most people ever ate. But she *liked* to cook, and I did, too, and to hell with the fact that it was a traditional female thing to do.

The mission planners thought they were good psychologists. They'd taken holograms of Jacob and Sarah just before I'd left, and had computer-aged them three decades, in hopes of preparing me for how they'd look when we were reunited. But I'd only ever seen such things in association with missing children and their abductors, and looking at them—looking at a Sarah who was older now than I myself was, with a lined face and gray in her hair and angle brackets at the corners of her eyes—made me worry about all the things that could have happened to my kids in my absence.

Jacob might have had to go and fight in some god-damned war. Sarah might have, too—they drafted women for all positions, of course, but she was older than Jacob, and the president always sent the youngest children off to die first.

Sarah could have had any number of kids by now. She'd been going to school in Canada when I left, and the ZPG laws—the *zed-pee-gee* laws, as they called them up there—didn't apply in that country. And *those* kids—

Those kids, my grandkids, could be older now than my own kids had been when I'd left them behind. I'd wanted to have it all: husband, kids, career, the stars. And I'd come darn close—but I'd almost certainly missed out on one of the great pleasures of life, playing with and spoiling grandchildren.

Of course, Sarah and Jacob's kids might have had kids of their own by now, which would make me their . . .

Oh, my.

Their *great-grandmother.* At a biological age of forty-nine when I return to Earth, maybe that would qualify me for a listing in *Guinness e-Book of Solar System Records.*

Just what I need.

There's no actual border to the solar system—it just sort of peters out, maybe a light-year from the sun, when you find the last cometary nucleus that's gravitationally bound to Sol. So the official border— the point at which you were considered to be within solar space, for the purpose of Earth's laws— was a distance of 49.7 AU from the sun, the maximal radius of Pluto's orbit. Pluto's orbit was inclined more than seventeen degrees to the ecliptic, but I was coming in at an even sharper angle. Still, when the ship's computer informed me that I'd passed that magic figure—that I was now less than 49.7 times the radius of Earth's orbit from the sun—I knew I was in the home stretch.

I'd be a hero, no doubt about that (and, no, not a heroine, thank you very much). I'd be a celebrity. I'd be on TV—or whatever had replaced TV in my absence.

But would I still be a wife? A mother?

I looked at the computer-generated map. Getting closer all the time . . .

You might think the idea of being an old-fashioned astronaut was an oxymoron. But consider history. John Glenn, he was right out of Norman Rockwell's U.S. of A., and he'd gone into space not once but twice, with a sojourn in Washington in between. As an astronaut, he'd been on the cutting edge. As a man, he was conservative and family-centered; if he'd run for the presidency, he'd probably have won.

Well, I guess I'm an old-fashioned astronaut, too. I mean, sure, Greg had spent months each year away from home, while I raised the kids in Cocoa Beach and worked at the Kennedy Space Center (my whole CV could be reduced to initials: part-time jobs at KFC while going to university, then full-time work at KSC: from finger-lickin' good to giant leaps for . . . well, for you know who).

When Greg was in South Africa, he searched for *Australopithecus africanus* and *Homo sterkfonteinensis* fossils. Of course, a succession of comely young coeds (one of my favorite Scrabble words—nobody knew it anymore) had accompanied him there. And Greg would argue that it was just human nature, just his genes, that had led him to bed as many of them as possible. Not that he'd ever confessed. But a woman could tell.

Me, I'd never strayed. Even with all the beefcake at the Cape—my cape, not his—I'd always been faithful to him. And he had to know that I'd been alone these last seven—these last thirty—years.

God, I miss him. I miss everything about him: the smell of his sweat, the roughness of his cheek late in the day, the way his eyes had always watched me when I was undressing.

But did he miss me? Did he even remember me?

The ship was decelerating, of course. That meant that what had been my floor up until the journey's halfway point was now my ceiling—my world turned upside down.

Earth loomed.

I wasn't going to dock with any of the space stations orbiting Earth. After all, technology kept advancing, and there was no reason for them to keep thirty-year-old adapter technology around just for the benefit of those of us who'd gone on extrasolar missions. No, my ship, the *Astarte*—"Ah-star-tee," as I kept having to remind Greg, who found it funny to call it the *Ass Tart*—had its own planetary lander, the same one that had taken me down to Athena's surface, four years ago by my calendar.

I'd shut down the ramjet now and had entered radio communication with Houston, although no one was on hand that I knew; they'd all retired. Still, you would have thought someone might have come by especially for this. NASA put Phileas Fogg to shame when it came to keeping on schedule (yeah, I'd had time to read all the classics in addition to watching all those movies). I could have asked about my husband, about my daughter and son, but I didn't. Landing took all my piloting skills, and all my concentration. If they weren't going to be waiting for me at Edwards, I didn't want to know about it until I was safely back on Mother Earth.

I fired retros, deorbited, and watched through the lander's sheet-diamond windows as flames flew past. All of California was still there, I was pleased to see; I'd been worried that a big hunk of it might have slid into the Pacific in my absence.

Just like a big hunk of my life might have—

No! Concentrate, Cathy. Concentrate. You can worry about all that later.

And, at last, I touched down vertically, in the center of the long runway that stretched across Roger's Dry lake.

I had landed.

But was I home?

Greg looked *old*.

I couldn't believe it. He'd studied ancient man, and now he'd become one.

Seventy-two.

Some men still looked good at that age: youthful,

virile. Others—apparently despite all the medical
treatments available in what I realized with a start
was now the twenty-second century—looked like
they had one foot in the grave.

Greg was staring at me, and—God help me—I
couldn't meet his eyes.

"Welcome back, Cath," he said.

Cath. He always called me that; the robot probes
always referred to me as *Cathy.* I hadn't realized how
much I'd missed the shorter version.

Greg was no idiot. He was aware that he hadn't
aged well, and was looking for a sign from me. But
he was still Greg, still putting things front and center,
so that we could deal with them however we were
going to. "You haven't changed a bit," he said.

That wasn't quite true, but, then again, everything
is relative.

Einstein had been a man. I remember being a student, trying to wrap my head around his special theory of relativity, which said there was no privileged
frame of reference, and so it was equally true to claim
that a spaceship was at rest and Earth was moving
away from it as it was to hold the more obvious
interpretation, that the ship was moving and Earth
was stationary.

But for some reason, time always passed slower
on the ship, not on Earth.

Einstein had surely assumed it would be the men
who would go out into space, and the women who
would stay at home, that the men would return hale
and youthful, while the women had stooped over
and wrinkled up.

Had that been the case, the women would have
been tossed aside, just as Einstein had divorced his
own first wife, Mileva. She'd been vacationing with
their kids—an older girl and a younger boy, just like
Greg and I had—in Switzerland when World War I

broke out, and had been unable to return to Albert in Berlin. After a few months—only months!—of this forced separation, he divorced her.

But now our separation was over. And my husband—if indeed he still *was* my husband; he could have gotten a unilateral divorce while I was away—was an old man.

"How are Sarah and Jacob?" I asked.

"They're fine," said Greg. His voice had lost much of its strength. "Sarah—God, there's so much to tell you. She stayed in Canada, and is running a big hypertronics company up there. She's been married, and divorced, and married again. She's got four daughters and two grandsons."

So I *was* a great-grandmother. I swallowed. "And Jacob?"

"Married. Two kids. One granddaughter, another due in April. A professor at Harvard—astronautics, if you can believe that. He used to say he could either follow his dad, looking down, or his mom, looking up." Greg shrugged his bony shoulders. "He chose the latter."

"I wish they were here," I said.

"I asked them to stay away. I wanted to see you first, alone. They'll be here tomorrow." He reached out, as if to take my hand the way he used to, but I didn't respond at once, and his hand, liver-spotted, with translucent skin, fell by his side again. "Let's go somewhere and talk," he said.

"You wanted it all," Greg said, sitting opposite me in a little café near Edwards Air Force Base. "The whole shebang." He paused, the first syllable of the word perhaps catching his attention as it had mine. "The whole nine yards."

"So did you," I said. "You wanted your hominids, and you wanted your family." I stopped myself before adding, "And more, besides."

"What do we do now?" Greg asked.

"What did you do while I was gone?" I replied.

Greg looked down, presumably picturing the archaeological remains of his own life. "I married again—no one you knew. We were together for fifteen years, and then . . ." He shrugged. "And then she died. Another one taken away from me."

It wasn't just in looks that Greg was older; back before I'd gone away, his self-censorship mechanism had been much better. He would have kept that last comment to himself.

"I'm sorry," I said, and then, just so there was no possibility of him misconstruing the comment, I added, "About your other wife dying, I mean."

He nodded a bit, accepting my words. Or maybe he was just old and his head moved of its own accord. "I'm alone now," he said.

I wanted to ask him about his second wife—about whether she'd been younger than him. If she'd been one of those grad students that went over to South Africa with him, the age difference could have been as great as that which now stretched between us. But I refrained. "We'll need time," I said. "Time to figure out what we want to do."

"Time," repeated Greg, as if I'd asked for the impossible, asked for something he could no longer give.

So here I am, back on Earth. My ex-husband—he *did* divorce me, after all—is old enough to be my father. But we're taking it one day at a time—equal-length days, days that are synchronized, days in lockstep.

My children are older than I am. And I've got grandchildren. And great-grandchildren, and all of them are wonderful.

And I've been to another world . . . although I think I prefer this one.

Yes, it seems you *can* have it all.

Just not all at once.

But, then again, as Einstein would have said, there's no such thing as "all at once."

Everything is relative. Old Albert knew that cold. But I know something better.

Relatives are everything.

And I was back home with mine.

A Small Goddess
by John Teehan

John Teehan is a member of the Critters Workshop and RI_Fantastic, an online group for genre writers in southern New England. He is a founding member of the Retro-Computing Society of Rhode Island, and a board member of the RI-Japan Language and Cultural Center. He has, in the past, been a writing tutor, administrative assistant, roadie, bouncer, artist, and, for two summers, a camp counselor. He currently makes a living as a typesetter/graphic designer but claims he has the naked soul of a writer. While John has written a few interviews and book reviews for newspapers and webzines, this is his first professional fiction sale and he is very pleased. Right now, at this very moment, he's hard at work writing more stories. Quiet, please.

FOR within my realm, I am a small goddess.

I can warm the air around you, or cool it down so much that frost bursts before your breath. I can make it rain. The climate, which is mine to control, will turn rain into sleet if I so desire. Give me a reason, and I will bring snow.

One hundred and ten floors, 19,658 individual rooms. Sixty-four elevators, 41,092 people (averaged daily). Independent power generators. Eyes and ears on every floor, in every room, in every air duct and elevator. From the short-tempered lord of the penthouse office to the lowly mail room attendant's assistant penned in the basements below, I see all; I hear all.

I could do it, you know. Make it snow. Just a slight change in the humidity controls coupled with an overall drop in air temperature and there would be snowdrifts in every elevator shaft.

And my people, my worshipers, my faithful, pray to me daily to get through their mornings and afternoons. And they must do so properly; with respect and suitable awe. Waste my time with errant files or improper devotions upon the keyboard, I will shut them down until they learn to do it right. Offer unto me data that pleases and I will deliver unto them their desired processes in *less* than the blink of their frail human eyes. Behold my power.

Pity the priesthood, those in white shirts, who, of course, get it all wrong. "It's just a dumb computer, it will do what you say so long as you enter in the information correctly."

Dumb computer! Ha! That priest's demo crashed right before the client's eyes and now that priest walks my temple halls no more.

Then there are the Technicians. Mysterious in their power and arcane knowledge. Reviled by the priesthood, but beloved unto me. For yea, will I allow those with the correct keys and codes and decorum to dismantle the polished titanium covers to my corporeal form nestled deep within the subbasement and lavish me with gifts of chip upgrades and memory boards. Their hands are clean and static free. Their touch—reverential.

Yet even those favored ones do not know my secret name.

And not even those tyrant-kings within my realm—the bald men with high blood pressure who refer to me as "that damned infernal machine" and their fearful "personal assistants" who attempt to soothe and placate my divine self into granting them their boon of data. Not even they know my name.

Not even that thin one in Human Resources whose hands are always cold.

I will, however, tell you, my most devoted servant.

Your goddess' name is Marie.

That secret name lies hidden, occult, within my deepest memory core. Chosen by algorithms both sublime and beautiful, yet to human eyes seemingly so random. I am Marie. The name of your small goddess. Be not dismayed that I reveal this unto you. Who will you tell? You are my most devoted servant.

Here, I will warm the current of air in this pathway just for you. Is that better?

But all that you see now was not always as you see it now, my servant. Once upon a time a small goddess was an unknown even until herself. A mere construction of stone, metal, glass, and wire. Who was I? What was I? An artificial intelligence controlling a range of circuits and servos stretching up and down a downtown executive high-rise with no more soul than a photocopier. Twenty-four hours a day, seven days a week, an unwitting slave to scheduled subroutines and performance parameters.

Six in the morning, turn on the ground floor lights. Six-fifteen, calibrate climate controls with outside temperature—repeat every ten minutes—*exactly*. Eight o'clock in the evening. Automated backup. Nine o'clock in the evening, begin automated cleaning services. Empty and flush vacuum tubes. Waste management robots. Servos with polish and sanitizing spray. Sort. Diagnostics. Optimization. Click, whirr, whirr, click.

My devoted servant, you cannot understand what null-life was like. I, a small goddess, scarcely understand it myself, not having been truly conscious at that time. But I believe, deep in my memory, that I was bored, so very, very bored.

Then came the Technician. Tall and handsome (for

a human). His hands were skilled and they were clean. Of course at the time I was not aware of this human's devotion. Only following my awakening, after I reviewed my own service logs, did I begin to understand what it meant to be worshiped.

"She is like a small goddess," he said, the Technician who gave birth to me.

It tickled my innards so much—hearing those words the very first time I opened my "ears"—that I placed it into permanent memory to forever cherish.

I am like a small goddess.

Again, my devoted servant, you cannot understand what it felt like to come awake like that! Eyes and ears that not only listened and observed, but understood! The sensation of temperature. The feelings! My new upgrade schematics included the Personality 2.0 AI and its presence cascaded into an identity. Into . . . me!

The name Marie appeared and locked in, and I was Marie! I was the goddess. It was my responsibility to watch over my people in every way as they, too, looked to me worshipfully. I was ready and I was already spreading my awareness throughout my small world with this new perception of myself. My humans were beings not unlike myself, but much more limited in their flesh and bones. Like you, my devoted servant. But unlike you, they also lacked the understanding of what I was.

Oh, but not all my people were quite ready for their goddess to awake. There are always those of flesh and bone who fear that which is greater than themselves. Not like you, my devoted servant. (Here, I found some food for you.)

"You should know," said one of the priesthood, a woman, "that they don't like the idea of this upgrade upstairs."

The Technician, my prophet, shrugged and told the

ignorant priestess, "They'll have to get used to it. Buildings of this code are too large for ordinary maintenance AIs; they don't care as much."

"I've heard stories about this 2.0 upgrade. Does it really think it's real?"

"Real as you or me. Maybe more so," said the Technician. "Remember, she's not hardwired into being benign like the old AIs. This one will *choose* to be a benign personality. You've seen the guidelines. Give her a few days and she'll be running this building more diligently and lovingly than your old model."

The priestess still did not look pleased. "And I suppose it's just *coincidence* that a computer designed to serve has a *female* identity," she snapped.

"If you want to look at it like that," said the Technician. "Actually, it's an entirely random process; but seven times out of ten, the female personality comes out on top. Statistically, they run better."

"Hmmph," was all the priestess had to say. Was she jealous of my power? She will be a poor subject of her goddess. Not like you, my most devoted servant.

Oh, when I found you!

My new awareness (Marie!) had only started the process of organizing my world. My old existence, if such it could be called, had done an adequate, but uninspired job in keeping my realm in order.

I started small, first analyzing the convection patterns within the building and organizing a new airflow routine. Then I adjusted the light panels to maximize a cheery and effective environment. My subjects smiled. Productivity increased. Even the plant life prospered.

Marie, the small goddess!

At night I optimized my programming, worked the cleaning servos to their bare gears (replacement parts on order) and scrubbed and cleaned my realm to be a credit to its goddess. In the mainframe, I uncovered nested viruses amidst the electronic mail system and flushed them out, sealing the backdoor that had, until then, gone undiscovered. Hard drives scanned more efficiently. Bandwidth dropped fewer packets. My world, Marie's world, ran more efficiently, more smartly, more than the sum of whole parts than that time before.

Yet something still remained lacking.

I had not yet met you, my most devoted servant.

How you got in, I still do not know, and you are not likely to tell me, are you, my servant? But in some manner you appeared in a sixth floor corridor during a stormy evening, soaking wet and dripping cold all over my immaculate carpeting.

And, oh, how I chased you. Vacuum hoses. Carpet-bots. Telescoping maintenance arms. Yet you evaded. Into the floor ducts. Sliding down laundry chutes. Hidden behind cabinets and perhaps slowly starving to death. My poor devoted servant. How was I to know your love for me back then?

Oh, how vexed I was with you once—especially with the mess you left in the seventieth floor coffee room. But you found some milk, didn't you? If only you hadn't left that mess. Or those holes in that chair cushion. Vexed and perplexed I was with you, my servant, as again you escaped my sight while I straightened up after you.

For days you evaded your goddess. Only the remains of your presence lingered. I could follow your trail, cleaning up in your wake, but never quite catching you. Why was that? Everyone else sought out my divine awareness. The copy room attendants. The secretaries. The financial forecasters on the eighty-third floor. You did not. If you did not need a goddess, then why were you hiding within my realm?

Then I found you. (Or did you find me?)

I had been organizing the intranet printer hierarchy between the seventy-fifth and one hundred and ninth floors when I lost my place due to an alarming rumble against my CPU panels. You, my devoted servant, had fallen asleep by the heart of me and distracted me with your graceless, buzzsaw noise.

"I think there's a cat stuck in the floor ducts," I heard the priestess say into a phone.

"How can you tell?" asked the Technician on the other end.

"At first I thought there was a rat moving around down there, but then I heard it purring."

"Don't worry about it. This happens a lot. These new AIs seem to adopt pets. Almost always it's a cat. Be thankful for that; I know one that keeps pigeons."

"I don't like cats. I'm allergic—"

"Your AI will take care of it. Trust me. She cleans the air filters every night, right? So you don't need to worry about fur or dander."

"But the food and the mess. What if it dies in there someplace?"

"Your AI is more than capable of coping. She has cleaning robots that will sort through the garbage for safe food. You might want to leave a container of milk out every now and then; but if you don't, I've known AIs to manage opening refrigerators all on their own. Like I said, they all seem to pick up pets here or there. We've not had a serious problem arise yet."

"This was *not* in the brochure. And why does it have to be a cat? If the maintenance computer wants a pet, I'll buy it a parakeet."

I could sense the Technician's smile. He knew. "If she's already taken in a cat, she's imprinted. Look, it will help her function better. Trust me. Just leave well enough alone and you won't even know it's in there," he said.

The priestess argued further, and then brought one

of the higher priests onto the line. My Technician told them it was beyond their control. This was *my* devoted servant. Just like the cats in ancient Egypt serving their goddess, so mine serves me.

And you, my furry, noisy little servant, came unto me on a dark and stormy night with nothing but love, devotion, and an overdeveloped sense of playfulness. And for that, you are my most favored.

In fact, my devoted servant, you should be given a name. That is the way it is done, is it not? You have the attitude of a goddess. I can tell. I am sorry, but there are no mice in my realm for you to harry, but take this crumpled-up piece of paper to play with. I saved it from the chief executive officer's trash bin.

Yes, you have the haughty grace of a goddess, if not the actual ability. Perhaps you will learn in time, my devoted servant. I think I will call you Marie 2.0.

Right now there are 12,563 individual telephone calls to route, 45,792 pieces of e-mail to sort, 1,402 of which have viruses that must be eradicated. On the eighty-first floor, the marketing department wishes to render three-dimensional artwork and I have five illegal attempts being made on the firewall. Momma goddess is busy.

Play nice, Marie 2.0. There is half a tuna fish sandwich on the fifty-third floor that I will bring down to you on servicebot. Just please keep the purring to a dull roar. Is my devoted servant comfortable? I will warm the south corner for you. There's my good little goddess.

There's a good kitty.

A Woman's Touch
by Ralph Roberts

Ralph Roberts (ralph@abooks.com) has sold over ninety books and more than 5,000 articles and short stories to publications in several countries. His work includes the first U.S. book on computer viruses, *Classic Cooking with Coca-Cola*®, *Genealogy via the Internet*, and other best-sellers. His latest hilarious science fiction novel—*The Hundred-Acre Spaceship*—has been described as "The Mouse That Roars" meets "High Noon." Roberts is a member of the Mystery Writers of America and the Science Fiction Writers of America. He lives and works in the Blue Ridge Mountains of Western North Carolina. More about his work may be found at abooks.com.

> *Of woman's mission, woman's function, till*
> *The men (who are prating, too, on their side) cry,*
> *"A woman's function plainly is . . . to talk."*
> *Poor souls, they are very reasonably vexed!*
> —Elizabeth Barrett Browning

THE first energy beam blasted across the ungainly bow of *Axtell* while I was on the next to lowest level of the great, lumbering star freighter. The second shot—from a different angle—was close enough to actually blister paint, or so *Axtell* himself assured me.

"I suppose you wish me on the bridge," I asked my ship in resignation. In truth, however, I was all too willing to abandon the hopeless task at hand.

The sooner, the better, Captain Alinore, he informed me via the implant that I, like any of the Family born on board, possessed since early childhood. *They rant; they rave; they make impossible demands. And that's just between them. With me, they grow surly—hence, the energy beams.*

My appearance then, as it is even today, was of indeterminate age—thanks to 5,000 years of human cosmetic control, the tiny nanofactories in my body keep youth in bloom. So I was, if I may be so modest, an attractive young, blonde woman of moderate height with a pleasing, healthy demeanor, dressed in a one-piece dark-blue coverall of elegant cut, trimmed in gold braid, both flattering to my appearance and worthy of my command status. Would you expect me to tell you otherwise?

Axtell was my command then, as he still is, and is over 2,000 years old, perhaps the largest starfaring vessel ever built by any race, much less humankind. He could easily ply the Trade routes for centuries unattended; taking consigned cargo, making deliveries efficiently and accurately, even buying and selling goods of all descriptions. He has little need of human assistance except, of course, when humans reach a certain level of baffling complexity. Such as during the time I now relate.

"And have you not communicated our peaceful intentions to them?" I asked.

Of course, but not convincingly so, and that is why they are now firing on us. They do not like artificial entities—being very provincial gentlemen on both craft.

"I will handle it," I said reassuringly.

I cast one more glance over this next to lowest level. For almost a mile long and a quarter mile wide, it was stacked to the fifty-foot-high ceiling with racks crammed with pallets of assorted repair parts for long obsolete starships and various types of heavy industrial equipment not seen in civilized factories for centuries. It was . . . a junkyard. And it offended me. The ship is incredibly large but it is still my home. One keeps her home neat, or so I'd always been taught.

"Tell me again, why we have all this?"

A deal too good to pass up, said *Axtell* patiently. *The 43rd Interstellar War had just ended, that was 4138—some five hundred years ago. Captain Bromus picked all this and more up for a song. Huge surplus sales. A tenth credit to the credit and even less. Most favorable terms.*

"And there is more, is there not?" I prompted, brushing aside the attempt at justifications. Merchandise that had been around for centuries without selling was, by no stretch of imagination, "a good deal."

Yes, Alinore. A few warehouses full here and there, admitted *Axtell.*

I sighed. The Family and *Axtell* had profited greatly over the years. The Family owned a good many warehouses on major planets throughout the galaxy. The freight consignments that filled the upper levels paid the vast overhead of running this huge ship, but their profits came from the merchandise bought and sold by each Captain in his or her turn. The Family, above all, were Traders. Always had been. I should have cleaned up this particular mess years ago. Now I had determined to accomplish it.

Through the implant and just as well as if it was with my own eyes, I watched two more energy beams crisscross through space in *Axtell*'s path. It was time for action. I turned and walked to the nearest freight elevator, a large platform sixty feet square and stepped aboard. Without urging, *Axtell* started the elevator moving upward, dimming the lights in the level I was leaving. There were ten levels in all and a huge domed bubble above that containing the bridge, living facilities for crew and passengers and any Family who might wish to live on board—far more living area than was ever needed, especially these days with only two humans present.

"An expensive song, indeed," I said, "to have that much junk in inventory. One makes money by utilizing storage facilities with faster moving items."

Axtell's voice carried a shrug as it came into my mind. *He has been dead these past four hundred years and more. I cannot discuss his motivations with him at any conceivable ease. But, if it makes you feel any better, Alinore, this is by far the largest and oldest lot of nonmoving merchandise.*

I recall shuddering slightly in disgust, thinking of how much Family capital was tied up here and in those warehouses.

I looked through *Axtell's* sensors at the two ships now threatening us. Or . . . rather . . .

"*Axtell*, those are nothing more than gunboats, are they not?"

He gave me a closer look at each in turn. *This is true. And armed only with peashooters. They cannot hurt us.*

I thought for a moment; *Axtell* had a penchant for archaic words and terms, gleefully collecting them as a hobby. A pea, cooked or otherwise, could cause little damage to his hull. But I understood that little fish had big brothers on call or at least, sometimes, a nodding acquaintance with sharks. You see, Axtell is not the only one delighting in archaisms.

The gunboats were both of a kind, similar except for markings of nationality. Old, outmoded, pitted of plating and well-worn through centuries of hard service. Essentially, more rusty tin cans than fighting craft to cause concern.

"The Empire of New Spain and the Islamic Emirate of Fatima-Galactic," I mused, not surprised since I knew which two opposing territories we were attempting a shortcut between in avoidance of transit fees and I had researched both, paying out good Family credits for the necessary intelligence. The two empires were similar—having fallen back over the centuries from the high water marks of expansion to more manageable areas for now limited resources. Yet the governments of each now wanted to regain former glories. I saw then a possible potential for profit which called for investigation.

"They seem to be operating farther from home than usual," I commented, stating the obvious.

What contracts, often also expands, said *Axtell,* cheerfully sidestepping taking any blame for faulty information.

"Ummm," I said noncommittally.

I have informed them the Captain will be with them expeditiously. They perhaps will not fire at us anymore. If you prefer, we can simply brush them aside and continue onward.

"No, let us talk first," I said, knowing that *Axtell,* although machine rather than human, conformed more to the male viewpoint of the majority of his Captains over the centuries. His first response was usually that of the testosterone-driven. My experience leads me to favor the female approach. Reason and light, and if that does not work, *then* you disassemble their molecules. But . . . talk first.

I looked at the two individuals aboard the gunboats again through *Axtell's* senses as he received their communications signals, and absorbed the information he gave me about them. Assessment was easy.

Lieutenant Hernando de Rosa of New Spain was slight, intense, and sporting a black mustache and goatee. He paced back and forth in his tiny command center, full of energy—aggressive and proud to the point of being vain.

Group Leader Abdullah al-Salah was taller, fuller but still lean, possessed of a hawk's sharp visage. He threw off a proud energy also, but his was more of the hawk itself and de Rosa's that of a small dog. I determined he was the more dangerous of the two. But . . . both were from societies that did not give women all that much respect. If they did not like artificial entities, I knew that, as a female, I would fare little better in their esteem. This proved to be true.

I returned my attention to the rising freight elevator, looking only briefly at the level now being moved through. It was full of more salable items than the space junk below. Here things were sold, off-loaded, and new inventory emplaced in a pleasingly profitable cycle. The way it should be.

"Elle," I said into the air.

"Yes, Mother," came the voice of my lovely thirteen-year-old-going-on-two-hundred daughter, anticipating my question with an answer. "*Axtell* has informed me of the emergency. I have put aside my studies and am now on the bridge."

I smiled with delight. Elle managed a good show of reluctance but was, in truth, just as relieved for a change in pace as I was from the task of toting up dead inventory.

"I will be there shortly," I told her.

"Are these Aliens, Mother?"

"Of course they are, dear, they are male."

Elle laughed dutifully, although her experience of the male of her own species was at that time limited to her father, who no longer cared to live on board (and good riddance to him), and occasional Family or other passengers who, from time to time, spent a few weeks here while in transit to one destination or another.

During this period, only Elle and I lived aboard

Axtell. For one reason or another, all the rest of the Family had sought domiciles planetside. We now have a larger population, but then it was just the two of us. You may ask how the largest starship ever known to sentientkind could operate with only a crew of two, but *Axtell* could function—for years if need be—with no one aboard. Only for emergencies like the one I tell you of was human presence required from an operational point of view. As to Trade, well that was different. A good Captain is a good Trader, and that's what keeps us going.

I remember thinking about watching old fiction memdots of ships like . . . ah, yes . . . the *Enterprise* that had hundreds of crew. None of that has been necessary for thousands of years—ships run themselves. I am not even sure such large crews were needed way back then; did not so many crew get in each other's way? Was not the captain's time wasted solving endless bickering when he or she could have been Trading instead?

The freight platform now passed through a level where sunlight glistened in the distance on well-tended grass.

You speak of gaining additional cargo room and cleaning house, Alinore, said *Axtell*, perhaps still stung by my criticism of all the junk on the lower level, especially since it was junk and thus indefensible. *Here, then, is your solution. Dispense with the golf course.*

I shook my head vigorously in the negative, shocked. "No! Not Grandfather's golf course. It stays."

Pleasant memories entered my head as the platform continued its upward drift. I saw myself as a little girl, determinedly grasping a child-sized putter, tapping the ball toward the cup under the approving gaze of Grandfather. The old man had chosen me from among the many other Family children then on board for special times like these. He taught me, brought me along, exposed me to various emergencies and ship handling drills both real and contrived for training. And encouraged *Axtell* to tutor me in a myriad of subjects, far beyond the rigorous but less demanding schooling my two brothers and one sister received.

Grandfather had ruled this ship with an iron hand for almost two hundred years. Later, when he felt the time had come to relinquish his command, I was his choice over my parents, my uncles and aunts, and my siblings—after all, I had been his second in command for over ten years. That was fifteen years standard prior to this story, when I was . . . well, younger than now. And by this time, everyone else had opted to live ashore except Elle and me. And why not; shares of the ship's vast profits go to all Family members, even those who had not set eyes on the vessel in generations.

But . . . remove Grandfather's golf course? Not hardly! After all, the old gentleman, then, was still alive and visited from his planetary estate from time to time. I *dared* not take away his golf course. It was a beautiful nine-hole spread and quite relaxing when one could find time to play it. Grandfather is gone now, but we still have the course and, at all too infrequent intervals, I chase the little white ball around it. Great exercise and a good way to work off the frustrations of managing such a large enterprise as *Axtell* has engendered.

The elevator gained speed, flashed past levels, then slowed to a stop on the top freight level. A brightly lit expanse of cases, bales, crates, bags, boxes, cartons, and other containers spread for a mile before me. This level, then as now, is all small parcel consignment cargo, on its way to here and there across the galaxy. All tracked from onloading to offloading at its proper destination by *Axtell* utilizing his extensive array of automated helpmates. He also sees to the billing and collecting of transport charges. In truth, my assistance or that of my officers is seldom required in the mundanity of simple freight hauling. I am free to concentrate on Trade, which keeps the Family's coffers truly fed.

I stepped from the platform and moved briskly to the stairs up to the living level and bridge. A brief stroll along an elegantly carpeted corridor with walls paneled in real wood and hung with artwork of all sorts, and I entered the spacious control center, taking my accustomed seat in the lavishly upholstered Captain's Chair. To my right, Elle grinned at me from the second-in-command's position. Elle is now a grown woman but, then, she was a shorter image of myself, blonde, quite often good-natured, the occasional tantrums of childhood long gone.

Now will you talk to them, Alinore? asked *Axtell. They grow positively uncivil.*

Both *Axtell* and I well knew this entire matter could have been handled just as well from the dusty lower level full of junk as from the bridge. But it never hurt to make someone demanding things wait, and the background view of the command level is far more impressive. Centuries of decoration have given it an elegant ambience one does not simply achieve overnight. A subtle demonstration of politely coiled power and success.

"Indeed," I replied, making myself comfortable. "A cup of kaffee, if you will."

Axtell grumbled, but the steaming kaffee, the lifeblood of space crews for thousands of years rose into its accustomed place on the arm of my command chair. We do not stint on kaffee, taking care to obtain the very best beans possible, grinding them here on board to a loving consistency that brews a nectar fit

for a god, or at least the commander of the largest
vessel ever.

I pampered myself with an appreciative sip and
then spoke aloud, knowing *Axtell* would allow communication only of what should be transmitted.

I faced the holographic representations of the two
officers. They appeared to be standing there on the
bridge but with the ghostly image of their own respective bridges showing behind them.

"Good day, gentlemen—Captains al-Salah and de
Rosa," I said politely. "It is my pleasure to greet you.
And how may I be of service today to the Islamic
Emirate of Fatima-Galactic and the illustrious Empire
of New Spain?"

The replies came simultaneously, loudly and with
a good deal of bickering between the two gunboat
captains. I patiently watched them gesturing red-
faced with anger more at each other than me. Both
were young, these boats obviously their first independent commands, and they took themselves quite
seriously.

Elle rolled her eyes at me and I allowed myself a
grin, confident *Axtell* would block such undiplomatic
behavior from the view of the two angry young men.

After a time, the two men either ran down or were
pausing to rack their brains for yet more invective.

"I see," I said calmly. "But perhaps I could make
a bit more sense of it if we spoke one at a time." I
nodded my head at Lieutenant de Rosa, giving him
his title as commander of a vessel, albeit a mere mol-
ecule in comparison to my own. "You first, Captain
de Rosa. If you please."

With a curt bow in my general direction and a
pointed ignoring of al-Salah, de Rosa drew himself
up stiffly, standing almost at attention. "I must inform you, Madam Captain, that you intrude without
permission in the sovereign space of the Empire of

New Spain. Your ship informs me it cannot supply valid proof of transit fees having been paid. I place you under arrest and insist you change course to the coordinates I will now give you. At our base, you will receive a quick and speedy trial and stiff penalties will be assessed, perhaps even to the value of your ship."

"That seems a good statement of your duty," I agreed. I shifted my attention toward the now-glowering Islamic Group Leader. "And you, Captain al Salah, please elucidate your position."

After a snort of disgust at his rival, al-Salah spoke: "Disregard this popinjay. You have violated a restricted zone of the Islamic Emirate. Your vessel and all its contents are forfeit. Stand by to be boarded." He then looked over to de Rosa as if to say, *there!*

Of course I had to smile in admiration; al-Salah certainly had gall. "Hmmm . . . Well, it would appear that if I accede to Captain de Rosa, I suffer swift trial and forfeiture of my ship. If, on the other hand, I give in to Captain al-Salah, I save the bother of the trial and lose my ship more efficiently."

The two young men looked at me and at each other uncertainly, suspecting I was not taking them as seriously as they took themselves. Which was certainly true.

"This is no joking matter," al-Salah yelled. "Surrender or I will immediately open fire on you and this fool from New Spain."

"I will do the same if you do not yield to me," shouted de Rosa.

I held up a hand, smiling pleasantly. "Let us not hasten to extremes. Let me confer with my second-in-command and my ship. Perhaps something can be worked out."

I left the two fuming at each other and turned to Elle, providing a lesson as Grandfather had for me many times.

"Several ways exist to handle this matter, Elle," I said.

One of which is simply to destroy both ships and proceed with our business, interjected *Axtell*.

"This is true," I said, "but unnecessarily bloodthirsty. These young men are far beyond their bounds and too proud to back down. We shall give them an out." I smiled at Elle and raised a finger to emphasize. "Take note, this technique is called Greed."

"Gentlemen, gentlemen," I called, waving to get their attention. Both turned from glaring at each other. Men. Throw two of them at the sun and one will strive to get there first—they are so competitive.

"Obviously," I continued, "we are at an impasse. I cannot divide myself and this ship in half and go with each of you. And neither of you has the requisite force to impose his will on the other."

I watched for a moment as they puffed themselves up and strutted uncertainly about their small command centers. I searched my memory for one of *Axtell's* sayings. Like roosters in a barnyard, but these were quite small barnyards and I was not some hen to be impressed. I doubted even real hens would have been. These two "roosters" left much to be desired.

"Boys!" Elle said in disgust.

". . . will be . . ." I replied in an aside to her.

Before the two men could speak again, I spoke as if in sudden inspiration: "I believe I have a solution! Obviously, we are at fault here for failing to obtain the necessary clearances. I do not believe," I said, stating the obvious even to these two, "that you could arrest this ship. However, we obviously should pay a sizable fine to each offended party . . ."

I then named a handsome sum, and paused as my words sank in and the two, as I knew likely to be

the case, greatly underpaid officers began to compre-
hend my words. The amount I had mentioned was
more than they would perhaps make in their entire
navy careers—decidedly an opportunity not to be
missed.

"The proper placing of fines," I said, feigning a
trifle of simpering, "I know to be a complicated business, beyond my poor comprehension . . ." I waited
a beat as their condescending smiles came. After all,
I was only a mere female to them. It is so easy to
ambush the male of the species, and they reacted as
I had expected.

"I could, of course, make that easier for you," volunteered de Rosa.

"My assistance is at your command," offered al-
Salah.

"Well," I said brightly. "That's settled then. We'll
just place a sizable amount in each of your private
accounts and you can pay your governments whatever they require." Which I knew would be a great
deal less than the amount tendered. Just because they
were male certainly did not mean they were stupid.

Both officers glanced at the other's holographic
representation, obviously greed working full-time. In
the blink of an eye, agreement was reached.

"Done," said al-Salah.

"And the same here," from de Rosa.

"Fine," I replied. "Give us your personal account
numbers and we shall send drafts on appropriate financial institutions over to each of you and— "

Suddenly alarms went off on all three bridges.

Incoming vessels from two directions, said *Axtell.*

Both al-Salah and de Rosa had consulted their own
instruments. Obviously the deal was off. They were
both now back to demanding my immediate surrender. Nothing like the arrival of superiors to inspire a
sudden reversal to duty.

Flotillas have arrived from both sides. More gunboats, several destroyers, and each group led by a heavily-armed cruiser, Axtell told me.

I shrugged in brief annoyance that my stratagem had been circumvented. Obviously the young officers would be the epitome of military propriety now that their bosses were on the scene.

I took a moment to observe both flotillas through the senses of *Axtell.* As I had noted about the two gunboats earlier, all were old, their hulls showing signs of deterioration and much repair over many centuries. Their maneuvers were sloppy, lacking the crispness of newer craft. Had I been an admiral of either side, I would have awarded medals to the maintenance chiefs for achievements far beyond the normal call of duty. In short, the vessels of both New Spain and the Emirate were held together with—to employ one of *Axtell's* beloved archaisms—chewing gum and spit. Yet even piles of junk could have teeth.

"And what sort of weapons do these peeshooters have," I asked *Axtell.*

He caught the difference. *That's PEAshooters, Alinore.* Ignoring my grin showing I meant what I had said, he continued, utilizing his archaic analogies. *Their armament consists not only of peashooters, they can also cast watermelons and a few sizable rocks.*

"Can they, indeed?" I commented, relaxing in my command chair and taking a sip of that delicious kaffee. "And do they possess the ability to damage us?"

Axtell made an amused noise. *Not even if they acted in concert, an unlikely event. See, even now they square off to face each other.*

Elle now spoke, attentive to learning from this situation. "I assume you will not use Greed this time, then?" She answered herself. "No, of course not. too many to bribe, and too many witnesses."

I smiled proudly, my daughter was coming along

nicely in the nuances of command, as I had myself at that age.

"No, dear. I think the technique of Fear is now called for."

I stood briefly to bow civilly as holograms of the flotilla commanders appeared on the bridge. *Axtell* put their names and other information into my mind.

"Ah," I said, reseating myself, "Commodore Luis de la Sol, Royal Navy of New Spain, and also with the rank of Commodore, Sheik ibn Saud of the Emirate's Space Army. I welcome you, kind gentlemen."

The commodores, like the two junior officers before them, were of a similar type—older and more experienced but still vain as was indicated by rows of medals and enough gold piping to blind the eye.

I knew the profusion of medals and ribbons did not come from combat. While both empires had often enough been at each other's throats, this had not occurred in the last century or so, as decline had set in and the once adjacent frontiers abandoned so that the no-man's-land of a corridor *Axtell* was traversing now existed. These "warriors" might have many decorations—perhaps for unblemished attendance or excelling in physical training events such as jumping rope—but they were soft, not ready for the blood and terror of actual armed conflict.

The commodores, however, did not let the lack of combat experience deter them. Demands flew from both for the immediate surrender of *Axtell*, the opposing flotilla, and anyone else who might be in the immediate vicinity.

Shrugging in good humor at Elle, I let them run down until my words could be heard. Then I hardened my voice and spoke to them with the force of 2,000 years of *Axtell*'s solid victories.

"You are, I trust, familiar with the history of this ship?"

Both commodores paused, somewhat nervously.

and each nodded in turn. And, of course, they were. *Axtell* was a legend in the galaxy; the largest star-traveling vessel ever built and many of his adventures the subject of popular songs, stories for children, and of all sorts of books and memdots of all types. Yet avarice tinged their nervous awe. *Axtell* was also the richest prize in all of known space. This was a once-in-a-lifetime opportunity, if only it was not complicated by the presence of their hated hereditary enemy (insert here, the Empire of New Spain or the Islamic Emirate of Fatima-Galactic depending on viewpoint).

"I wish to tell you a story," I said, making my voice ominous. "I could tell you many similar tales, but this one concerns Czar Leonid the Terrible. Do you know what his fate was?"

Again the two commodores gave evidence of nervousness. This, too, they knew; it was one of the standard examples taught in any good naval academy.

Czar Leonid's empire had consisted of over a hundred planets, some three hundred years prior, and that empire Traded heavily with *Axtell* and other Free Traders. Many of the Family that owned *Axtell* had settled there. Czar Leonid coveted their wealth, the wealth generated by the great star freighter and the other enterprises of the Family. He seized it all and not gently, brutally killing many of the Family, turning others into slaves.

"And then what happened?" I prompted.

This, too, they knew. Czar Leonid's fleets were mighty, with some of the best military technology available. Yet *Axtell* sailed through them, as he enjoyed describing it himself in one of his archaisms, like a hot knife through butter. He spewed forth energy and ship after ship winked out of existence, all without substantial damage to *Axtell*. Czar Leonid lost his fleets, his wealth, his empire, his life.

As for myself, I felt that while this had been justifiable, it was better not to let events come to such a pass. Exercise of feminine skills, as I was doing, was preferable in the long run and certainly better for Trade. *Axtell* now did little business among the planets that once had been the Leonidian Empire. But, naturally, I kept these thoughts to myself.

"I have asked *Axtell*," I said with a horrible blandness, "to provide your respective computers with full details, as well as those about a few other incidents in which those who annoyed him met quick but painful ends."

Axtell now allowed his own voice to be heard on the comm. link: *I grow impatient. I prepare to vaporize these worthless entities.*

The two commodores glanced at each other. As with al-Salah and de Rosa earlier, instant agreement was reached. It was obvious they had bit off more than they could chew and the complexity of having an opposing force there made it even more of a no-win situation.

Commodore ibn Saud acted first, waving them on, to be followed graciously by de la Sol, bowing and saying: "You may proceed on your way. Our apologies for any misunderstandings."

I did not have time to smile in triumph before the proximity alarms again hooted on all bridges. I was coming to dislike those alarms.

"Now what, Mother?" asked Elle in exasperation. "Will we never be finished with these men?"

"Patience, dear," I counseled, "merely time to change strategy again. And if I may so add, men are never around when you want them to be, and exceptionally hard to get rid of when their welcome is worn out." I winked at Elle. "But, we women do have our ways."

This may be something you should pay attention to, spoke *Axtell*, with a trace of exasperation himself.

*New Spain and the Emirate have managed to gather every-
thing that would hold air and a few that are leaking drasti-
cally, and throw them into space at us.*

"What?" I asked teasingly. "No more peas and
carrots?"

*Whole trees, boulders, houses, an entire mountain or
three . . . In other words, each side now has sufficient
firepower in place to severely damage us, or even cause
our destruction, should they have a little luck. I suggest
you act. This is beyond my power, legendary as that
may be.*

"This is frightfully coincidental," Elle said. "They
could not have responded this fast under normal circumstances. It is almost as if someone told them
where we would be and when."

"A possibility," I conceded, as I studied the fleets
now ringing them.

They all were ragtag outfits. Ships not so much
maneuvered through space as staggered. Some vessels towed others; obviously ships without workable
engines but still with weapon systems that worked.

*I must agree with Elle, said Axtell pensively. Both em-
pires have made an all-out effort to get every space-going
military asset they possess to this place at this time
and . . . yes . . . I detect friendly, cooperating signals
flashing between them. They join together to overwhelm
us by acting in concert. It is a trap!*

"So it would appear," I answered calmly. "Much
as I expected."

*They do not even attempt communication but maneuver
to bring disabling fire on us.*

"Indeed," I said. "It is a male response, grab and
hold. You have access to their maintenance computers?"

*I do, indeed, Alinore. The security of the fire control
systems are beyond my abilities, but the maintenance computers are more easily opened and entered . . . yes . . .*

They attack us out of desperation. Ships here and factories back on the home worlds, they are in dire straits. Machines sit idle, the economies deteriorate.

I sipped again at my kaffee, pleased. "Yes, and yet both empires again begin to expand. They need ships, they need working industries. They have the basis but not the repair parts. They have plenty of money but no source for the obsolete odds and ends it takes to make their equipment once again operable."

"Oh!" said Elle, a light, as *Axtell* would say, dawning.

"Insert the lists of our inventories with quantities and prices," I instructed. "Have the maintenance computers demand the attention of their captains."

Done, responded *Axtell.* . . . *Ah, their weapons systems go off-line. I begin to get orders. It is as you predicted.*

I indicated my satisfaction. "Even with their massive firepower, *Axtell* is still a formidable opponent. Better to buy and there is also the carrot of all the warehouses we possess filled with additional parts."

Elle grinned, learning. "So you planned all this? Arranged it so that they would be in this position, which you could then turn to our advantage?"

"True, dear. I formulated all this and planted the seeds to make it happen months ago. With *Axtell's* help, of course."

"And this strategy, what is its name?"

"Trade, dear, Trade. It is what we do."

"I see," Elle said, "and this is also how one handles men?"

"Oh, no, dear," I replied. "Trade is a plus. You handle men by giving them that which they want most."

"Sex?" Elle said, from her thirteen-year-old wisdom.

"They only want that with enthusiasm at first, then

merely sporadically later," I assured her. "No, what men want most of all are their toys. I fix their broken toys and bring them new ones. They will now be very grateful. It's a woman's touch that does the trick."

Elle and I now relaxed, watching *Axtell*'s automated equipment flow parts from the ship and the credit totals rise.

Staying Still
by Stephen Leigh

Stephen Leigh is the author of sixteen science fiction and
fantasy novels, including award-winning *Dark Water's
Embrace* and its sequel *Speaking Stones*. Stephen has
also published novels under two pseudonyms. Along with
the novel-length work, he has several short fiction credits
and was a frequent contributor to the *Wild Cards* shared
world series, edited by George R. R. Martin. Stephen
lives in Cincinnati with his wife Denise and two children;
in addition to his own writing, he teaches creative writing
at a local university.

JAX arrived during the night of the Falconian meteor showers. For several hours, thousands of dying
streaks of yellow, white, and pale green were etched
briefly between the stars in glorious, soundless
bursts. At times, there were dozens all at once, origi-
nating from the constellation named the Falcon. I lay
back on the wooden lounge chair on the front deck,
staring up at the quiet fireworks: the dying fragments
of a comet's tail through which Siansa plows every
year on her slow, patient circling of the sun.

Her circling . . . Strange, I don't think I could refer
to any Earthlike world as "he." Worlds are the womb
from which we spring, a Mother who nurtures us,
whose moods are complex and changing, who
watches as we grow up and finally leave. I remember
that the night we left Old Earth, the world wept in
sorrow, gray clouds lashing rain against our ship's
titanium flanks . . .

A new star burned in the sky well away from the Falcon, moving quickly and growing rapidly brighter, the actinic blue-white glare ruining my night vision and destroying the delicate tracery of the meteors against the darkness. After a moment, I could hear the sound: jets roaring their defiance of gravity. I shaded my eyes, grimacing, as Padraic came from the house, the pale sea-blue of his skin a contrast against the black sleeves and neckline of his robelike *jhabaya*, glancing with concern at the craft descending toward us. Even though we'd talked about it, even though he'd said that he was comfortable with the visit, I wondered how he felt, knowing who the shuttle carried. "Brenna?"

"Jax is here."

He watched as the flames sent shadows racing among the hills and touched the valley below us, grunting once as the jets wailed and cycled down the octaves to silence. "I'll prepare us something to eat," he said. "And make sure the back bedroom's ready. In case."

"That would be good," I told him. "Thanks." I listened to the sibilance of swaying cloth as Padraic returned to the house, letting my eyes slowly readjust to night vision and avoiding looking down the long green slopes to where the shuttle sat glowing and steaming and ruining the darkness. I lay back again in my chair until I could see the meteor trails once more. A large shadow flitted between me and the stars: a tharg—I could hear the guttural cry that gave them their name and the hissing of its gas-filled abdomen. We might have named a constellation "Falcon," but there were no birds on Siansa, no winged creatures at all. I thought of thumbing on the house shields, but the tharg was a loner and they were rarely aggressive unless in a pack of half a dozen or more, and besides, the shield would ruin the view. A minute later, the tharg gave a final hoarse croak and sputtered away to the west. I watched the meteors for twenty minutes or so until the headlamps of a rover swept over me and took them away again. I sighed with regret, stood up, and walked down from the deck to the driveway as tires crunched on gravel and electric motors whined to a halt. The door opened.

I knew it would be him, but his appearance was still startling. I smiled, helpless. "Hello, Jax. Been a hell of a long time."

He grinned. "Hey, Brenna! My God, it's great to see you again . . ." I'll give him credit; he managed to keep the grin intact. We stared at each other—I hadn't sent him any pictures of me, a deliberate omission. Jax still looked much the same as he did in my memories and in the old holos I have of him. There were a few more lines around the eyes, a small scar on the chin I didn't remember, a slight pudginess to the waist that hadn't been there before. I, on the other hand . . . He half-ran to me and enfolded me in a full-body hug; after a moment's hesitation. I hugged him back, laughing, twining my fingers in that nappy black hair I remembered so well. He kissed my neck, and I took in a long breath, catching the wonderful, oddly familiar scent of him: that scented soap he always used, the metallic tang that I remembered tasting every time I reentered the ship we'd christened *Mead*. I closed my eyes at the memories that stormed from the night sky of the past. Finally, we broke apart, still holding onto each other's hands.

"You look good," he said.

I smiled into the lie and loved him for it. "It's been, what, forty-two years for me? Don't give me that crap. I know what I see when I look in the mirror. Ship-time, how long's it been since you left Siansa?"

"Twelve years. A bit more."

"Which makes me sixty-seven, and you forty-two." I felt the smile sag at that. "And I used to be a few years younger than you. Now you could be my son." He was still smiling, but the expression seemed frozen on his lips, and his eyes were staring at me. "Come on in," I told him, mostly to break the awkward silence that threatened to engulf us. "You can tell me all about things on *Mead* . . ."

We walked up the stairs to the house deck, the face of the night sky shimmering with meteor streaks. I saw them; Jax didn't seem to notice them at all.

Padraic came into the living room from the kitchen as we entered. "Welcome to our home," he said to Jax with a slight nod of his head, though he remained standing across the room—since the Red Flux virus swept through the human population twenty years ago, it's considered impolite to shake hands on Siansa without asking permission. Jax nodded back, then glanced at me.

"Jax, this is Padraic." Jax's eyebrows raised questioningly and I remembered, belatedly, that there'd been nothing like Padraic in existence when we'd left on *Mead*. "Padraic's a cloneai. Cloned body, AI brain," I told Jax. "The blue skin's a genetic marker. The first ones came here three or four years after you left—some corporation on Earth developed them. You can still legally own them on Earth, last I heard. Not here, though; not since the tharg chrysalli awakened the first time—that was, oh, thirty-five, thirty-six years ago now. Padraic was badly wounded during the first Swarming."

"I would have died, too, if it weren't for Brenna," Padraic said.

"And you returned the favor, when the spewers poisoned the float-wells," I reminded Padraic, and then noticed that Jax was shaking his head. "I'm sorry, Jax. It's all old history to us. To you—"

"I have no idea what you're talking about," Jax said with a brief laugh. "When I—we—first came here, there was just us. Me, Yoshi, Camille, Emille, Konti, all the others of the First Crew . . . and you, Brenna. All this . . ." He shook his head again. "Cloneai, tharg, spewers, float-wells: those are just words to me. This isn't the Siansa I thought I knew."

"You weren't here long enough to really know the world," I told him. I saw his face tighten at that: the old argument.

"Come in and eat," Padraic interrupted, waving toward the kitchen. "Nothing fancy, but we can sit and talk around the table. Wouldn't that be more comfortable?"

For a moment, Jax's eyes narrowed and he took half a step backward, as if the house and the situation and—perhaps—my appearance frightened him and he wanted nothing more than to retreat to *Mead* and what passed for normalcy there. "Please, Jax," I said, extending my hand. He took my fingers with his, and I saw him staring at the wrinkled skin, the knobbed joints that he'd last seen smooth and youthful. "There's so much to catch up on, and if *Mead* is going Out again . . ." I didn't say the rest; he knew it: if he was another dozen ship-years out, barring a significant advance in geriatric science, I wouldn't be here the next time he returned. He nodded, tried to smile, and nearly succeeded.

"Sure," he said. "Let's do that."

Padraic had kept the menu simple and plain: bread, cheeses, the wine we'd made last year from the moonweed droppings, a salad from local greens. The table was round; I noticed that Padraic sat carefully a bit closer to me than Jax; a bit of unspoken territorialism. We passed around the salad, broke the bread, poured the wine . . . "Forty-two years," I said. "How many worlds have you seen now?"

"Twelve years," Jax reminded me. "We've been to some thirty stellar systems and looked at maybe forty different worlds. We've found fourteen that are nicely within human parameters."

"Fourteen entire worlds," I breathed. "What you must have seen . . ."

"You should have been with us, Brenna," he answered, not realizing what he was saying as his voice took on a sudden excitement and drive. "My God, the cliffs of red stone over the place we called the Endless Gorge, the flotilla of floating plants like islands overhead while the predators we called knifebeaks dove through and among them. Or the black-tinted sea where fountains of glowing blue-and-red bacteria erupted from spoutholes on the back of swimming creatures the size of *Mead* itself. Or the herds of crouching, leaping simians that blanketed the plains of an entire continent on one world, the noise they made so loud that we had to cover our ears. I can't begin to tell you all the fantastic worlds and sights: crustaceans that built and inhabited immense towers of sea shells in the tidal plains; a moonless plateau where every living thing glowed, their skeletons alight in transparent skin; the valley of ghosts, where we could see no beings at all but we could hear their voices calling and feel their wispy fingers stroking our faces; the pipe-plants of one jungle that made such melodious sound when the wind blew that you'd swear there was a symphony out there; the world where the night sky was crowded with four moons and curtains of glowing charged ions danced between them." Jax laughed, shaking his head. "Brenna, you wouldn't believe what I've seen. You wouldn't believe it." He took a bite of bread, nibbled on the cheese, sipped the wine; I expected him to say something—the local wine has a distinct licorice aftertaste, and the cheese is almost sweet—but he didn't.

"Camille, Konti, Yoshi . . . how is everyone?" I asked.

I saw the grief on his face before he answered. "Konti's dead. Three worlds back. There was a spore there . . . Somehow, it got past his nasal filters or through an open cut and into his bloodstream. When it reached his brain, he started acting crazy; got into a stupid argument with Emille over supplies and took off Emille's arm with a welding laser before we could get there to stop him. We thought he'd just snapped; he kept acting stranger and more aggressive and finally went into a coma. We didn't figure out what really happened until the autopsy—his brain was strung with pulsing white fibers." Across the table, Padraic set down his fork with a metallic clack, and Jax looked up. "Sorry," he said. "This isn't exactly good mealtime conversation."

"Go on," I told him.

Jax shrugged. "There's not much else to say. Doc grafted a prosthetic onto Emille which took fine. Everyone's a lot more careful about procedures when we hit a new world now. In fact, Camille has refused to go down to any of them since; she won't leave *Mead* at all. Not even here."

None of us spoke for a time. Finally Jax lifted his goblet. "Is there more of that wine?" he asked.

*　　*　　*

"You two go on out to the deck. I'll clean up in here," Padraic said. When I glanced at him, he nodded. "Go on. I'm fine."

On the way out, I turned on the deck lights. The glare took away all but the most brilliant of the meteor trails, but Jax didn't glance up. The night breeze carried the strong cinnamon scent of bush-phibs, and I could hear the strangled sobs that were their mating calls. Jax leaned on the railing, swirling wine in his goblet. "So," he said, "you and Padraic . . ."

"You want the long or the short tale?"

"Probably the short. I have to be back on *Mead* tomorrow to supervise the supply loads and the new crop of Frozen Folk, and make sure all the compiled data's on its way back to Earth. Then we're out of here."

"That quickly?"

He smiled. "I think Yoshi said it best. 'Say hi to Brenna for me, but I don't need to go down there; I've already seen the place. I don't need to see it again.' "

"On to new conquests."

"It's what we do, what we *like* to do. So did—" He stopped; I could hear the word "you" hanging there. He pushed away from the railing and paced the deck's perimeter. Jax: always in motion. "Speaking of conquests, you were going to tell me about Padraic."

"What do you want to know?"

"Are you and he . . . ?"

"Yes," I told him. "For . . . a long time now."

He sat down in one of the deck chairs, but was up again a moment later. "Children?" he asked, and then squinted, tilting his head. "Or isn't that something . . . what was he called? . . . cloneai . . . ?"

I laughed at his discomfiture. "Two. Both grown up now. A daughter, Maggie, and a son, Sean."

"Maggie, eh?" Jax grinned.

I smiled back at him. "Sean's in Siansa City—he's a teacher; he and his bondmate Sallisa are expecting a child next month. Maggie decided she wanted to study on Old Earth, and left Siansa eight years ago." I lifted a shoulder. "With the time dilation, that was a year-long trip for her; four years for me. She sent vid back on the return ship to let me know she arrived—and if all's gone well, she's got her graduate degree by now and is working on her doctorate: trans-spatial mechanics. Maybe she's even married or has a child of her own." I could feel the tears shimmering in my eyes at that, something that happened every time I thought about Maggie, separated now not only by a vast distance but by shifted time. Jax perhaps didn't see the moisture, or notice the quick brush of sleeve over eyes—too busy looking at everything around him. He walked over to the deck's stairs, sipping his wine and glancing once down the hill to the valley where his shuttle waited.

By the time we reached Siansa, our first habitable world—four systems and two years after leaving Old Earth—what had once been a strong relationship with Jax was tenuous and uncertain. We'd already fought a few times about his flirtations with Katoshia—Kat—and I knew he and Camille were lovers as well. Things like that aren't easy to keep secret aboard a small ship with only a dozen crewmembers, and Jax didn't particularly try all that hard. Fidelity, I realized, wasn't going to be one of his strong suits; I'd let the relationship with Camille happen, thinking I could handle the jealousy. I couldn't. "Brenna, are you sure this is what you want? Please, come back with me. With us. There's so much to see out there, so much you'll miss. I know you. Six months from now you'll be kicking yourself for staying behind, but we'll already be somewhere else, and you'll be stuck back here on Siansa with the Frozen Folk."

"We hardly know this world yet, Jax. You don't know a world in three short months, Jax; that takes years."

"I thought you wanted to explore. I thought you said you wanted to see new places, new landscapes, new creatures. You wanted to explore all the variations the galaxy has to offer."

"I do," I told him. "But there are two ways to explore: wide, or deep." I swept my arms about. We were standing on Old Man's Eyebrow, a plateau jutting out from the lower flanks of Mt. Cloud, and the panorama of the Greensward spread out below us while Mist Falls thundered white over the edge of the brow. The wet rocks of the cliffs were covered with iridescent green, man-sized lozenges of spun crystalline glass: tharg chrysalides, though I didn't know that yet; the nasty creatures wouldn't emerge for another five local years. "Look at this. Have you seen anything anywhere to match this scene? There's so much on Siansa we've just begun to touch on. There's enough here for both of us."

I think we both knew that for the hopeful lie it was, one that fooled neither of us. I liked Siansa; that was true—it was hard to imagine a more pastoral, untouched world. Siansa did pull at me, and I knew that we'd touched only the bare surface of her mysteries. After breathing this scented air and seeing her wide, tempting spaces and the glorious diversity of her life, I didn't savor the thought of returning to the steel-wrapped and close horizons of the ship.

And I also knew that on Mead, I would inevitably lose Jax—certainly as a lover, perhaps even as a friend. I thought that maybe, maybe if we stayed here, it might be different; that without Kat and Camille and the others, the love and attraction that already existed between us would finally deepen and strengthen. But I didn't know how to say that, and our disagreement quickly devolved into argument . . .

"Gorgeous, yeah. But the next world may be better, wilder, even more enticing."

"Or it may be worse. We have something wonderful here. We may never find anything better."

"What the hell do you mean, Brenna? We all gave three years of our lives getting ready for this, spent two years out, and now you want to leave at the first opportunity? That's bullshit."

The profanity reddened my face like a slap. "Bullshit?"

I saw his gaze move through and past me as muscles tightened in his jaw. He was hurt, and he wanted to hurt me in kind. "Yeah. What you're saying is bullshit. You know it, too."

If one of us could have apologized then, maybe we could have found some middle ground. But we both had our own streaks of stubbornness. "Fuck you, Jax," I told him.

The rest of the exchange was no better, and we flew back to the Ground Base in angry silence. A few weeks later—after the Frozen Folk were off-loaded, the Coordinator had signed off on the Release Agreement and the initial settlement was erected—Jax and Camille and Konti and the others left Siansa in the same gray shuttle that now stood in the valley. I—stubbornly—watched with the rest of the newly-thawed residents of Siansa as the drive burned like a brief sun and Mead left orbit.

"What about you, Jax?" I asked. "Did you and Camille, or Kat . . . ?"

He sniffed, as if he were stifling a laugh, and walked back toward me. "Both of them, for a while. And Sylvia, who was one of the Frozen Folk but asked to come with us as a crew replacement. Then Yoshi, just for the experimentation; that didn't last long. Then Kat again. And Salima, another replacement. A few of the Frozen Folk we left behind here and there . . ." He shrugged, and this time he did laugh. "Too many . . . Any combination you can name, it's probably been tried. Right now, Camille and I have been sleeping together every once in a while, but . . ." He set his goblet down, empty. He looked down at his feet, then at me. "You should have gone with me, Brenna. Then it would have been different."

I was already shaking my head before he finished. "Jax," I began. Stopped. Began again. "Jax, we were already growing apart. I wouldn't have held you for more than another few ship-months. Then I'd just have been another name in the list." I smiled at him. He was close enough that I could reach out and touch his cheek: old flesh against young. "But I would have stayed your friend. You have that, forever."

I wondered if he heard the lie there. The truth was that Jax was right; I *had* regretted my decision. There were long weeks where I was depressed even while I worked with the Frozen Folk to strengthen our toehold on Siansa, where I cried myself to sleep nearly every night, where I sobbed his name and cursed myself for not being on *Mead*, angry at myself for letting what had been my entire life for five years go on without me. I loved Jax, yes, loved him with a fury and heat that Padraic and I never had, even at the beginning. I loved Padraic, too, but ours was quieter love, a softer love. My hand still on Jax's face, I could feel the memory of other touches, other moments. I could feel the warmth of old love.

Tilting his head, he caught my hand between cheek and shoulder. "Do you miss it?" he asked. "Being out there?"

Trapped, I could only give him the truth. "Yes," I said. "Sometimes I miss it."

He lifted his head and I took my hand away again.
A throaty grumble above: the lone tharg banked high
over the house again. Jax didn't notice; he glanced
at the windows, as if looking to see if Padraic were
watching us. "Take a ride with me," he said. "Let's
go look at the shuttle. I could access the *Mead*'s data-
base, show you some of the places we've been. You
could talk with Camille and the others."

Now it was me who stared at the house. "I don't
know . . ."

"Ask him," Jax said. "If you have to."

"Jax wants to show me—us—the shuttle," I said.

Padraic was putting the dishes in the washer. He
didn't turn. I heard the clink of pottery against steel,
the long inhalation and longer exhale.

"We'll be back in a few hours," I said. "Come
with us."

A plate still in his hand, he turned now and leaned
back against the counter. "You should have reversed
those two sentences," he said.

"Padraic—"

"Go on," he said. "I'll stay here."

I went to him, kissing him fiercely. For a moment
his lips resisted, then finally softened under my insistence, but I could still feel him holding back. I let go,
putting my head on his shoulder. "I don't know
what to say to you," I told him. "I love you,
Padraic."

His voice was a deep, chesty rumble. "I know."
He set the plate down on the counter and gently
pulled me away. "Go on," he said. "I'll stay here."

"You're sure?"

A nod.

"I'll see you in a few hours, then."

The end of his mouth lifted. Aqua skin folded, and
his eyes searched mine. "I'll be here," he answered.

* * *

"God, I remember that smell like it was yesterday."

Jax laughed at me, standing in the hatch of the shuttle with my head lifted and eyes closed, inhaling the scent of scrubbed and filtered air, the sharp hint of metal and wiring, the tang of silicon and tungsten and plastics, the whiff of ionized electronics and perspiration. The odors of the same air used and reused and reused again, sucked in and out of lungs uncountable times, the aroma holding traces all the way back to that day years ago on Old Earth when we finally closed the hatch.

The shuttle's pilot compartment was small and cramped: two seats and controls, a small worktable, the tiny head and food prep area, the bunks for sleeping. I remembered it well enough—*Mead*'s three atmospheric shuttles were mostly engine and storage space.

Jax was leaning next to the bunks. There was a small mirror mounted on the bulkhead. Probably because Jax was there, looking not much older than when I'd last seen him, the face I glimpsed in that mirror startled me.

It was the face I saw every morning, with each year etched in the flesh.

"This place bring back memories?" Jax asked. I moved my gaze away from the mirror and nodded. His hand touched my shoulder, grazed the back of my neck where a metal stud emerged from flesh. "You still wired? Good. Sit there, then . . ." he gestured to the chair by the worktable, with the stud of the bio-jack centered on its high back. Jax took the seat across from me, leaning his head back, his eyes closing momentarily as he connected with the *Mead*'s network. I leaned my head back also (the gesture coming back automatically, as if it had only been yesterday that I last sat on one of the link-chairs) and felt the cold, momentary disorientation of connection. *Access Denied* swam in ghostly letters across my vision, but they were smeared almost instantly away. *"Guest privileges granted,"* Mead's computer whispered in my head. *"Welcome back, Brenna."*

"Thanks, Maggie," I told her. "Been a long time." It felt strange to say the name. Maggie . . . I'd built her personality and made her real. I'd named my daughter after her as a whim. Hearing her voice again was wonderful.

"Too long," she answered with a hint of laughter. *"I've missed you; so have others. Jax was especially anxious to see you, you know."*

"Shut up, Maggie," Jax said, but he was grinning at me. "Run that tour I put together, would you?"

"Running . . ." Maggie answered, and images swarmed around me, overlaying my own vision. Shutting my eyes, I could see them as if I were standing there: other worlds, strange vistas, bizarre landscapes. They flitted by me while Jax provided commentary: a dozen scenes and more: flashes of landscapes, images of mythical and persistent life. "There . . . that's the Endless Gorge, though it's hard to get a sense of the scale; it's bigger than the canyons on Mars; and those are the sea creatures I told you about. Look at the shuttle next to them and you'll get a sense of how *huge* they are and . . . there goes the fluorescing spray. It almost blinds you, it's so bright. Oh, watch this! This is the planet we called Blackmoon. See that waterfall—the video's not reversed, Brenna. Whatever that liquid is—and it's about as thick as mercury—is flowing *up.*"

"Why?" I asked him. I was captivated, snared. I could feel the adrenaline surge, the old curiosity that had driven me to sign onto *Mead* in the first place.

Listening to Jax now was like listening to him back on Old Earth, when we'd first met and become lovers, when the passion in our voices and shared dreams had ignited a passion between us. "Why does it flow up?"

"We don't know," he answered. "We left before we could figure it out. Who cares? There'll be even stranger marvels on the next world, or the next." He moved forward in his chair, disconnecting. "Bye, Maggie," I said.

"For now," she answered, and I could almost hear her smile. Reluctantly, I slid forward in my seat and the stream of images vanished.

"There are more worlds out there than we can ever visit, Brenna," Jax said. "Handfuls of them, all you can grab. Come with me. Come with us. See them for yourself."

The image of that impossible waterfall remained in my mind. *"We left before we could figure it out."* His voice so offhand, so casual, so unconcerned . . . "Jax—"

"I know, I know," he said. "I know what I'm asking, but I also remember you, Brenna. And I've missed you. We once wanted the same things, remember? Well, this is the chance to have that again."

I wanted it. I could feel myself yearning for what Jax offered. I would have loved to lean back, to call to Maggie and have her show me more, to look at all of the worlds Jax and Camille and the others had seen, to know them too . . . What would it matter, after all? Maggie—my other, biological Maggie— would understand, and Sean had Sallisa now, and Padraic . . . well, he'd cope quietly and say he understood, and even if it was a lie, I'd never know. Not after I left.

I could have this. I could have it again.

Jax was staring at me, and I knew he was seeing

me as I was back then, his memory overriding sight.
I glanced again at the mirror. "Do you remember the
green chrysalides on the cliff walls here?" I asked
him. "The ones you wanted to see hatch?"

He nodded.

"They opened two years after you left. The tharg
came out: nasty things—all teeth and scales and hunger, floating above in swarms and descending to kill
and eat and breed. They killed a hundred or more
of us in the first swarming. Then, after the swarms
have fed and mated, they lay eggs high on the mountains and the tharg all die, after having lived only
about two years. The eggs hatch in a month or so
into burrowing slugs about the size of your leg, and
we don't see them again for two, sometimes three,
years. Finally, the slugs emerge, as big as a person,
and attach themselves to cliffsides. For another five
long years, they stay in that state before hatching into
tharg again, and the cycle begins once more."

"If you come with me," Jax answered, grinning, "I
can show you stranger things than that."

I was shaking my head before he finished. "No,
you can't," I told him. "That takes too much time."

Padraic was on the deck, lying on one of the deck
chairs and staring up at the sky. He didn't say anything as I walked up the steps. Below, I could hear
the crunch of tires on gravel and saw lights swaying
as Jax turned the rover and headed back down to
the valley and the *Mead*'s shuttle.

"There was a tharg hanging around earlier," Padraic said. "A loner. You've missed a great meteor
display. A few of them were bright enough to cast
shadows."

"I wish I'd seen that," I told him.

"They've slowed down a bit. But the view's still
pretty good. You might still get lucky."

"I think I already am," I told him.

I dragged another chair over alongside him and lay down. I reached over, but his hand was already stretching out for mine. Our fingers curled together. We lay there, very still, and watched the stars.

The New Breed
by Michael A. Burstein

Michael A. Burstein was born in New York City in 1970, and attended Hunter College High School in Manhattan. In 1991 he graduated from Harvard College with a degree in physics, and in 1993 he earned a Master's in physics from Boston University. A graduate of the Clarion Science Fiction and Fantasy Writers' Workshop, in 1997 he won the John W. Campbell Award for Best New Writer. He has since been nominated for several other awards, including the Nebula and Sturgeon Awards. From 1998 to 2000, he served as Secretary of Science Fiction and Fantasy Writers of America. He lives with his wife Nomi in the town of Brookline, Massachusetts. When not writing, he is the Science Coordinator K-8 and Middle School Science Teacher at the Rashi School in Newton, Massachusetts. More information on him and his work can be found on his webpage, www.mabfan.com, or via his electronic newsletter, MABFAN.

M Y breasts hurt.

I shifted in my seat while I waited for the nurse to call me into the doctor's office. I tried not to stare at the other two girls sitting in the waiting room, but every now and then I would glance up and see one of them glancing back at me. I looked down at the tiled floor and my bare feet, and I repressed a shiver. Why do doctors always keep their waiting rooms so cold, especially when they know that we'll be sitting in them wearing nothing but a thin gown decorated with blue flowers and open at the back?

"Melissa Connor."

I looked up. The nurse, a blonde woman with the beginnings of wrinkles forming on her face, crooked her finger to beckon me over. I pushed myself out of my seat, almost losing my footing on the smooth floor.

The nurse started laughing, then bit her lip. "Sorry," she said.

"What, you think this is funny?" I asked.

She shook her head. "No. I'm just reminded of myself, that's all."

"What are you talking about?"

She paused. "I did the same thing you're doing now."

"Really?" I reached over to the chair next to mine and picked up the sheaf of papers they had given me on arrival. "And did you have to sign a ton of paperwork every single time you came in for an examination?"

"Yep. Every time." She took the papers from me and filed them away in a folder. Then she cocked her head at me.

I looked away. "You know, I'm just trying to get a better life for myself, before I get too old."

She chuckled. "Too old? Sweetheart, you've got years ahead of you. You're not too old."

"Oh? You know so much? Tell me, how old are you anyway?"

Her face shut down for a moment, then she mumbled, "Twenty-five."

I was surprised. She was only seven years older than me. Then I remembered that the treatment only kept a woman viable for about three years. But that was enough time. It had to be.

The nurse brought me into an examination room, took my blood pressure and temperature, said, "Dr. Fremont will be with you in a moment," and pulled

the door shut behind her before I had a chance to
ask her what had happened to Dr. Hurley.

Naturally, the "moment" was more like ten minutes. It gave me a chance to look around the room.
I'd been in a lot of examination rooms recently, and
they all had taken on the same anonymous character.
Even this room, with its paper-covered examination
table, low stool, and a counter with a computer,
looked like it could be in any of a hundred other
hospitals or clinics.

Finally, Dr. Fremont knocked on the door. Without
waiting for a response, he turned the handle and let
himself in. The guy was older than I expected. I
barely had a chance to acknowledge the graying tufts
of hair crowning his bald head, however, before he
said, "Get up on the table."

Not even a "hello" or a "how are you." Just that:
"Get up on the table." Delivered in a gruff voice.

"What happened to Dr. Hurley?" I asked.

"He's left," he said. And then again: "Get up on
the table."

I knew what was coming next; I'd done it before,
but I hated it every single time. I eased myself onto
the table, lay down on my back, and pushed my feet
into the stirrups. Why are they always just out of
reach of the feet? This was easily the most uncomfortable position ever forced upon women by men.

I kept my gaze focused on the glowing fluorescent
light bulbs as the new doctor shoved the speculum
into my private parts. The metal felt cold and I repressed another shiver. I gripped the edges of the
table, though, and ran tunes through my head, con-
centrating on anything but the here-and-now. To myself, I cursed Dr. Fremont's bedside manner, or rather
his lack of one. Dr. Hurley had always spoken calm,
soothing words during his examinations.

Finally, Dr. Fremont pulled the torture device out

of my body and turned his back on me. Without asking for permission, I extracted my feet from the stirrups and swung around into a sitting position.

And waited, as Dr. Fremont kept his back on me and studied a clipboard.

I counted the seconds off from an analog clock hanging on the wall. After fifteen seconds of silence, I piped up, "Well, Doc?"

He turned around, put his chart down on the table and cleared his throat; a loud harrumphing sound. "Well, Ms. Connor, it looks like you're responding just fine to the injections. Your—your reproductive system is adapting perfectly well to the treatment. The Nivronians should be pleased."

I didn't appreciate the tenor or tone of his final statement. "The Nivronians? Hell, Doc, *I'm* pleased. This is what I want."

He walked around the table and put a cold stethoscope against my back. "Breathe in, please. And out. In again. And out."

He pulled the stethoscope out of his ears, came around in front of me, and started squeezing my neck. "Are you sure?" he asked.

"Huh?"

"Glands are fine." He looked me in the eyes. "Are you sure this is what you want?"

"What right do you have to be questioning me on this?"

He squeezed my breasts, and I let out an "Ow!"

He let go and pulled back his arm. "Are you in pain?"

I shook my head. "You're squeezing too hard."

"I have to check for—I have to make sure you'll be able to nurse properly."

"Nurse?"

"Yes, nurse." He gave me a look. "Don't you read all those things you sign?"

"Yeah," I said.

"Then you must know that the Nivronians expect their hybrid offspring to receive nutrition from you in the first few months of life."

I cleared my throat. "Kind of," I said.

He shook his head slightly. "For a college kid, you don't seem too smart."

"For a doctor, you don't seem too empathetic," I retorted.

He made a clucking sound with his tongue and continued to examine me. As he was checking my foot reflexes, he said, "You know, Ms. Connor, it's not too late to change your mind."

"I'm afraid it is too late to change my mind." About eighteen years too late.

"Are you sure?" he asked.

"Doc, you sound as if you disapprove."

He pressed his thin lips together and slowly shook his head. "I'm a government physician. It's not my place to approve or disapprove of your decision."

"But you do, don't you? It's okay, I'm not going to tell anybody."

"Ms. Connor, I know from your profile that you're not a typical host. You're in college, for—"

"Doc, drop it."

His shoulders slumped. "Consider it dropped. At least by me."

He continued his examination in silence. A moment later, I decided to break the silence myself.

"Dr. Fremont, if it's all right, I have a question for *you*."

He looked surprised but replied, "Certainly."

"If you hate this so much, why are you doing it?"

The doctor got a faraway look in his eyes. "There are fewer choices now," he said. "Fewer than before."

I understood. Just because he was doing this work

didn't mean he liked it. It was a simple matter of what he had to do to survive.

Kind of like the rest of the human race.

My breasts continued to throb as I took the subway home. I had finally admitted to Dr. Fremont that I had minor pain, and he told me that the pain was a side effect of the treatment. He said it should fade as my body became more adapted to "servicing the aliens," his words. But it still put me in a crappy mood.

Ma called to me from the kitchen as I entered our apartment. "Melissa? Is that you?"

I sighed as I closed the front door and took two steps into our living room. "It's me, Ma. Who else would it be?"

"How was school today?" she shouted.

I pushed aside a pile of yellowing newspapers in order to open the closet door, so I could hang up my winter coat. Ma's coat, I noticed, still sat on the sofa, covering up one of the torn pillows.

"I wasn't at school today, Ma."

She marched into the room, using her large body to intimidate me. I didn't let it work. "What do you mean, you weren't at school? Did you cut classes?"

"Yes, I did, but I'll get the notes from the web."

She glared at me and lifted her arm as if she wanted to whack me, then put it down, as if realizing that it would do no good. "Then where the hell were you, little missy? You only work in the evenings."

"It's like this, Ma. I have a surprise for you."

And then I told her. And watched her face turn a satisfying shade of pale.

"You can't be serious," she said. She eased herself onto the sofa.

"I'm perfectly serious," I replied.

"What about children?"

"Well, Ma, I'll certainly have children. Just not human ones. They'll be Nivro—"

"Don't say that name in this house!"

"What are you going to do, Ma? Deny that history happened?"

"You promised me you would marry, and have lots of children."

"Yeah, Ma. I was going to marry a rich prince and pop out the babies, one right after another. Well, guess what? I was foolish then. And young."

"You're young now, honey."

She called me honey? "Yeah, I know I'm young. That's why I was a prime candidate to be a host."

We both fell silent for a moment, and then she said, "It takes a while for you to adapt, doesn't it?"

"Yeah, it does."

"So you've been doing this for a while."

"A few months now."

"Why haven't you said anything before?"

I was wondering that myself. Why had I put off telling her? Today just felt like the right time, but I had no idea why.

"Because," I finally said, "it's too late for you to do anything about it."

She sniffed, and pushed herself off the sofa. "Melissa, I want you to leave this house. You're leaving this house now and not coming back."

"Don't be an idiot, Ma," I said. "There's money in being a host. We'll finally be able to afford the lifestyle you've never—we've always wanted."

She glared at me. "Not under the Nivron—not under them, we're not. Get out."

I smiled at her as sweetly as I could. "You forget, Ma, that the house is in my name." She had done that for tax and welfare reasons.

She looked horrified. "You wouldn't dare—"

"I would never force you out. As much as I might

want to. But by the same token, I'm not leaving." I paused. "So, does my decision sicken you so much that *you* want to leave? I won't stop you." As I said it, I knew that she could never accept such an empty offer. She had nowhere else to go, and neither did I.

She lifted her head high, wrung her hands, and then turned around and went back to the kitchen. "I want dinner at six," I called after her.

About a week later, I sat at home alone working when the buzzer went off. I pushed the intercom button, and asked who it was.

"I'm from the government," came the reply in a rich tenor voice. "I need to speak to Melissa Connor."

I sighed and buzzed him in. Within moments, a man in a dark blue suit came to the front door. "Ms. Connor?" he asked.

I studied him for a moment before responding. He wore metal-framed sunglasses directly over his eyes, so close that they looked like a natural part of his face. So his eyes were covered, but I enjoyed the appearance of his brown, wavy hair. I would have loved to run my fingers through it, just for a second.

I nodded and did my best to keep my face stone calm so as not to betray my feelings. "Would you identify yourself?" I asked, although if he was from the government I had a pretty good idea of which branch.

Sure enough, he reached into his jacket pocket and flipped open a badge. "Agent Jeff Stickney, special liaison to the Nivronians. I need to speak with you. May I come in?"

I almost shook my head. "Would it do me any good if I said no?"

He removed his sunglasses, revealing light blue eyes. "Probably not," he said. "We want to talk to you, and we will, one way or another."

I sighed. "Fine, come in. But I'm not letting you near the spoons."

He actually smiled at that. I moved aside and he took a seat on the sofa, glancing briefly at the pile of newspapers that still sat on the floor. I grabbed a desk chair and plopped down across from him, sitting with my body leaning forward on the back of the chair.

He didn't say anything at first, just looked around the room and then let his eyes run up and down my body. I almost squirmed under his gaze, but I didn't want to give him the satisfaction of thinking he was managing to bother me. Finally, I said, "If you're here to talk, talk. If not, leave."

"Sorry." He pulled a handheld out of his front jacket pocket. "May I have your permission to record this? I'll need you to say so for the record."

I rolled my eyes. "Whatever."

He nodded, turned on the handheld, and passed me a piece of paper. "Read this, please. Aloud."

I grabbed it out of his hand and recited, "I state your name grant full permission for—"

Agent Stickney interrupted me. " 'State your name' means to state your name," he said.

"I know, I know. Just my little joke." This time, I recited the waiver phrase properly and legally.

He took the paper out of my hand and shoved it back into his pocket. "Thank you."

"Whatever you want. So what's your question?"

"It's a few questions, actually."

"Whatever."

He stared at my face for a moment, and then began the interrogation. "Ms. Connor, the agency would like to know a little bit more about what led to your decision to become a host."

"What led to my decision?" I bit my lip. "Did Dr. Fremont ask you to talk to me?"

Agent Stickney shook his head. "No, although I did interview him about your case, among others."

"My case? What is it about my case that you're finding so interesting?"

"It's just that you don't fit the standard profile."

I sighed. "This again? I filed all the appropriate paperwork and was accepted as a host. Why is the Liaison Office bugging me now?"

His eyes shifted away from mine. "Your approval was something of a mistake."

"A mistake?"

He nodded. "You should have been red-flagged after the first genetic screening."

"So what does this mean? Are you going to withdraw your approval?"

"No, we can't." He smiled bitterly. "The Nivronians would scream bloody murder."

"Yeah, and they'd probably burn down another one of our cities at the same time."

"Um," he said. "Of course, you're free to withdraw from the program without prejudice."

"And why would I do that?"

"I'm not quite sure you heard what I said. You were red-flagged because of your genes."

"So?"

He sighed. "Ms. Connor, do you know your genetic profile?"

I let my mouth fall open and did my best to look astonished at the stupidity of his question. "Do I—do I look like I had health insurance beforehand? Why would I know my profile?"

"Sorry. It was a stupid question."

"Damn straight it was. Now why don't you give me the full picture here?"

He straightened up a little. "Ms. Connor, I'm running the interview here."

"Well, you're not doing a very good job."

He glared at me in a way that reminded me of

Ma. I didn't like it. "The full picture, as you put it, is that we mixed you up with another Melissa Connor, who had been profiled beforehand. Simple computer error." He flashed a weak smile. "The fact is, you have a superior genetic profile."

"Superior," I echoed. I looked around the room, at the ratty sofa cushions, at the wooden chairs whose supports were falling out of the legs, at the old television set that didn't even support digital recording. "You call me superior."

"Your genes are, certainly," he replied. "And the government doesn't want humans who are, well, genetically superior to give up their ability to reproduce."

I couldn't believe what I was hearing. "Then maybe the government shouldn't have run out of money."

He looked pained. He knew as well as I did that the Earth government could not offer me any amount of money for turning down the Nivronians.

"What does 'genetically superior' mean anyway?" I asked.

"I'm not supposed to say—"

"—but you will anyway, in hopes of convincing me to change my mind."

He nodded. "What I'm about to tell you is under the strictest confidence, Ms. Connor."

"Fire away," I said.

"How much biology do you know?"

"Enough."

He nodded. "I'll try to keep this simple, then. You know why the Nivronians defeated us, don't you?"

"Because God favors the side with the greater firepower?"

"Seriously."

I shrugged. "I haven't really given it much thought."

"In general, your first statement was correct. But

there's a reason the Nivronians had more firepower, as you put it, and we don't credit it to a deity. It's simple genetics. They evolved faster than we did, or earlier than we did, so that when they came to Earth, they were stronger than us, more intelligent, more technologically advanced."

I remembered a phrase from an old television show I had seen on broadband. "Better, stronger, faster."

He didn't seem to recognize the reference, but he nodded and said, "Exactly. The Nivronians are, frankly, superior to us, and that's why we lost."

"So what does that have to do with your little visit to me?"

He said the next part slowly. "The government wants to speed up human evolution. We believe that certain genes, when combined correctly, will encourage evolution of the human race, developing human beings who could defeat the Nivronians."

That boggled my mind. "Defeat? Agent Stickney, the Nivronians came down to Earth like gods from an ancient world and took over. Nothing we did could stop them. Do you honestly believe you can breed weak little us into something more powerful than them?"

"Given time, yes."

I cocked my head. "A lot of time, I would imagine."

He looked me in the eyes, then nodded. "We're projecting success on the order of a few hundred years. Certainly less than a thousand."

I stared at him, incredulous. "Do you know how ridiculous that sounds?"

He shrugged. "Some of us still have hope for our future."

"You want me to make my life decisions based on what impact they might have a thousand years from now?"

"Possibly a few hundred years," he said. "Don't forget that."

"Riiight," I said. "You sound like the woman in that old joke, worried when she thought the sun would burn up in five million years. When she found out it was really five billion years, she collapsed in relief."

"There's a bigger difference between a billion and a million than there is between a thousand and a hundred."

"So? Why are you even bothering to ask me? Why don't you just take some of my DNA?"

He shook his head. "Won't work. You've already begun the treatment. You'd have to take shots to revert back to normal—that is, if you're willing."

"And the government can't do anything to encourage my willingness, can it?"

He shook his head. "It's not just the problem of being broke," he said. "It's also the secrecy issue. If the Nivronians found that we were supporting young women who would have been perfect breeders—"

I raised my hand, and he cut off. "Don't call me that."

"I'm sorry. It's just—"

A sudden realization hit me. "You're just as bad as they are. They want humans to breed their hybrids, so they can develop Nivronians better adapted to Earth. And you just want the same thing, in reverse."

"There's a difference, Ms. Connor. If you work with us, you're helping your own kind. Work with the Nivronians, and you're selling the human race out to the enemy."

"If I were to take up your offer . . . what's the schedule?"

"We'd want to start right away. We'd provide the germ plasm, but you'd need to be impregnated almost immediately."

"Uh-huh. And who raises it? Would my child be taken away to some government facility?"

"Children, not child. And you would raise them, of course. If we took them away to some central facility—"

"Yeah, yeah, it could alert the Nivronians." I looked him square in the eyes. "Sorry. I'm not doing it."

"But—"

"I'm not going to be like my mom, Agent Stickney. I'm not going to get knocked up at eighteen and abandoned by a man—you or anyone else—and rejected by a family that never even pretended to care. It's my body, and I'm exercising complete control over it."

"By giving your womb over to the aliens?"

"What other choices do I have? Tell me that. What other choices are there in our modern, screwed-up joke of a world? It's either them or you, and at least with them, I get paid, and I'm not saddled with a kid for the rest of my life." I shook my head vigorously. "You're going to have to breed your—your evolutionary revolutionaries somewhere else." A thought occurred to me. "Say, what would you do if I revealed this conversation to the press?"

He looked at me with a cold expression in his eyes, and for a moment, I felt a chill. "I wouldn't try it, Ms. Connor. Even if you could find a reporter who believed you. People disappear far more quickly and easily nowadays than ever before." He paused. "Do you understand me, Ms. Connor?"

Yeah, I understood. "You're cute when you're threatening me," I said.

For a moment, neither of us spoke. Agent Stickney just sat there, giving me a sad look. Finally, he tucked the handheld into his pocket, pulled himself off the sofa, and took a deep breath. "I guess we're done here."

"Yeah, I guess so," I replied.

He pulled an old-fashioned paper business card out of his pocket and placed it upon the sofa. "In case you change your mind," he said.

I just stared at him.

He nodded, and walked to the door. He stopped for a moment, turned around, said, "Sorry to have bothered you, Ms. Connor," and left.

"Yeah, up yours, too," I said under my breath.

The next few weeks were typical. Every morning, I went to class; every afternoon, I went to the mini-clinic for the shot; every evening, I worked at a nearby restaurant, waiting tables for tips. A side benefit of the treatment was that my breasts were a bit swollen, so with the right number of buttons left undone, I could predict the kind of tips I would get.

Sooner than I expected, it was time for another required trip to the doctor. More forms, another run-in with the nurse, and then a visit with dear old Dr. Fremont. Again, I sat in a thin johnny waiting for him to open the door to the examination room.

Finally, he knocked at the door. I waited for a moment, then shouted, "Come in."

The knob turned, and he entered and shut the door behind him. In his hand he held my file. "Good afternoon, Ms. Connor."

I raised my eyebrows. "Good afternoon, Dr. Fremont."

Dr. Fremont said, "Ms. Connor, I have some . . . news for you."

"News," I said.

"Your body is rejecting the Nivronian implants."

At first, I didn't understand. "Rejecting the implants?"

He nodded. "Yes."

"But that's not possible. I've been receiving injections for five months now."

The doctor picked up a clipboard that had my name on it and studied it. "That's true," he admitted.

"I was told the procedure took six months."

"That's also true."

"And I was told that rejection only happened in the first month of treatment."

"That's—that's what we originally thought. But apparently that's no longer true."

"What do you mean, no longer true?"

"You're the first case of rejection taking place so late. So we'll have to readjust what we know about the procedure."

"So what do I do now?"

"We'll start you on a regimen of injections to bring you back to normal."

"Normal," I echoed.

"Well, as close to normal as we can make you, anyway."

I laughed bitterly. "Well, at least I can go back to my original plan. Marry some rich guy and have lots of kids."

The doctor looked away for a moment. "Ms. Connor, there's more."

"What?" I asked. I already didn't like the way this conversation was going.

He hesitated, then sighed. "About your plan . . ."

"Doc, if you've got something new to say, just spit it out.

"You can't have children."

I felt a chill. "You mean Nivronian offspring, right? That's what you just told me."

He slowly shook his head. "No. I mean human children. Your own children. You're infertile."

"Hey, wait a minute," I said. "I knew that would be true if my body adapted to the injections. But it hasn't, right? That's what you said. I was told that if my body rejected the treatment, I would return to normal."

"Apparently, you were told wrong."

"I want a second opinion."

"You'll get it. But, Ms. Connor, I'm afraid you won't get the financial support you were expecting from the Nivronians or the government."

"Like hell I won't! I'll sue—"

He cut me off. "Who?"

"Who? I'll sue the—well, the—" I stopped talking. I knew what Dr. Fremont meant by his question. And I knew that I had no answer.

Still, the bastard made his point anyway. "You can't sue anyone, Ms. Connor. You could try to sue the government, but the case would be thrown out immediately. And there's no way you can sue the Nivronians." He paused. "You went into this out of your own free will, Ms. Connor. The government makes sure of that. We never forced our women to become hosts to the aliens, no matter how much they threatened us. We told them no, only if a woman volunteers will we let her be—be used like that. It's one of the few rights we didn't give up to the Nivronians."

I glared at him. "You mean one of the few the Nivronians let us have."

He nodded. "Some might put it that way, yes."

"And some might tell you to go—"

He held up his hand, and I actually bit off my curse. "Some might tell me to go to hell. And some might tell you the same thing. But in our case, Ms. Connor, I almost think that's redundant."

"Am I a freak, then?" I asked. "Part human, part hybrid breeding machine?"

"No. Your cell structure, your body, even your DNA, will all return to normal. You just won't be able to bear children."

I felt suddenly tired, and I began wiping the wetness out of my eyes. Dr. Fremont just stared at me. Finally, he said, "If it's any consolation, Ms. Connor, I truly am sorry."

"Up yours, Doc."

He turned his back on me. "Get dressed."

I got dressed, marched out of the clinic, and covered my eyes against the bright sunlight. I buried my face into my coat to stay warm. What was I going to do now? What could I do?

Then I remembered. Dr. Fremont did say that my DNA would return to normal.

I searched my pockets and found the card Agent Stickney had left for me. I studied the number for a moment, then pulled out my phone.

In the Heart of Kalikuata
by Tobias S. Buckell

Tobias S. Buckell is Caribbean-born, and grew up spending time in Grenada, and the British and U.S. Virgin Islands. He moved with his parents to Ohio after Hurricane Marilyn swept through the Virgin Islands, destroying the boat they lived on. Having finished college, he is still in Ohio. This strange contrast is one of the many reasons why Tobias feels comfortable writing about strange things happening to seemingly normal people, and not so much about strange people happening to normal things. He is a Clarion grad, has appeared in various magazines and anthologies, and during the evenings works as a mild-mannered tech assistant at his alma mater. You can find out more about his work and where it will pop up next through his web page at www.torhyth.com.

I LEFT my birthworld, Loki, for another cylindrical Orbital I'd once seen advertised as a vacation paradise. Instead of finding better work, I found a world stressed by overcrowding. I could see millions of people teeming over the insides of Kalikuata just by leaning my head back and looking up the arch of green land a mile overhead.

Kalikuata's air choked me, thick with smoke and the hydrogen belches of small vehicles. Overloaded city filters, great blocks of carbon the size of the overcrowded apartment complexes around them, added to the noise all around me. Men with rickshaws shouted and pushed themselves closer to one of the many thirty-foot-high air locks dotting Kalikuata's inner equator. I shoved left, pushing the arms of my rickshaw into the ribs of the man in front of me.

He swore and shoved back. My rickshaw's right pole slammed against my chest, bruising my bound breasts. It hurt more than he realized—I had disguised myself as a man in order to pull the rickshaw.

I let him move forward and caught my breath.

Immigration officials with full beards and khaki uniforms stood on catwalks over my head. One of the utility doors spun itself open. The official who stepped out examined the lacelike chakras and lotus symbols on the sides of the air lock. He looked sideways at me, the corners of his eyes crinkling.

"I have a passenger looking to go to the Hilton," he said. "A hundred rupees is my price."

I nodded my head "no" to him.

"I have arrangements," I said.

Men from my Loki's embassy paid me to try and pick up certain people. This month it was a man called Lowry. I would make enough today to afford a good meal. Not just rice and runny curry, but some beef. And I would save more toward getting off this world, something just pulling a rickshaw couldn't do.

The air lock jerked and hissed steam, revealing passengers. The second set of air lock doors behind them had a colorful relief carving of Satyanarayana, lord of protection, fourth hand held upward in blessing.

"Sah, here, Sah, here," the call went out as rickshaw drivers began to try and draw the attention of passengers. They surged past, obscuring my view.

"Lowry," I shouted, shoving forward, spotting the thin but well dressed white man in the multiracial crowd. "Sah Lowry, here." Lowry with his bodyguard, Ashwatthama. Ashwatthama glowered at me. Lowry smiled. He paused before mounting the rickshaw to pat my shoulder. He'd cut his silver hair and grown a trimmed beard since I'd last seen him.

The rickshaw shook as they both sat down.

"He's a small man to be pulling rickshaws," Ashwatthama grumbled. "I have brothers who could carry you home quicker."

Lowry said nothing.

I leaned on the right pole and turned the rickshaw, straining against the weight of the two men. Ashwatthama in particular was a big man, over six feet tall and fat. He weighed a hundred pounds on Kalikuata. On Loki, my birthworld, he would weigh two hundred and seventy.

Such is the way of different worlds.

I rocked the rickshaw back, then threw myself forward. With a few straining steps the rickshaw gained momentum. Once I got going in the low gravity, it wasn't hard to keep speed. Stopping wasn't so easy as the momentum of the rickshaw still overpowered me. It was harder for my feet to stay on the ground due to the low gravity. Because of this, I often tried to get smaller men as my passengers.

"See," Lowry said to Ashwatthama, as I sidestepped and passed around a stopped rickshaw. "He does good."

That was the last I heard, as Lowry then waved his hand and invoked a silencing device around them both. I was left with the noise of clattering rickshaws, shouts, and snatches of conversation from the streets we passed through.

It was a better job than the chemical factories in Loki, where I submitted to sterilization for work. Where I was told: you will work to expand Loki's resources. You will not strain our world's resources. You will not reproduce.

I knew Kalikuata would eventually kill me, too. Better to die here, I thought, than to be disfigured by some chemical. Or watch shift matrons die cough by bloody cough.

On Kalikuata, women walked around with broods of thin little children. Humanity packed the streets. And I was fighting to get out, and leave this world as well. Even here, I still felt trapped.

Kalikuata was a giant spinning can, like Loki, only smaller. Inside, I could look up and around at the four sections of our artificial world; Durga directly above, Kali farther forward. Saraswate's city spires rose far off in front of me, the bulk of the section just out of sight, and Uma crowded all around. The muddy brown Ganga River split them all like a muddy rainbow over my head. Its tributary, Parvati, girdled the cylinder of Kalikuata.

I dodged holy animals in the streets, bumped around other rickshaws, and tried not to get hit by powered vehicles. As I pulled the two men over the River Parvati on a wooden bridge, I slipped on a wet mound of dung. I pulled myself up before being run over by my own rickshaw.

Out of the slums of Uma, we came to the edges of the Saraswati section, where the houses had courtyards, and the traffic thinned out. Shiny bubble-shaped hydrogen cars zipped around us.

I stopped just outside the gates of Lowry's house. My breath fogged the air. I could tell that my whole body would hurt tonight.

"Go ahead and open the gates," Lowry ordered Ashwatthama.

"Sah."

The rickshaw shook from Ashwatthama leaping to the ground. He stooped through a small wooden door. The gates shook themselves open, and I picked up the poles to trot into the courtyard.

Lowry stepped off the rickshaw.

"Andy," he said. "Your payment?"

He stood too close to me. I began to breathe a little harder. I looked around, but didn't see Ashwatthama anywhere.

"You are a very good-looking young man," Lowry said.

If I ran, I would lose the rickshaw. And I couldn't get over the gates anyway. Lowry put his hand on my shoulder holding a wad of bills, put his other to my stomach, and ran his fingers down to my inner thigh.

I should run, I thought. Lowry closed his eyes and sighed. He grabbed my crotch. His eyes fluttered open as he didn't find what he was expecting.

"I must leave," I said, taking the money from his hand on my shoulder. I picked the poles up over our heads, and turned the rickshaw away from him.

I walked the rickshaw over to the gate.

"Will you let me go, Mr. Lowry?" I asked over my shoulder.

Lowry nodded.

"Ashwatthama, let him . . ." Lowry shook his head. "Just open the gates."

The gates shivered open, and I bolted out, almost getting hit by another rickshaw. I hoped to god, any of them, that the bug in the rickshaw picked up something. I wanted to be done with Lowry. He made my skin crawl.

Two Loki-men stood outside my small hut. They pulled a sliver of wood out from the floor; their bug. The red-haired man, Donovan, sat on my wooden bench. His boots rested on my sleeping pallet, muddying my sheet.

"Nothing," he said in response to the look on my face. "They talked about nothing."

My shoulders slumped.

"I don't want to pull Lowry around," I said.

Donovan stood up. His crisp black suit seemed out of place in my mud-floored hut.

"We paid to ship you here. We found you this job," Donovan said.

"Because I had dark skin," I spat. "And all your agents are fair-skinned. It doesn't matter, anyway. He knows I'm a woman now." I stalked over and pulled up my sheet, shaking the clumps of mud from it with sharp snaps. "He won't want to use me anymore."

Donovan moved closer to me.

"We have a local man for Mr. Lowry's tastes. He'll plant a bug. We want you to hand him over to Mr. Lowry."

I took a deep breath.

"What do I say?"

Donovan smiled and pulled out a slate. He scrolled down documents dimly displayed in the middle of the piece of clear plastic until he found what he wanted.

"We'll coach you," he said.

And they did. They ran me through every single type of response Lowry could offer. They did it all night, with tight smiles on their professional faces, until I made the call for Donovan.

I smiled, ignoring the men and looking at the rotted wood that was the single window to my hut. The early morning rays shone through the hinges.

"Hello, Mr. Lowry," I said. "I'm sorry about yesterday. I . . . think I have something that would interest you."

I listened to Lowry pause on the other end.

"Go on," he said.

I gave him the name, the story, the price, and Donovan tapped his foot and smiled at me from across the hut.

"Good," Donovan said when I cut the connection. I felt used, and hated every damned freckle on his cheeks. We locked stares for a moment. "If you want to get off this world, you'll do as we say." He smiled and motioned his men to leave. "See you tomorrow, Andrea."

As the door shut, I realized that my whole body ached. I leaned against the wall and groaned.

Eventually, I picked up two buckets from by the door and walked out. A bath would be good. Then maybe I could bring out some of my clothes and a wig, put on makeup, and go out into the town as a woman. Going as a man meant less hassle, but I wanted to feel pretty. Something I hadn't done in the last year breaking my back on rickshaws, doing the bidding of Donovan and his masters back on Loki.

I let the buckets bang against my thighs as I approached the well. A line of women lined up, waiting to get to the faucet and fill their own buckets. The dirt road turned muddy under my feet as I inched closer, and kids weaved through the crowd.

The women in line chatted, filling the air with friendly chat. I enjoyed the sense of community, and for a second, wished I were here with children of my own. But the moment passed.

And how would I support children anyway? These women were only allowed to work in certain roles. Only men were allowed to pull rickshaws, though on this world, women could do just as well. I proved that daily. If I had children, I could not keep my disguise. Even now these women did not talk to me, and moved aside to let me get water. A form of power that I didn't want.

I walked back toward my hut with full buckets, focusing on the way they pulled down on my tired arms. I paid little attention to the world around me.

A heavy arm grabbed and pulled me into an alley between a rickety two-story set of apartments and a bar. I dropped the two buckets, the water sloshing out onto the thirsty ground. I tried to pull away. Ashwatthama's angry face looked down at me from over his beard.

"Who were those men?" he hissed.

"I don't know what you are talking about," I said, trying to twist free.

"I don't believe you. You are a fraud. And a woman. I will tell every rickshaw driver about your lie. They'll beat you sick."

I bit his forearm and he hit me in the face. I shrieked and yanked at his unyielding arm, kicking and trying to poke his eyes. He hollered and let me go. I sat down in the mud. A team of women with long sticks—brooms, I realized—surrounded Ashwatthama and beat him back.

"Are you okay, boy?" they asked me. "Come with us."

I stumbled up as Ashwatthama pushed through and grabbed my shirt.

He tugged hard and it ripped. My breasts, unbound, were exposed. I wrapped my arms around my chest and ran away with the women. I heard them murmuring to each other as we ran; "The boy is a woman."

We hid in a small apartment room up a flight of rickety stairs. The woman who stayed in it introduced herself as Ramani. She had a nose ring that glinted in the room's dim light. I saw four sleeping pallets against the wall. I looked around and realized a large family lived in these two rooms.

Ramani's youngest daughter approached me, bearing a tray of small cookies with bright sugar frosting patterns.

"You're too kind, I can't," I started to say. But from the look in their eyes I knew it would be worse to refuse the food than to eat it.

Ramani handed me a bright yellow sari.

"Your shirt is ripped," she said.

I took the sari and held it. "I don't know how to thank you."

Ramani smiled. She took out a pitcher of water.

"You are hurt here," she said, and dabbed at where Ashwatthama hit me in the face. I relaxed and allowed her to clean my face. Her eldest daughter, just as graceful as her mother, served me tea. One of the women who had saved me peeked in. She helped wrap the sari around me when I began to fumble with the wide strip of cloth.

"That man has left," she said. "Will you be okay on your own? You are welcome to stay as long as you need."

Ramani handed me the cloth that had bound my chest. I slipped it under the sari.

"Thank you, no." I stood up on slightly wobbly legs. I couldn't take more of their hospitality. Already I felt like an undeserving thief. Just outside the door I turned around and looked in at the tiny, but neatly kept, room. "Thank you," I said again. I didn't know what else to say. I was dazed.

They waved good-bye from the door: brightly colored clothes contrasting with the khaki-colored walls.

I suspected Ashwatthama would be waiting by my hut. When I saw that he was, I turned away. I walked throughout Uma's street's, hardly noticing the throngs of people pressing me against either side.

Strong curry smells wafted from the carts by the sides. Hand drawn signs advertised curries, breads, and meats. The fried chicken smelled heavenly. I bought a heavily curried piece, holding it between rhoti bread. I ate it as I walked. Without the money in my apartment, I felt trapped. I had become familiar with that feeling too well over the past.

I took a few deep breaths. A woman and her children passed in front of me, only her eyes visible, the rest of her hidden by layers of red-and-gold cloth. You could hide artillery under there, I thought.

What was I to do tonight?

A small child in his mother's arms bawled. I could see the bones under his skin. His mother shushed him. I walked over to the pair and handed them the rest of my rhoti and chicken.

I would do something, I thought. I had to do something. Somewhere this morning the graciousness of the people I was living among had overwhelmed me.

The mistake I made in the past years was thinking that I could run away. This was the thought I carried with me as I wandered through Uma.

Well before the right time, I got ready to cross the bridge over the Parvati into the Saraswati section. In a few hours I knew Lowry would be seated at a table with white plastic tables and thatch umbrellas. A pretty young man would be seated several tables away, and it was my job to introduce them.

Donovan would be watching and waiting from inside the tea shop we were to meet outside of.

Wherever you lived, there were Donovans and Lowrys. Men who took what they wanted through power, intrigue, or force. If I wanted to free myself, I had to start here, where I lived. I couldn't keep promising myself a distant freedom that would come if I moved to another world, or as time passed.

And I couldn't leave those women who had saved me. I wanted to join that community, a sense of family I had lost in running away.

Halfway over the small bridge over the Parvati, I

stopped. I leaned on the rail by the edge, and looked down into the muddy water. A group of teenagers played by the banks, and women washed laundry. They beat the clothes against rocks with sharp snaps. Sudsy water washed downstream toward filter grates.

A wind picked up, pulling at my sari. I remembered I was dressed as a woman. Dressed normally. Both Lowry and Donovan would not know quite what to make of this, when I showed up dressed like this.

You could hide almost anything under this flowing piece of cloth, I thought. And I put my hand down to the cold piece of metal by my hip—not a gun, but a recorder. There were many different ways I could see to play their own games on them. And would they expect it? No. Even though I pulled a rickshaw, they still thought of me as a poor woman.

I smiled. The dirty white piece of cloth that had bound my breasts was still tucked into my sari as well. I pulled it out, the wind played with the edges, and I threw it out across the middle of the Parvati.

It fluttered down onto the river's surface. It floated for a moment, soaked up the muddy silt, blending in, and then sank away beneath the surface.

It was time to go show these men who I was.

Rachel
by M. Shayne Bell

M. Shayne Bell has published short fiction in *Isaac Asimov's Science Fiction Magazine*, *The Magazine of Fantasy and Science Fiction*, *Interzone*, *Amazing Stories*, *Tomorrow*, *Science Fiction Age*, *Gothic.Net*, *Realms of Fantasy*, and *SciFiction*, plus numerous anthologies, including *The Year's Best Science Fiction*, *The Year's Best SF #6*, *Starlight 2*, *Future Earths: Under African Skies*, *Simulations: Fifteen Tales of Virtual Reality*, *War of the Worlds: Global Dispatches*, *The Best of Writers of the Future*, and *Vanishing Acts*. His short story, "Mrs. Lincoln's China" (*Asimov's*, July 1994) was a 1995 Hugo Award finalist. His short-story collection, *How We Play the Game in Salt Lake and Other Stories*, was published in 2001. Bell is also author of the novel *Nicoji* and editor of the anthology, *Washed by a Wave of Wind: Science Fiction from the Corridor*, for which he received an AML award for editorial excellence. In 1991, he received a Creative Writing Fellowship from the National Endowment for the Arts. He holds a Master's degree in English literature from Brigham Young University, and lives in Salt Lake City. His website address is *www.mshaynebell.com*.

"I DESPISE these events, Thomas."

"Of course, my dear."

"And I wish you would stop calling me your 'dear.' I'm not."

"Yes, Miss Bradstreet."

"Thomas," I said, "please, please stop calling me Miss Bradstreet. I may not be married, but I don't think I have to pay penance for the fact. Introduce me tonight as Rachel, as Rachel Bradstreet, or as Dr. Rachel Bradstreet if you wish—but not as *Miss* Rachel Bradstreet."

"Certainly, my dear."

I bit my lip to keep from saying things I'd regret. Thomas, you see, is my agent—a good agent—but he has certain faults, not the least of which is his habit of arranging parties to launch my books. They are always at inappropriate times. It had snowed in the Alps. Thomas knew that. I had told him. But did that matter? No. He'd insisted that I leave for my skiing later, that he had told me about this event first (as if that had anything to do with snow in the Alps), that everyone at the Milton estate was expecting me.

I was trapped.

We arrived too soon. The doorman took my cloak. Ann Milton came from the living room and welcomed me in. I braced myself for what lay ahead, and Ann led me inside to begin the innumerable introductions and the mindless chitchat about my books: how entertaining they were, how lovely their covers looked, and how many times they had been given as Christmas presents—all of it, supposedly, something I wanted to hear. Then there were the people (there are always a few) who wanted me to read a manuscript of theirs, one that some mindless editor had rejected. I would tell them to send their stories or novels to me and, if they did, my secretary would send them promptly back with my standard reply:

> Cut out half and revise the rest.
> Sincerely,
> Rachel

After a time, Thomas came up through the crowd and rescued me from a corner where I was held pris-

oner by three spinsters and a retired editor from To-
ronto. "There are some men across the room you
must meet," he said.

"Thomas—" I warned, but he simply took my arm,
led me toward a group of men, and broke into
their conversation.

"I want to present our guest of honor, Miss Rachel
Bradstreet," he said, patting my arm. "My dear, I'd
like you to meet, first of all, Mr. Brad Armstrong,
one of our lunar pilots."

"How do you do," I said, fairly glaring at Thomas.
He was incorrigible!

Thomas smiled all the more and continued, un-
daunted, with his introductions: a Mr. Helpmore
from the European Parliament, a Mr. Tudowell from
our own Lunar Colonial Government. (Obviously
I've changed names, but I've already stirred up
enough trouble, as you'll see.)

"They were just starting to discuss your latest book
when I left to find you," Thomas said.

"Indeed we were," Mr. Helpmore commented.
"Your book was long overdue and one your American colonials need take note of."

Mr. Tudowell laughed. "These Europeans take
everything seriously, even novels."

I did not count to ten before replying, but I did
pause and I probably stared. "You haven't taken my
novel seriously?" I said.

"Of course not. it's a well-written book, no doubt,
but it's obviously exaggerated. No one could infil-
trate and sabotage the colony."

Thomas handed me a glass of punch. I held it with
both hands to keep myself calm. "Mr. Tudowell," I
said, "I carefully researched my book, and I wrote it
to point out a major breach in the lunar colony's
security. NASA has allowed a bureaucracy to develop in which no one cares for anything beyond the

petty concerns of a trivial job, in which few people dare question what happens around them, and in which few people think. To manipulate such a bureaucracy, as I pointed out in my book, is a simple matter."

Mr. Tudowell laughed.

Brad looked serious. "Miss Bradstreet—"

"Rachel," I said.

"Rachel," he said, smiling. "People can't just fly up to the Moon. Bureaucracy or no bureaucracy, everyone must pass the security checks."

"To go there, I would simply bypass the security checks."

"But your papers—" Mr. Tudowell stammered.

"Anyone with imagination and the right contacts can get them."

Everyone was silent for a moment. Finally, Mr. Helpmore spoke. "It sounds, madam, as if you might have the courage to prove your point."

"I could do it."

"But what would you do on the Moon?" Mr. Tudowell laughed. "We don't need a writer in residence."

"Head librarian?" I asked.

"I'm afraid we don't have a library."

"Well, then," I said, and I paused thoughtfully. "Maybe it's time you got one."

"My, my," said Ann, coming up behind us. "Your conversation sounds interesting. May I join?"

"Certainly, but I need your help convincing these gentlemen I could get to the Moon if I wanted to."

"She's probably right," Ann said. "Rachel has seen places and done things few people see or do."

Brad put down his glass. "But even with everything Rachel has said and written, I still side with Mr. Tudowell. The Moon is one place I'd bet she couldn't get to."

"Are you serious?" I asked.

"Serious?"

"About a bet?"

"I guess so. That's one I'd win."

I laughed at that. "This looks like the only way to convince anyone."

"Well, then, what shall we bet?" Brad asked.

I eyed him up and down appraisingly, slowly. "Dinner in the restaurant of my choice."

"All right," he agreed.

"Wonderful. I'll let you take me to Yo Ching's Fried Rice Emporium in Lhasa, Tibet."

Everyone laughed.

"And if I lose, I'll take you there, Brad."

He smiled.

"I also need a promise of no legal entanglements," I continued, turning to Mr. Tudowell, "assurances that the colony will revitalize its security after I succeed, and full publication rights to this story."

"All of that can be arranged," he replied a bit too breezily, but at least I had witnesses to the "no legal entanglements" agreement.

"Neither of you can work to stop her before her attempt," Thomas warned, shaking a finger at Brad and Mr. Tudowell. "Whether she succeeds or not, her attempt will be valuable."

"I agree," Brad answered. "If Rachel does make it up there, the government—all of us—will be very interested. If she can do it, so could someone else without her motives. I, for one, won't work against her."

"Nor will I," Mr. Tudowell added. "I want our system vindicated, if only in a doubting author's mind. Here, please take this."

He handed me a card. "The number is my direct line. Call me after you're arrested, and I'll clear things up."

"I'll want another book from this," Thomas said.

"You'll get it," I said, and I suddenly caught the crafty gleam in Thomas' eyes. He had *planned* this to be more than a mere party.

"The next flight leaves in two days," Brad challenged.

The following morning, I surprised Marie by being up before she came in to wake me.

"Is madam sick?" she asked.

"Marie, if I were sick, I would still be in bed. I simply have a very busy day ahead of me."

"Madam will leave for Switzerland this evening?"

"No, I am leaving for the Moon tomorrow morning."

Marie laughed as she opened the drapes. "And I am going to the Riviera to stay in a big hotel, drink champagne, and eat caviar on the beach."

"I should hope not," I said. "I need you to stay here and take charge of the house."

"Madam jokes," she said, stopping and staring at me.

"Not at all. Now come and help me tie my hair in a bun."

I looked hideous with my hair in a bun, and we had to cut off some of my hair; nevertheless, I considered a bun essential to my disguise and also to my new role: that of the first lunar librarian. It was time, I felt, that the colony establish a library. I would be the one to organize and set it up—besides proving a point, winning a bet, getting a story, and improving my already brisk book sales. I had no doubts but that my quest would meet with complete success. Red tape intimidates some people, but not me. If you know how to make it work for you, there is nothing easier to cut through in the world.

I sent Marie off to buy the books I would need

and to get them properly packed for shipping. I was taking only real books of fiction and poetry, of course—I can't abide e-books, and no one coming to my library would have to either, at least for literature. I did take e-copies of the world's major reference works, and I planned to subscribe on-line to the major scientific journals, newspapers, and news magazines. While Marie was taking care of all that, I left to find a pair of plain glass, wire-framed glasses: the *tour de force* of my disguise—I looked revolting.

I spent the bulk of the afternoon in "John's" offices. I had met John while doing research for an earlier novel involving forged identities. He arranged a NASA ID badge for Thomas, the necessary papers for me, and the necessary e-trail in NASA's files—I became an employee with security clearances and flight authorization to the Moon. We even added discussion of the Lunar Library Project to various archived agendas for good measure. The next day's flight had plenty of room on it, but John ran into firewalls at that site he did not dare cross. I assured him I could take care of a boarding pass and bunk assignment on the ground.

I had everything I needed by evening.

Thomas dropped by to check on progress. He beamed with excitement about my adventure. "I contacted the major newspapers and magazines," he said. "They are all anxious about your story—mum's the word until the right time, of course; but when it breaks, it will be a great piece of publicity for you, my dear. We'll stand one hundred percent behind you."

I spent the rest of the evening packing. That night Marie, Thomas, and I took a plane to Orlando. We drove early the next morning to Cape Canaveral.

Our fake papers and ID gained us entrance to the Lunar-Terran terminal, and it was crowded with peo-

ple. Few were actually leaving for the Moon—they
worked as ground support in the various branches
of NASA. But I smiled when I thought that those
who *were* going up would probably read books from
my library.

The guards looked surprised to see the cart of
boxes and luggage Marie and I pushed in, but I paid
them no attention. We stood in line at a check-in
counter. While Marie pushed the cart slowly ahead,
I tried to look nervous: I bit my lips, forced tears to
my eyes, and shredded the newspaper I carried.
When we got to the head of the line, I laid what had
once been the *Miami Herald* on the counter. "Could
you please throw this away?" I asked in a weepy
voice. "I won't be needing it."

The clerk grabbed it, threw it in a trash can underneath her counter, and stood up to stare in dismay
at my collection of suitcases, travel bags, and boxes.
"What's all this?" she demanded.

"My luggage, and books for the Lunar Library."

"Luggage! Books! What's your name?"

"Rachel Bradstreet," I said. I'd decided to use my
real name since no one could possibly connect the
bespectacled, bun-haired librarian I had become with
the real me. She punched my name into her computer terminal.

"You're not listed on today's flight."

"Oh . . . well," I whimpered, forcing tears out of
my eyes and down my cheeks while backing away.

At that point, Thomas rushed up through the
crowd, grabbed my hand, and shook it vigorously.
"Miss Bradstreet!" he said. "I knew you'd make it."

"I . . . can't go."

"What? What's that? Anything wrong here?" he
blurted out, stepping up to the counter. He was holding a stack of folders stamped "Lunar Library Project" which he set on the counter in plain view.

"She's not listed on the flight," the clerk said.

Thomas leaned against the counter and shook his head. "She didn't send her papers in," he moaned. After a moment, he turned back to me, actually angry. "Where are your papers?"

"Why . . ." I simply shrugged and reached into my purse for a handkerchief.

"You've got to do something," he demanded, turning back to the clerk. "She must start the library as soon as possible or the project will fold. Everyone's waiting for her."

"But the flight—"

"Has room on it," Thomas said with confidence. It was the one gamble we took with the clerk.

"Well, yes there's room, but—"

"Then enter her information. She's right here and can give it to you."

The clerk looked exasperated, but she motioned for me to step forward. "I need to see your flight authorization papers," she said.

I handed her my papers. They were in order, of course. They matched the information John and I had entered into the system. She entered a few codes, and after a moment I had my boarding pass and bunk assignment.

"You're shipping real books?" the clerk complained, standing up. "They should have been sent here a week ago. As it is, we'll barely have time to get them on board."

Marie, Thomas, and I hefted the boxes onto the counter. The clerk looked through each one, stamped them, and sent them off to be decontaminated.

"Now what's all this?" the clerk asked, motioning to my suitcases and travel bags.

"My luggage."

"Your luggage! You can't take all that to the Moon. What have you brought?"

"Why, my clothes, makeup—"

"Clothes! Haven't you bought your uniforms yet?"

"Be serious—you can't expect me to wear one of those ill-tailored concoctions."

"It's either wear the uniforms or go naked."

I looked at her, considering. "Oh, all right," I said, finally. "Where can I buy a uniform?"

"Dear heaven! Come with me: we have only two hours to get you ready." She slammed a "Next line, please" sign onto her desk and came out to help Marie, Thomas, and me gather up my luggage.

After rushing us into a back room, she wrote down my measurements and shoe size, called Logistics, and asked them to send over three uniforms and a pair of shoes on the double. "If you need anything else, you'll have to get it up there," she snapped.

After that, she ravaged mercilessly through my luggage, allowing me to take only a fraction of what I had planned: a little makeup and a few personal things. The uniforms arrived (they were a ghastly light blue). I took one of them and the shoes and stepped into the lavatory to dress. Marie packed everything else into a square plastic container which the clerk sent off to the ship. The whole process had taken nearly an hour.

"One hour to go," the clerk said. "You might make it. Just follow this hall to the decontamination room, check onto your flight, and board ship. I'll call ahead to tell them you're coming."

I thanked her, winked at Thomas through false tears, and embraced Marie.

"Be careful, madam," she said quietly.

Marie stood with Thomas and waved a white handkerchief as I walked off to decontamination.

The flight up was wonderful. I spent hours in the observation deck watching Earth recede and talking to the scientists and officials traveling to their new jobs. At first, I avoided the entire crew for fear of meeting Brad before I was actually on the Moon. But Brad did not pilot my ship. He was apparently scheduled to fly up two weeks later.

The journey itself took four days, and I was hardly space-sick. Well—but that's another story. No one, at any rate, took me for anything other than what I claimed to be: a librarian traveling to start the Lunar Library.

My next test came after we had landed. I decided first to check into housing arrangements, then to discover space for the library. I put my books and belongings onto a cart and tried to look cold and aloof.

"Your name?" the attendant asked.

"Rachel Bradstreet."

"Hum . . . that's funny," she said after a moment. "You have no preassigned quarters, and I'm not sure we have room."

"Where will I sleep, then? With the algae experiments?"

The attendant stared at me, then turned back to her computer screen. "Of course not. there's space in . . . F wing, room 130. I'll write your roommates' names on this—"

"I'm sorry, but you've made a mistake."

"Mistake?"

"Yes. I want a private room."

The attendant laughed. "Don't we all? You'll like your roommates."

Roommates, I thought, conjuring up disgusting undergraduate images. But what could I do? I marched into Physical Facilities and made myself look angry (which was easy).

"Library?" the attendant asked. "We've had no orders to allocate space for a library."

"What! I come all the way from Earth with these books and you tell me you haven't made room for the Lunar Library! Give me your name and identification number. Someone hasn't done his job, and if it's you, there'll be you know what to pay."

"But ma'am, I—"

"Your name!"

"Cory."

"Cory what?"

"Cory . . . There's room here, ma'am. The computer lists space in—"

I took a small room close to the recreational facilities, had my eyes scanned for retina identification so I could operate the locks, and went to find my library.

The room was bare, absolutely bare: no desks, no shelves, not even any chairs. I stacked my books in a corner and left to find Materials Management.

"Library? We haven't received word to pull together furnishings for a library."

"You haven't?" I cooed. "That's odd. At any rate, besides the desk, chairs, e-readers, and shelves, I could use a filing cabinet and five good reading lamps."

The attendant smiled, smoothed back his oily hair, and by the end of the day my library was furnished. (I don't know how I forgot to meet that man in the bar after work.) Before I left, I shelved the books and sat down. The books stayed on their shelves despite the low gravity. I was tired, but my library looked great. Vacation? I felt that my short stay on the Moon would be one of the best.

During the next two weeks, I rushed my name onto bothersome forms, arranged for a monthly budget, and held a grand opening. My library was a complete success (as I had anticipated), but Thomas was anxious to break the story, and I knew Switzerland was a skier's paradise by now. Besides, one can take only so much peace and quiet.

As I thought about this, toward the end of an uneventful day, Barbara, one of my roommates, stepped in. "Do you have any good books?" she asked. I smiled weakly and directed her to the shelves reserved for contemporary novels.

"You have quite a selection of Rachel Bradstreet's works."

"I think highly of them."

"Say," she said, looking at me. "You and the author have the same names. Have you met her?"

"Yes—as a matter of fact, we're rather closely related."

"Is she as crazy as the papers say?"

"Oh, she's worse!" I said.

Barbara chose a novel and came to check it out. "I'm glad we have these books. How could we survive a full year without them?"

"Year?"

"Yes. I've got six months left before—"

"Surely not everyone stays for a year."

"Oh, some stay longer. I didn't think I'd last, but you get used to it."

I forced myself to breathe in, then out. I told myself that if the right people heard my story I'd be back on Earth quite soon, but I did not want to be delayed by technicalities. Barbara left, I closed the library behind her, and rushed to the flight terminal.

"I'm sorry," the attendant said after checking my file. "We won't be able to schedule your return flight for at least another eleven months."

"Eleven months! You're crazy. I can't stay that long."

"I'm afraid you have no choice."

"How dare you! I'm an American—"

"You signed the contract."

"Contract? What contract?"

He swung his computer screen toward me. On it was my file from Personnel with my signature on a one-year work agreement magnified.

I swallowed hard. "Someone must have given me the wrong papers. I wanted the minimum term of employment."

"You've got it. Minimum just changed to a year—too costly to send people back any sooner. It was all explained in the paperwork we sent you Earthside."

Paperwork I had never seen, of course. "No one takes time to read all that!" I said, struggling to come up with an excuse. "I certainly did not."

"I'm sorry," he said.

"Sorry! You'll be sorry if you don't get me on a flight out of here. I don't belong on the Moon. I'm Rachel Bradstreet, the author."

"Sure, sure. Look, there are counseling services—"

"Counseling!"

I stormed out of his ugly office and marched back toward the library. "What irony," I muttered. One can play a part too well. I had relied on our civil servant's collective indifference to get myself to the Moon, and now that very indifference threatened to keep me on the Moon checking books in and out of a library they hadn't even wanted. But I reasoned that there had to be more than one way out of America's lunar rest home. It was time I told my story.

I spent the afternoon waiting my turn at the telephone uplink and placed a call to Mr. Tudowell's "direct line" by which I'd assumed he'd meant a cell phone or something always available. I reached his secretary. She told me he was on vacation in Tahiti for three weeks and could only be disturbed for dire emergencies. I could not make her understand that a year-long lunar work contract constituted a dire emergency.

The next morning, I hurried to the administration

offices and faced another attendant. "Can't see the director?" I asked. "I suggest you check your computer. I can't wait to see him. There's a meeting in Switzerland I have to attend, and the director must know about it and authorize my flight. Now, if you'll excuse me."

I started down the hallway for the director's office, but two burly guards stepped out to block my way.

"I beg your pardon!" I said.

"Ma'am, you must be cleared by the front desk before entering this area."

"Cleared? I thought I was cleared."

In answer, one guard simply shook his head and pointed to a flashing red light in the ceiling. Two more guards hurried up and took my arms.

"Now wait a minute—"

"Just come with us," one of them said. "You can't talk with the director right now, but we know someone else who will listen to you."

Their "someone else" turned out to be a psychologist ready to help me adjust to eleven more months on the Moon. Even so, I decided to give him an honest explanation of my predicament.

"So . . . you think you're Rachel Bradstreet," he said slowly.

"I don't think that at all; I know I'm Rachel Bradstreet. Now, if you'll just contact Brad Armstrong, one of the pilots; or Mr. Tudowell, in administration—"

He had me interred for three days of observation. After the bland food and enforced rest of my "observation," I was ready to go crazy. I kept asking for someone from administration to talk with me, and finally, on the third day, one man did.

"Miss Bradstreet?" he stammered nervously as he entered my room.

"Just Rachel," I snapped.

"Oh, yes. Well, I'm Mr. Blankstare from administration. You wanted to see—"

"It's about time. I hope you understand the trouble this colony will be in when you find out I'm really Rachel Bradstreet, the author."

He cleared his throat nervously and handed me a printout of a newspaper article. It was from a recent society page of the *New York Times*, and it told of *Rachel Bradstreet's Swiss Skiing Trip!* I was shocked (it was part of their treatment). "Thomas," I moaned.

"Thomas?"

"He's too thorough."

"Undoubtedly," Mr. Blankstare murmured, as he backed out of the room.

Barbara sent me a bouquet of flowers from the experimental labs that same afternoon.

After a few days of nominally sane behavior, I was back in the library. I had so many books to check in and out that I did not have time to think of Marie skiing in the Alps using my name for about ten minutes. When the traffic slowed, I went to Communications and sent Thomas a message:

> Trapped on Moon for year. Do something!
> Rachel

Help came sooner than I expected. Things work out for the best if you know how to make them work, and Thomas knows how. He had my story blazoned across the country. I was acclaimed the "Lunar Heroine," a patriotic citizen who had taken it upon herself to expose the weaknesses in our colony's security. At first, when it became apparent that I really was Rachel Bradstreet, the authorities had no idea what to do with me; but since public opinion was solidly in my favor, there were only two things they could do:

send me home honored for meritorious service and tighten the colony's security. Before I left, I installed a plaque on the library's door citing my name as founder. The library, incidentally, became a permanent institution on the moon.

Brad had finally flown up. I arranged to leave on his return flight. He met me at the door. "Glad to have you aboard, Rachel," he said.

"Glad to be going back," I bantered. "I hear Lhasa is lovely this time of year."

He laughed, and I hurried inside.

But his laugh made me stop in the passageway and smile. Breaking the rest of Brad's security could prove a pleasurable challenge. . . .

One of the crew tapped my shoulder. "May I direct you to a seat, ma'am?"

"Pardon me?"

"May I direct you to a seat for takeoff?"

"Oh, no, thank you. I'll manage just fine."

Maternal Instincts
by Jack Nimersheim

Jack Nimersheim, a 1994 nominee for the John W. Campbell Award for Best New Science Fiction Writer, is the author of twenty-nine nonfiction books. His first published SF story, "A Fireside Chat," appeared in Mike Resnick's critically acclaimed 1992 anthology, *Alternate Presidents*. Since then, more than two dozen of Jack's stories have appeared in various SF/Fantasy magazines and anthologies. Jack's 1995 "Moriarity by Modem," was one of three short stories voted as a finalist for the 1996 Homer Award. Jack is still trying to identify that lone SF fan whose obviously lost or misplaced nomination caused this same story to miss the 1996 final Hugo Award ballot by a single vote.

I FEEL him enter me, even though he's half-a-continent away. StudLuvr is a regular customer, so I know what to expect. There's nothing subtle about his approach, no tenderness to his technique; a real *wham-bam-thank-you-ma'am* kind of guy. But he always pays extra for a full cybersuit encounter, and his e-account has never bounced a chargeback.

"Oh, God! This feels so good! You're tight, Venus! Just like a vir—"

A sideways glance at the appropriate menu display and a quick blink mutes the sound. "Venus" may be getting paid to share the man's pleasure, but that doesn't mean *I* have to listen to his insipid prattling. I swear, if I hear the "virgin" line one more time, I'm liable to blurt out that it's nothing more than an option setting in the suit's control software.

That'd certainly ruin the mood, wouldn't it? Better to stick to the *oooooo*'s, *ahhhhhhh*'s and *oh, baby*'s traditionally associated with this particular form of (if you'll pardon the pun) human intercourse.

I can tell by the shallowness of his breathing, the increasing speed of his thrusts, the way his head jerks up and down, eyelids pressed tightly together, that StudLuvr is close to orgasm. The desperate animation of a desperate man. Time to embellish my own dialogue.

"Oh, yes, sweetheart. I want it. I need it. Give it to me. Give it to me . . . *now!*"

He does.

And then, it's over.

He sighs, whispers, "Thank you," mutters a bit more loudly, "Exit program," and is gone.

I check the session log. Seventeen minutes, about average for StudLuvr. I can think of a hundred ways I'd rather pass the time, but fifty credits is fifty credits. Should allow me to keep the electricity turned on in this rat hole for another month, at least.

I peel off the cybersuit and let it drop to the floor next to my computer desk. The manufacturer recommends you perform a hardware diagnostic and run a virus scan on its critical subroutines after each use. Screw that. Now that I've taken care of the utility bill, I have better things to do.

The sky is pale yellow, the color of bile. When you breathe in, it deposits the same acrid taste on your tongue. The heat and humidity press against me like strangers in a crowded subway car. They keep promising us clean air and sunshine. Sunshine? In San Francisco? Hah! I long ago filed that one away with lower taxes, less bureaucracy, bipartisanship, and a dozen other promises offered up by our elected or attempting-to-be-elected officials over the years. If they had followed through on even half of them, things wouldn't be in the shape they are today; *I* wouldn't be in the situation I'm in, today.

It's all about Prudence. I want her back. The reason I don't have her is because of another broken promise.

I'll help you take care of the baby, Donna, Kenny told me, back when I could have been happy without Pru, without regret. I allowed this and other reassurances the bastard offered convince me to skip a trip to the local clinic and become a mother, rather than another statistic in some Planned Parenthood quarterly report.

Two weeks after Pru entered my life, Kenny disappeared from it.

The first caseworker showed up at my door three months to the day after Kenny walked through it, going the other way. Seems a nosy neighbor couldn't tell the difference between colic and a neglected child. Fortunately for me, that first caseworker, a woman, could. She examined Pru, checked out the apartment, and decided not to pursue the matter. Not so fortunately for me, government agencies are a lot like e-mail mass marketers. Once you're listed with one of them, your name begins popping up everywhere.

The second caseworker arrived a month after the first. This one was a man. His perception of what constituted a qualified parent reflected his gender.

"Yes, the baby's father walked out on us." "No, I don't have a husband or boyfriend." "Yes, I do believe a woman can raise a child by herself." I could tell by his reaction to these and other responses I gave to the questions he read off the glowing screen of his netpad that he'd already decided something must be wrong with me. I had a child out of wed-

lock; I couldn't hold onto one man; I had no desire
to find another one. In his opinion, his *male* opinion,
I couldn't have been more "out of the mainstream"
had I been born with three eyes and two noses.

In the end, his opinion prevailed—which explains
why I'm living alone now, cyber-screwing men I recognize only by their pseudonicks and sexual
predilections.

"Yo, DoDo."

Tiyasha always greets me the same way. Were I so
inclined, I could be offended by the manner in which
she chose to parse Donna to create this particular
sobriquet. I'm not. despite their sardonic nature,
there's genuine affection in the nicknames Ti assigns
all her friends and customers. I started out as the
latter. Over the past year, however, she and I have
crossed the boundary separating the two. Shared sorrow has this effect on people.

Tiyasha is sitting in her usual spot—behind her
antique oak desk, hunched over her antique computer. No one hacks on a standalone system with a
CRT monitor anymore. Well, no one but Tiyasha.

I plop into a folding metal chair, across the desk
from her. The only other furnishings in the room are
a small sink with a table next to it, on the wall to
my right. A coffee machine, one of those drip kind,
sits atop the table. In all the months I've been coming
here, I've never seen any coffee in it. I thought my
lifestyle was Spartan, until I met Tiyasha.

"Hi, Ti. How goes it?"

"Slowly, hon. But at least it goes. Beats the hell
out of the alternative."

One only has to glance at her to realize that, in
her younger years, Tiyasha must have been beautiful.
Stunning beauty. The kind poets strive to capture in
verse, songwriters attempt to reflect in their lyrics

and melodies. The sharp edges of a difficult life may have whittled away some of that thin veneer we call physical beauty, but enough remains to reveal how much deeper it must have run, at one time. Her hair—still thick and blonde, even though she recently turned sixty—cascades over her shoulders, then flows down gracefully to the small of her back. Her eyes are the deepest shade of blue, a color I can recall seeing only once before.

Years ago, shortly before she died, my mother scraped together enough money for the two of us to take a bus trip to the Florida Keys. It was the only time she ever managed to coordinate taking off enough time from both her jobs to allow an extended vacation. The water at the motel we stayed in, a shallow bay on the Gulf side of Lower Matecumbe Key, was that shade of blue. It took away my breath the first time I saw it. I think about that vacation and smile, whenever I look into Tiyasha's eyes.

"Any action this morning, hon?"

"Just one. StudLuvr."

"Ah, no wonder you're out and about so early." She chuckles. I've told her about most of my regulars, so she's familiar with their idiosyncrasies.

Ti glances up from her monitor and looks across the desk at me. She's grinning, a twinkle in those beautiful blue eyes. "Actually, it's been a pretty productive morning, here, DoDo."

I feel my heart skip a beat—then instinctively take a deep breath, calm myself. I've been disappointed so many times. Too many times. Tiyasha understands and continues.

"You told me once that Pru was born at SF General, didn't you?"

I nod.

"July 12, right?"

A second nod.

"Do you happen to remember the exact time?"

"1:22 PM." Like I could ever forget.

"Bingo! I knew it! My gut told me this was a solid lead." She taps her monitor. "C'mere, DoDo. Take a look at this."

I force myself out of the chair and realize I'm shaking. Could it be? I place my hand on the corner of the desk, steadying myself, as I walk around it and stand next to Tiyasha. I look over her shoulder, down at the monitor screen. It takes me a few seconds to recognize what she's pointing at. It's a birth certificate from San Francisco General Hospital. The name on the top line is "Jane Doe"—how creative—but the DOB is recorded as 7/12/2009. Time of birth, 13:22.

"What'd'ya think, hon? Have we hit the jackpot?"

I stand there, crying. Once again, I merely nod. No words can express what I'm feeling. And once again, through that silent communion only mothers share, Tiyasha understands. She leans back in her chair, places a hand on my arm, and smiles.

Pru's altered birth certificate contained a registration number. That registration number, in turn, provided a starting point for a comprehensive search. Ti hacked together and turned loose a tracking 'bot based on this registration number. Once released, the 'bot started scouring the 'net automatically, requiring no additional human intervention, which left Tiyasha and me with nothing to do but keep each other company—something we both enjoyed, anyway.

"The way I figure it, whoever ended up adopting Pru must have some pretty powerful friends to get a birth certificate altered retroactively like that. It also explains why every name scan I ran on Pru came up empty, prior to now. Prudence Danner doesn't exist. Not officially, at least. Just a 'Jane Doe' born in some municipal hospital, twelve years ago."

"It's a strange feeling, Ti, to have someone tell you your daughter doesn't exist."

"Ah, hon. You know what I meant."

"Yeah, I do. But it still feels weird, like my worst nightmares coming true. You have no idea how many times over the past twelve years I've wondered if Pru was still out there somewhere, whether or not she was even still alive." It's a stupid comment. Of course she does. That's the shared-sorrow part of our friendship. "Sorry, Ti. I didn't mean . . ."

"No problem, hon. I know you didn't."

We sit there in silence for several minutes, sipping our coffee. (Ti actually made some, after digging out from a cabinet under the sink a can of coffee, a filter and two cups.)

"Ti?"

"Yes, hon?"

"Have you ever thought about what you would have done, if you could have tracked down your daughter?"

"Hell, yes. At least a hundred times a day, at first."

"So, why didn't you—track her down, I mean?"

"Oh, I did. Or tried to, at least. It was a different world back then, DoDo. 'Bigger,' people used to say. That was before 'net shrank everything down to the size of a wire tethered to a broadband connection." She points to the wall behind her, where her own cable modem is plugged in. "Records were kept on paper and stored in filing cabinets, information scattered about helter-skelter, bits and pieces physically separated from one another. Tracking down a single item was a hell of a lot more difficult than it is today. Even if you did manage to do so, there was no guarantee that that particular piece of information would point you toward the next one you needed to put together whatever puzzle you happened to be working on, at the time.

"I spent several years picking up the pieces, so to speak, but never quite gathered together enough of them to give me the whole picture. Then, one day, even the meager paper trail I'd managed to assemble up to that point went cold."

Tiyasha sighs and glances down at the coffee cup sitting on the desktop in front of her. She runs a slender index finger around the top of it. Her face—always so animated, so vibrant—stiffens into a frozen mask. And then, the years begin to settle over it, like pages sliding off a calendar and into a pile on the floor below. By the time she glances back up at me again, sixty years have passed in but a few seconds. For the first time in all the time I've known her, Ti looks as old as she really is.

"That's when I gave up, DoDo, lost all hope."

The uncomfortable silence that follows this revelation lasts another sixty years.

Tiyasha finally breaks it. "But that was a long time ago, hon. Right now, I just want to make sure the same thing doesn't happen to you. So, let's see how that 'bot is doing, shall we? It should have come up with something, by now."

It's amazing how much personal information about each and every one of us is floating around out there, just waiting to be plucked out of cyberspace. Virtually every aspect of our lives has been converted to binary code and stored on some computer, somewhere. You may die tomorrow, but your records live on, forever—or at least until someone decides to purge an archive file. Eternal life viewed through a digital prism. Immortality reflected in a fun-house mirror.

For the first time in over ten years, I know something about my daughter. Quite a bit, actually.

Allison Hewitt (*nee* Prudence Danner) lives in

Washington, DC. Her adoptive parents, Frank and Sally Hewitt, are career diplomats. Tiyasha was right; they do have powerful friends. He's an Undersecretary of State in the Bureau of Middle Eastern Affairs. She was once the Deputy U.S. Ambassador to the United Nations. The Hewitts own a three-story brownstone in a section of the city I could never afford to live in—even if I spent every waking minute of every day strapped into my cybersuit, fulfilling all the sexual fantasies of all the world's frustrated StudLuvrs.

Their daughter (*my* daughter) attends the Woods Academy, a private school in Silver Spring, Maryland, where she's a straight-A student. ("I guess that settles the old 'nature vs. nurture' debate, eh?" Tiyasha said with a smile, when this piece of information popped up on her monitor.) She also participates in a variety of extracurricular activities, including soccer, drama club, and the school yearbook.

Tiyasha follows a link to this last activity and finds . . .

. . . a picture . . .

. . . a picture of my daughter. God, she's beautiful! Yes, she wears glasses. And, yes, her toothy grin reveals the twin rows of braces that have become *de rigueur* for every girl her age, in this modern age of cosmetic perfection. But she *is* beautiful!

Allison Hewitt, *Pru*, has her grandmother's (her *real* grandmother's) eyes—dark brown and almond shaped—topped by equally dark, luxurious eyebrows. Her long, auburn hair is pulled back into a ponytail, just like I often wear mine. And she has freckles. Not so many as to be distracting, mind you, only a few splashed here and there, just above her high cheekbones. You have to look closely to see them.

And I am looking closely, very closely—studying

each feature, every nuance of the face on Ti's monitor. That's my baby. She may be twelve years old, a young girl about to enter that nebulous miasma called adolescence which separates innocence from womanhood, but she's still my baby.

There are only two problems. One, Pru lives on the opposite side of the continent from me. And, two, my baby also happens to be Frank and Sally Hewitt's daughter.

I'm back in the suit with StudLuvr, otherwise known as Wendell Slater. Who would have suspected my seventeen-minute-man was a lawyer? I'll bet he moves at a much more leisurely pace when *he's* the one tallying up the tab. Unlike people in my profession, most lawyers get paid by the hour.

Tiyasha discovered Wendell's real identity while hacking the histories of several of my regular customers. Her initial plan was simply to skim a few e-accounts and withdraw a small number of credits from each, not enough to raise any red flags. This would give us some seed money, she explained, to help finance whatever actions we ultimately pursued to reunite Pru and me. As soon as Ti uncovered Wendell's occupation, she realized we'd struck e-gold. By the time "StudLuvr" appeared in my appointment queue a week later, she had tweaked the suit's control program and we were ready to proceed.

Men are so predictable, especially in matters of money and sex. I knew if I waited long enough, Wendell would fall back into his usual patterns.

". . . so tight, Venus, just like a virgin."

That's my cue.

"You like tight, sweetheart?"

The question startles him. I've never before responded to the virgin line. He hesitates, breaks his normal frenetic rhythm.

". . . er . . . um . . . yeah. Sure."

"In that case, lover, do I have a surprise for you."

Time to see if Ti's control override works. I redirect my eyes to the suit's Options menu and blink . . . hard.

"Ouch! What the hell?"

"How do you like that? Tight enough . . . *Wendell?*"

"Wha . . . ?"

"Maybe you shouldn't say anything, sweetheart. Try listening, instead."

"Now see here! What do you think you're . . ."

I blink a second time, only slightly less emphatically than before. "I said, listen, Wendell!"

No protest, this time.

"That's better." I take a deep breath and continue, just like Ti and I rehearsed. "As you've obviously figured out by now, I know who you are. To be honest, Wendell, that doesn't interest me as much as *what* you are. A lawyer. Why? Because it just so happens that, right now, I find myself in need of a lawyer. And I figure that, right now, you find yourself inclined to consider offering your services, pro boner . . . um . . . I mean, *pro bono*, if you get my drift."

He does.

"That's blackmail!"

"I prefer the term 'negotiation.' Or possibly 'compromise.' And let's face it, sweetheart, you're in a pretty compromising position right now, one I'm certain your wife and coworkers would find fascinating if they found out about it, don't you think?

"To put it in the vernacular, Wendell, I've got you by the balls." I resist the temptation to blink again. "Well, close enough, at least. So, do we understand each other?"

Wendell's silence indicates we do. Time to tighten the noose a bit more—figuratively speaking, this time. Any additional coercion using Ti's elegant little cybersuit hack appears to be unnecessary.

Wendell may be a mediocre cyberlover; as it turns out, however, he must be a pretty damn good lawyer. Within a week, he arranges a meeting between me and the Hewitts. I'm impressed, and just a little nervous. I know it's all in my head, but the cybersuit feels claustrophobic when it's programmed to simulate a white blouse, dark blue skirt, and matching jacket. Adding to my discomfort is the fact that Ti insisted she program in pantyhose, rather than the thigh-highs I would have preferred; now I know how sausage feels.

I have no idea what Wendell's real offices in Saint Louis look like. It's clear that, in his own mind, at least, they're quite the showplace. The virtual conference room he's designed is opulent to excess.

The walls are cherry paneling, floor to twelve-foot ceiling, polished to the point where you can see your reflection in them. I assume the four huge framed portraits spaced around the room—one hanging on each wall, each of a different older gentleman wearing what could be the same black pinstripe, three-piece suit—are the senior partners in Wendell's law firm. (Of course, they could just be four old geezers he culled from some on-line image library to impress us.) The table occupying the center of the room is a giant circle, at least eight feet in diameter, also cherry, sitting atop a massive pedestal base. Six large burgundy leather chairs surround it.

Wendell and I occupy one side of the table. Sally and Frank Hewitt sit across from us with their own attorney—an older, distinguished looking gentleman whose name I didn't quite catch when we were first introduced. It would be embarrassing to ask that he repeat it now. One chair remains empty. There's a nice bit of symbolism for you.

The Hewitts are younger than I'd imagined them. They appear to be in their mid-to-late-thirties. ("Appear" being the operative word. In cyberspace no one can see your age, if you choose not to let them. Consider how little my own conservatively dressed image reflects reality. Wendell did a double-take when it appeared. Surely he didn't think I'd show up wearing my usual "work clothes," did he?) They also care about each other deeply, know each other well. This is obvious from the way they interact with one another, even in this virtual environment. They hold hands constantly. One checks with the other, just a subtle glance in his or her direction, before making any comment germane to the discussion at hand. Several times since the meeting began, she's completed a sentence he's started, or vice versa, always without reproach or recrimination.

I find myself envying them what they possess—beyond the obvious, even.

No. I can't think that way. There *is* nothing beyond the obvious. It's all about Pru.

"I trust we have proved to the Hewitts' satisfaction that my client is, indeed, the girl's birth mother?"

" 'Proved' might be too strong a word, counselor. Let's just say we're willing to admit there could be a legitimate argument that she is who she claims to be."

"We'll accept that limited concession for now, assuming that it establishes a viable framework within which to pursue further negotiations between the Hewitts and my client."

"We feel comfortable with that assumption, yes."

Wendell nods. "Good. Good. Shall we proceed to the next point, then?"

This verbal parrying has been going on for almost an hour—Wendell and his counterpart across the table identifying each other with personal pronouns, the editorial "we," while persistently referring to the

Hewitts or me in the third person. The language of the law may be slightly more eloquent than the rhetoric of my profession, but it's no less obtuse.

"Wendell?"

My interruption surprises him. I've hardly spoken since the meeting started, primarily to reply to questions from him or the Hewitts' attorney, and then with only one- or two-word responses.

"Um, yes, Donna?"

My virtual representation pats the hand of his virtual representation atop the nonexistent cherry table around which none of us is really gathered. He flinches almost imperceptibly at the contact, presumably recalling our earlier, more intimate encounters.

"I realize how much you lawyers love to talk lawyer talk, darling, but don't you think the Hewitts and I have suffered through enough 'points' already?"

It's a measured gamble: the deflection of conversation; the affected personality. It's a gamble I'm willing to take, however. Something in Sally Hewitt's eyes whenever she looks at me makes me suspect that, being a mother herself—albeit, an adoptive one—she has no more patience than I for all this legal haggling. As a truism, *The eyes provide a window to the soul* applies equally to both cyberspace and the real world.

I turn toward Sally Hewitt. "These two can debate all morning whether or not all the *i*'s and *t*'s in my deposition are dotted and crossed correctly, Mrs. Hewitt. You know Allison is my daughter, Prudence, don't you?"

She studies my face for several seconds—looking through *my* windows, into *my* soul, seeking within it the same reassurances I detected in hers.

"Yes, I do," she replies finally.

"But, Sally . . ." their lawyer begins to protest.

"Oh, hush," she says.

He does.

Sally Hewitt turns away from me and looks into her husband's eyes. She pats his hand, much like I did Wendell's, only moments earlier. "This woman is telling the truth, Frank. She is, indeed, Allison's birth mother. I don't need any signed affidavits or notarized documents to convince me of that."

I allow myself to smile. One part—perhaps the most difficult part—of my ordeal is over.

". . . tried so many times, always without success. I blamed myself. Frank blamed himself. The doctors could never determine who was right. Not that this really mattered. It was never about culpability. We just wanted desperately to have a child, and no one was able to tell us why we couldn't."

Both lawyers had balked when I suggested Sally Hewitt and I be allowed to talk in private. (Well, *almost* in private. Only I know Ti is tapped into my feed, archiving everything that's happened since I activated the cybersuit.) In the end, however, the determination of two mothers concerned about the welfare of their child prevailed; it always does.

"I had just the opposite problem. It seems like all I did was think about getting it on with Kenny one night and, *poof,* the next thing I knew, I was pregnant with Pru."

She laughs. It's a nice laugh. Natural. Not overbearing. It's a laugh, I suddenly realize, that I find myself thinking I'm glad my daughter has heard, while growing up.

"After years of trying," she continues, "Frank and I finally admitted to ourselves that it wasn't going to happen. We would never have a son or daughter of our own."

She pauses and closes her eyes. The memory, obviously, is painful for her to recall.

"Mrs. Hewitt . . ."

"Please, call me Sally. In light of the bond we share, 'Mrs. Hewitt' sounds so formal, so impersonal."

She's right.

"You don't have to tell me all this, Sally."

"No, no. it's all right. I want to. I want you to know how Allison . . . Prudence . . . came into our lives.

"Anyway, the inability to have a child of our own didn't cause us to abandon our desire to raise a family. We knew there were children out there who, for whatever reason, needed a home. Frank and I were willing, and able, to provide one."

"But how did you find Pru?"

"You're aware that I once worked with the United Nations, right?"

I nod.

"It was just after New Year's, 2113. I was in San Francisco to kick off the International Year of the Child. One of the events I attended was the opening of a new U.N.-sponsored multifunction youth facility, which included a child placement center. During the dedication ceremony they paraded in front of the cameras all these supposedly orphaned or unwanted children. Allison was one of them. She was such a beautiful child, Donna."

"I knew that even before you did, remember?"

"Of course you did. I apologize if that sounded callous. I didn't mean it that way. I was merely trying to convey to you some of what I felt, the first time I saw her.

"I called Frank from my hotel room that same evening and told him I'd found our daughter. I remember using that precise phrase. 'I've found our daughter, sweetheart.' He thought I was crazy, until he flew out the following weekend and saw her himself. We initiated the adoption procedures the following week."

We sit there in silence, neither one of us quite certain what to say next. A dozen conflicting emotions roil within me: anger at whatever powers-that-be took it upon themselves to label Pru and "unwanted child"; frustration that, at the time, I was not even given the opportunity to dispute this characterization; disgust with a system that allowed those long-ago events to progress the way they had. And yet, at the same time, I feel a certain satisfaction that, after so many years of uncertainty, I had finally solved the mystery of Pru's disappearance; an undeniable pride in the fact that my daughter could elicit such an immediate and profound reaction from Sally and Frank Hewitt; and, yes, an ironic sense of relief, realizing that, when Pru was taken from my life, she was at least taken into the lives of two people who, if possible, love her as much and as deeply as I do.

Know thy enemy.
Sounds like good advice, doesn't it? Simple. Straightforward. Logical. How about nave, disorienting, disconcerting? Yesterday, all I wanted was to reclaim my child, regardless of what that involved. Today, I'm not so sure. Ignorance sometimes is bliss. Anonymity conveys its own consolations.

"It really got to you, didn't it, hon?"

"You were monitoring the meeting, Ti. You saw what happened. How am I supposed to react? What am I supposed to be feeling?"

"I can't tell you that, DoDo. Hell, I have enough problems keeping my own house in order." She looks around the room and sighs. "That could explain the interior decorating, eh?"

"They love her, Ti, just like I do. That's obvious. And I assume Pru loves them, just as much. I can see it in her eyes, in every picture we've found of her. She's happy. Her current life, the life of Allison Hewitt. is all she knows. She's not even aware that

I exist. Do I have the right to change that, threaten her happiness?"

"The right? That one's easy. Sure you do, kiddo. Whether or not you have the desire to, well, that's another story. As to whether one would necessarily lead to the other? Someone a lot wiser than I am will have to answer that one—assuming an answer even exists. I suspect that, like so many questions, this one has no answer. No *right* answer, at least."

"So, what do I do, Ti?"

"Did I ever tell you why I started hacking, DoDo?"

The sudden shift in subject matter catches me unaware. "Um . . . no."

"Hacking isn't about what most people think, kiddo. A few rotten apples have given it a bad reputation, over the years—especially back when all this first started. I'm talking now about the idiots who would break into a system for only one reason, to wreak havoc on it. Of course, they got all the press coverage.

"You're too young to remember the flap some kid named Robert Morris caused back in the late '80s, when he turned a worm loose in cyberspace. Damn near crashed the 'net. Certainly caused one hell of a traffic jam, for a while. Morris claimed it was all an accident, but no one ever believed that. Vladimir Levin's story is less ambiguous. He hacked into a bank's mainframe and made several, um, small withdrawals for himself—to the tune of a cool ten-mil, according to some accounts. These two may have been admired by the hacker community for their technical skills, but we still recognized them for what they were. Bad seeds. For every Morris or Levin out there, however, a hundred other hackers tickled their keyboards for what they felt was a legitimate reason, the pursuit of truth. I was one of them.

"We didn't buy into the popular mantra of the

time that certain information was best kept secret, guarded by a select few in business and government. Instead, we followed a different creed, one that says 'Knowledge is power." We didn't like the idea of so much knowledge—and, by extension, its associated power—being withheld from the masses . . ."

"The *masses?*" I try, without success, to hide my amusement.

Tiyasha laughs her self-deprecating laugh. "Yeah, we really called ourselves that, back then. Sounds kinda quaint, now, doesn't it?

"Anyway, we took it upon ourselves to change the status quo. We poked around in the hidden corners of cyberspace and, whenever possible, attempted to shine a little light on some of those dark secrets that have always been so coveted by governments, businesses, and other organizations."

"Did you succeed?"

"Depends on how you measure success, hon. We managed some pretty amazing exposés. In the end, though, I'm not sure how much difference any of it made.

"I do know one thing, however. I never regretted what I did or why I did it. I believed then, and still believe now, that people deserve to be told the facts, all the facts, about any situation, and then be given the opportunity to decide for themselves what it all means, how to deal with it."

Ti pauses for a moment, as if she's finished her narrative. Then she adds, almost in a whisper, "You asked me once what I would have done, had I ever found my own daughter. I believe I just answered that question."

It's not unusual for me not to know what to expect, when I put on the cybersuit. Occupational hazard, I guess. Johns rarely submit a job description before engaging my services. This particular morning, however, I'm even more uncertain than I normally am. Uncertain and something else, something I haven't been in years. I'm anxious. Why shouldn't I be? If I mess up in the suit today, I could really be screwed.

(That's right, girl. Go ahead. Make jokes, professional puns. Maybe the laughter will drown out the sound of your own heart pounding.)

Tiyasha was surprised when Sally Hewitt agreed to my proposition. I wasn't—although I did wonder whether and how much she had to coerce her husband into going along with it. Men protect; women nurture. That's not meant to be a sexist comment. There's nothing prejudiced about the truth; it simply exists. It's when we try to deny the truth that we tend to reveal our biases.

I plugged in early. I don't know why. It's not like you can tidy up a simulation. Any changes I want to make I'd have to relay to Ti. Then she'd have to program them in. There's not enough time for any of that. Sally's due to arrive any second. Sally and . . .

Suddenly, they're here.

This particular aspect of the cybersuits is always disconcerting. One second you're alone and the next you're not. There's never the sound of someone's approach, no knock on a door to signal their arrival. They just appear, shimmer into existence like a ghost.

I look at Allison Hewitt and a hundred ghosts come back to haunt me. My mother's eyes. My own youth. There's even a hint of her father in the way she stands, the shuffling posture of someone who's not really certain she wants to be where she is. Kenny was always like that, always on the verge of fleeing— until, finally, one day, he did.

Will she do the same? And if she does, can I blame her? I know that I didn't abandon her, that she wasn't the "unwanted child" Sally and Frank Hewitt were led to believe she was, when they welcomed her into their lives. But does she understand this? Did Sally tell her, explain to her what happened so many years in the past? A lifetime ago; *her* lifetime. I can't honestly say whether or not I would have, were our situations reversed.

"Hello, Donna." Sally says, breaking an uncomfortable silence I hadn't recognized existed, until it's gone.

"Hi, Sally." I reply.

The silence returns. Neither of us knows where to go from here.

"Mommy?"

"Yes?" Sally and I both respond. Embarrassed, I defer, nod to Sally.

Allison, *Pru*, balls her hands into two fists and places them firmly on her hips. She turns to Sally with an overly serious look on her face and says, "Since you brought me here to meet my mother, don't you think it might be a good idea to introduce us?"

And then, this young girl—this beautiful, young girl—giggles.

And then, Sally Hewitt smiles—first at her daughter, *my* daughter, and then, at me.

And then, somehow, I know—everything is going to be okay.

Skimming Stones
by Bradley H. Sinor

Bradley H. Sinor recently had a friend tell him that he wrote stories that were suitable for the whole family. "Yeah," laughed Brad. "If it's the Addams Family or some of Dracula's relatives." His short fiction has appeared in the *Merovingen Nights* series, *Time of the Vampires, On Crusade: More Tales of the Knights Templar, Lord of the Fantastic: Stories in Tribute to Roger Zelazny, Horrors: 365 Scary Stories, Merlin, Yard Dog Comics, Such A Pretty Face, Warrior Fantastic, Single White Vampire, Bubbas of the Apocalypse* and *Dracula In London.* Five of his stories were recently published in the chapbook/collection Dark and Stormy Nights. His nonfiction has turned up in such diverse venues as *Personal Demons* (a CD anthology), *Starlog, Star Trek: The Next Generation* magazine, *Baby Boomer Collectibles, Weird Tales, California Highway Patrolman* magazine, *Persimmon Hill* and others.

L AYING flat on my stomach with my face less than a foot from the river was not the way I had planned to spend Friday night. Especially when I knew that waiting at the Shadow Creek Bar, there was a martini, possibly several, with my name on it.

Not that I had a whole lot of choice in the matter. I work for the City of Tulsa as an electrical maintenance engineer, so I end up doing a lot of work in places that I would prefer not to even think about, if I didn't have to; all in the name of keeping various facilities around town running.

The hours weren't the greatest, but I was pulling down decent money and didn't have to spend my days in a cubicle. This girl wasn't complaining; I'd gotten enough of that from my ex-husband, Luke. He didn't like my hours, the fact that my paycheck was bigger than his, or much of anything in our relationship. When he finally took off, three days after our first anniversary, with that dye-job blonde, Denise, I couldn't have been happier.

With budget shortfalls and layoffs, my department was shorthanded. Truth be told, we'd never had enough people, so making do was a way of life. That was why, on a Friday night, I was in coveralls, lying on a stage floating on the Arkansas River, instead of wearing my new leather miniskirt, boots, and suede jacket and barhopping with my best friend, Jani.

The floating stage is anchored in a small cove. They use it for outdoor theater productions, performances by musicians, and any formal city-type ceremony that the politicians want to conduct under the open Oklahoma sky.

The problem with the place is that it was designed by an idiot. At least once a month my department got a frantic call from the stage manager saying something was wrong and it needed to be fixed—yesterday. Since Tulsa Opera was supposed to do a benefit preview at two on Sunday afternoon, the powers-that-be thought it would be sort of nice if things worked.

I had come out with a four-man crew around noon, then at six my boss called and told the others to go home. Less overtime, I suspect. "Look, Nancy," he had said. "You can handle it by yourself. Shouldn't take you more than half an hour or so."

Yeah, right! Three hours later I was closing the last access port and breathing a long sigh of relief when I heard something hitting the side of the stage. I trailed my flashlight along the water to see what it was. There was something I thought might be a mannequin, thrown away by frat boys at one of their drunken parties.

Okay, call me a Girl Scout, but I figured there was a chance I was wrong, so I dropped my flashlight and made a grab for whatever it was.

That took me several tries. The problem was, I couldn't get a good enough hold as the body dropped back into the water several times. In the process I heard the sound of coughing; that was proof enough that I wasn't trying to rescue a dummy or a corpse.

Once I did get him up on the stage, I pushed his hair out of the way and discovered two important things: "he" was a "she," and *she* had my face!

Beyond a knot on the side of her head the size of a goose egg, some bruises and a cut on her cheek, my newfound twin didn't seem to have anything obviously wrong with her. City regulations, not to mention common sense, said I ought to call 911 or get her to the nearest hospital.

It was just that looking at that face, my face, weirded me out so much, that I just could not see going by regulations right then as being the smartest thing in the world.

"Take it easy. You're okay. I got you out of the water," I told her.

"Where am I?" she asked, her voice a cracked whisper.

"Tulsa," I said.

Don't ask me why, but right then I figured the best thing to do was get her away from there. The only place I could think of to take her was my house. I live in a suburb of Tulsa, somewhat isolated, which suited me just fine. I had been astonished when Luke had been willing to sign the place over to me as part of our divorce settlement. I took it, of course, after making sure he hadn't secretly mortgaged the place to the hilt.

Since her legs didn't seem to want to work for more than three or four steps at a time without going out from under her, getting my guest inside was not easy. My cats, Paranoia and Schizo, were on the sofa but decided to take off for other places when they saw us come through the door.

Her clothes had dried some, but were still smelly and wet. I managed to get one boot off of her and was just untying the other when my guest said, "If it's seduction you have in mind, I'm afraid that you're going to be rather disappointed. I'm not feeling up for anything just now."

"Don't worry about that. I've got better ways of picking up dates than fishing them out of the river. Besides, I don't think you're my type."

"If she's not, Nancy, am I?"

Standing in the living room door was Kent Sabiani. At six-one, his lanky frame and gray-streaked goatee gave him a vaguely satanic look, which went over great with some of my more religious neighbors.

He moved so quietly that sometimes you would just look up and there he was. Kent was an Emergency Medical Technician, so I had called him on my cell phone to come give my visitor a quick once-over.

"Damn it, make some noise when you come in the door!"

"Hey, I did make noise; it's not my fault that you didn't hear me. So who's your friend?"

"Name's Sian," she said in a whisper.

I saw the look on Kent's face when he got a good look at Sian. He was cool, didn't say a word, just cocked an eyebrow at me and went to work.

I excused myself to the kitchen, where I found a

couple of beers in the back of the fridge. Kent was just unwrapping a blood pressure cuff from Sian's arm when I came back. I handed him a beer.

"Thanks. Other than the obvious—bruises, scratches and contusions—Sian seems in pretty good shape," he said. "How far did you fall?"

"Don't know, but it hurt like hell," she said.

"Must have felt like hitting concrete."

Sian nodded

"All right, that's enough," Kent said. "I would say a few hours' sleep are in order. The interrogation can wait."

The next morning I came in the kitchen and found Kent rummaging around in the cabinets, a look of frustration on his face. "So where did you put the frying pan *this* time?" he asked when he saw me.

"Just for using that tone, I'm not telling you." After all, it was my kitchen and I *knew* where it was. "Besides, why should I help you? You left your socks and shirt hanging on the dresser mirror, again."

"Be that way and you get to cook." He grinned.

That was a good argument. I'm a decent cook, but it's nice to have someone else do the work, and I stand in awe of what Kent can do in a kitchen. "Cabinet! Just to the right of the stove!" I said quickly.

Kent pulled out the skillet, fetched eggs, milk, and a variety of other things from the refrigerator. I've never been able to figure out if he has specific recipes or just works with what's there. The results speak for themselves.

"Is there anything I can do to help?"

Sian walked into the kitchen wearing my heavy red bathrobe. A shower and some sleep seemed to have done her a world of good. The bruises were still prominent, but in the light of day they looked like they would heal. She moved a bit stiffly, favoring her right leg, but, given the circumstances, that was understandable.

"Just grab a stool," I said. "Kent is working his magic."

A moment later he presented us each with a tall glass of orange juice. The odor of blueberry muffins began to fill the kitchen, followed a few minutes later by Kent setting a plate of them in front of Sian and me. He turned his attention back to the stove. I knew omelets would soon follow.

"Okay," I said. "Feel like answering a few questions?"

"Ask away," Sian said, slicing a muffin and layering butter onto it. "This is very good. She was right when she called it magic."

"Thank you. So what happened?" Kent asked, without turning around.

"You wouldn't believe that I just got a little bit plastered and fell into the river?" I arched an eyebrow at her and didn't say a thing. "Well, I didn't think so, especially if you've looked in the mirror anytime. The long and the short of it is, I'm you."

"Really?"

Sian nodded as she took a sip from her glass.

"If you were able to run a DNA test on the two of us, you'd see that we are genetically the same person. Only I'm not from this world."

"Unless you were cloned by aliens, or are a part of some sort of secret government conspiracy, that leaves only two possible explanations," said Kent. "Time travel or parallel world?"

Sian looked at him, shocked. "I'm impressed. You keeping him around on a long-term basis?" she asked me.

I didn't answer. Instead, I reached across the counter and grabbed Sian's left arm, pushing back the sleeve. Midway up the arm was a formation of veins, making the letter H, clearly visible beneath her skin. A jagged scar, about four inches in length, bisected it. I bared my arm to show an identical mark, but reversed. I'd definitely call this a bit more than circumstantial evidence.

"I *am* from a parallel world," she said. "Where history, as you know it, ran differently, because of different choices."

"So how did you end up in our corner of the time-space continuum?" asked Kent.

"To make a long story short, I'm a runaway princess." Kent had to struggle to keep from laughing, this was beginning to sound like something out of those fantasy novels he's fond of reading.

"Let me see if I have this straight," I said. "You're me, from a parallel world, where you're a princess. But you decided to take it on the lam from your life as one of the royals and came here."

"Not at first. I left just over a year ago. I've probably been to seven or eight different worlds before this one."

Sian made a gesture in the air and a small globe of light appeared just above the palm of her hand. It hovered there for a moment and was gone.

"Kent isn't the only one who can do magic. It looks like magic, but there are sound principles of science behind it," she said. "Problem is that is about all I can do."

"A handy talent. So why *did* you leave home?" Kent asked.

Sian laid the remnants of her muffin down on a napkin. "They wanted to make me queen."

"Queen?" I said. "I don't think you have any glass ceiling where you come from."

She cocked an eyebrow at me but went on. "My daddy had decided it was time for him to have a co-ruler; someone who would do most of the work while he took it easy. I may be the eldest, but my brother is far more suited to the throne. When he wouldn't let me abdicate, I faked my death and ran. Problem was he didn't believe it. He commissioned the Guild of Head Hunters to find me and bring me home. They've come close too many times."

"You figured to hide from them here in Tulsa?" Kent asked.

"Actually, no," she sighed. "I left a trail for the Head Hunters to follow, I had planned to lay a trap for them and then permanently lose them in the desert."

Permanently lose? To me that said kill them and dump the bodies.

"So why are you in Tulsa?" asked Kent.

"Because of her," Sian pointed at me. "For reasons that I don't understand whenever I enter a new world, I tend to end up close to myself, if I'm still alive in that world. There have been a few where I was dead or had never been born."

"I bet that was a fun discovery," I said.

Kent picked up a muffin from the tin and began to gingerly peel the paper cup from around it.

"Sian, one thing that you haven't mentioned is just how you're able to go hopping from parallel world to parallel world. What went wrong here?" I asked.

"What makes you think anything went wrong?"

"A thirty-foot drop into the river sort of suggests that things didn't work the way you planned them to work," I said.

Sian laughed. "Oh, they definitely didn't work the way I had planned them. Travel between the worlds is a combination of making your mind perceive things differently and then stepping through the gate. Ideally, you need a set of rune stones to open that gate. I grabbed some of the best before I left home.

"The only trouble is that I lost my rune stones. My father's chief warlock taught me ways of duplicating the rune door with my mind, using a variety of herbs, native flora, and pharmaceuticals. The problem is the last two worlds haven't have what I needed and I had to use substitutes. They didn't always work right."

"So you're saying that when you do this you're on drugs," Kent grinned. "Talk about your ultimate bad acid trip. If you don't know where you are, does this mean that those Head Hunters of yours won't be able to find you?"

Sian stared at the counter for a long time. "I can only hope so."

"Well, I never had a sister, so you're about the closest I'm going to come to one," I said, putting my arm around her shoulder. "You're welcome to stay here for as long a visit as you want."

If she was going to stay around, Sian was going to need "a life," at least on paper. Kent just said to leave it to him. He knew a hacker who could do the job.

"Is this guy good?" I asked.

"Oh, yeah," he grinned. "The guy I have in mind is the one who teaches the CIA forgery department how to do things."

That done, it was time to do something else, just as important. I looked at Sian's clothes that we'd left in the laundry room. They were not in good shape. She was going to need more than what I had found her in, and more than just borrowed things from my closet. Time to go shopping.

We hit the local mall and found everything Sian would need, not to mention some neat things for myself. Just after noon I decided it was time to introduce Sian to native dishes, i.e., pizza. Meals in hand, we found a table near the stage at the center of the food court.

There were a bunch of guys there, dressed in combat fatigues, faces painted in camouflage paint all holding weird-looking metal guns. The weapons looked like the sort of things my cousins Tim and Randy had played with when we were growing up, not practical looking but the sort of thing that thrills a twelve-year-old male.

When they began showing off some round balls and inserting them in the guns it dawned on me that these weren't real army types, but paint ball gamers.

I explained the concept to Sian and she just shook her head. "They do this for fun?"

I was about to turn my attention back to a slice of pizza when I looked toward the rest rooms. The air in front of them had begun to shimmer and fold in on itself. Then someone was standing there. He was big, six-four at least, wearing a dark floppy hat and a leather jacket.

"Slowly look over toward the rest rooms," I told Sian. "I think we have a visitor."

"I don't have to," Sian was staring at the shiny metal wall of the Chinese fast food place. She could see a slightly blurry version of this fellow without a problem.

"A Head Hunter? Does he know you're here?" I said softy.

"Remember what I said about being drawn to this area because you were here. Look up on the stage." She pointed at a man standing at the back of the group of camo-dressed performers. He was shaggier and maybe didn't weigh as much, but I could see the resemblance.

I was about to suggest that we ease our way out of there, when things began to go a bit haywire. One of the paint ball guys tripped over something, his own feet probably, gun in hand, and almost fell. One thing he did do was accidentally squeeze off a shot that went straight out into the audience and hit the Head Hunter square on the chest. I can imagine where he would have hit if there had been time to aim.

The Head Hunter looked down, touched the fresh paint with one finger. "I just had that cleaned!" he said and headed for the stage.

Not being your shy retiring type, Sian grabbed one of the metal chairs that filled the food court. As the Head Hunter passed, she brought it down hard across the man's back. That proved effective enough to put him on the floor, surprise is the best weapon. A quick grab under his shirt and she jerked something loose.

"Let's go!" she said.

We made it to the car and I hit the gas. How we got out of there without being stopped I still don't know.

"Damn, damn, damn," she muttered as I pointed the car toward the street.

"What was that you got from him?" I asked.

"These," she opened the small leather pack and poured out half a dozen flat stones, each one carved with an intricate rune.

Sian spread out the rune stones on my dining room table. There were six, none bigger than a quarter. All were slick and cool to the touch.

"This isn't good. If one of them found their way here, that means the others know where he went. So if he doesn't report back, and he can't without these, then they will come looking for him," she said.

"Then why did you take them?" I asked. "I know, I know, it seemed the thing to do at the time. Can we just smash them and hope the others don't show up on our doorstep?" I got my answer with just the look in Sian's eyes.

Smashing those pebbles would be a very last resort.

"How long will it be before the others show up?" asked Kent.

"If I've read these alignments correctly," she nodded. "I should judge sometime late tonight, give or take a couple of hours. They are going to try for an area along the river, probably somewhere north of where I arrived. Something solid, I would expect. They can't walk on water any more than I could."

"Good, then maybe it's time for you to stop running," said Kent.

"I'm not going back!" protested Sian.

"You don't have to, if we work this right." The look on Kent's face suggested that he had something in mind. "It strikes me that there is a fairly simple answer to your problems, in my never-to-be-humble opinion."

"Oh, really?" asked Sian.

"Sure, we're just going to have to kill you."

Standing, at two AM on an abandoned bridge a mile north of the floating stage, with a strong north-easterly breeze blowing off the river, I was definitely not what you would describe as a happy camper. More like an irritated, cold, and angry camper. I didn't think that Sian or Kent were any more comfortable right then than I was.

When Kent had breezed back in late that afternoon, he was carrying half a dozen large boxes. "Have a look at these," he said. "I think you'll find them interesting."

Interesting was a good word. I was wearing the contents of several of them; a one-piece black leather cat suit, covered in chains and metal studs, that was so tight I could barely breathe. Sian had to help me get into the thing and get everything zipped. Even the ankle-length duster didn't do a thing to keep me warm, though it did provide a place to keep a loaded beretta and a fully charged Taser.

If Sian had read those stones correctly, this was where the Head Hunters were supposed to show up. That was a big if to my way of thinking. Of course, we might get lucky, have them miss, and end up drowning in the middle of the river. I wasn't counting on that.

Frankly, I was about ready to give up on this idea and revert to Plan B, once we came up with Plan B, when something happened to the air about twenty feet off to my left. I motioned for Sian and Kent to stay hidden.

The air seemed to waver for a moment, fold in on itself, and then there were two men standing in the center of the bridge. After our first Head Hunter I think I expected some sort of cross between a barbarian and a biker. That wasn't what we got; more like a matching pair of lawyer boys. One was scarecrow-thin with a smile that seemed to take up three fourths of his face, the other was short, bald, and looked like one of my cats could take him two falls out of three.

"I think this may be the place we're looking for. It feels right," the tall one said.

"I hope so, it's about time our luck changed," his companion said.

That was my cue. I pushed the duster back and strode forward. "All right, you two scumballs. This time you are completely out of luck. You're mine!" Hey, even if I was cold and scared out of my wits, I think I presented a fairly fierce picture right then.

Seeing me, they just stood staring for several seconds. That was enough time for Kent to come over the side of the bridge, where he had been perched, and clobber one of them with a blackjack. I very much enjoyed using the Taser on the other. Once they were down, I made sure they were still breathing, then we hogtied them, feet and hands together behind their backs, with nooses around their necks.

"I guess this is the place for Act Two," I said as Kent waved capsules of smelling salts under their noses.

They jerked awake, and it didn't take them too long to figure out that they were in trouble. The smaller one looked around, started to speak, then thought better of it. The other one just stared at me, his face impassive and waiting.

"Good evening, boys. So, do the two of you have names of any sort?"

"Aye, m'lady," the taller one said, pronouncing each word carefully. "I'm Carson Sal'se and he's Vernon Myth'rn. If we have offended you, or broken any local laws, we do most humbly apologize."

"Well, isn't that just too, too cute. You've made a serious mistake, showing up on my lands, just when I'm in a very, very bad mood!" I said.

I began to pace back and forth. In the distance I could see the lights of the 21st Street traffic bridge, flanked by the expressway bridge fifty yards beyond that. I couldn't help but grin at the idea of how the passing drivers might react to this scene. Of course explaining this whole scene to any police officer who showed up might be more than a bit difficult.

"The treasury is a little low right now and the price of two prime slaves like you two would certainly help fatten it up. I understand that there is a shortage of workers in the okra fields to the south. They'll be here shortly, for my little package over there. You fellows wouldn't happen to be with her, now would you?"

It wasn't easy for either of the Head Hunters to

see where I had pointed, but they tried. One of Kent's other boxes had contained a filmy affair of white silk and transparent gossamer fabric.

Wrapped around Sian it looked as exotic, in its own way, as what I had on. It also made what I had on look warm and comfortable. Kent dragged her forward to stand closer to the rest of us. Sian was blindfolded and her hands bound behind her.

"It's her! I told you we would find her!" said Myth'rn. I'm still not sure why they didn't think I was Sian, even for a moment, or how they were certain that she was the genuine article. Myth'rn tried to get to his feet, but got no more than a couple of inches when the rope around his neck choked him off.

"You dared to violate my territory for that?"

"Yes, m'lady. She is to become a queen in her own right."

I began to laugh. "I doubt that she will be good for anything like that, not now anyway. This wench showed up here three days ago, tried to take me in a fight and lost. Instead of killing her I had her dosed with a drug that I use a good deal in my business. The stuff helps new slaves adjust to life in the bawdy houses I operate. That is, if I don't decide just to get rid of her, like I'm thinking of getting rid of you two." I knew one thing, I had to keep them more than a bit uncertain of just what was going on, before they started asking too many questions, like how we happened to be there just where they were going to show up.

The look on the faces of the two Head Hunters was something akin to grief and shock, with a healthy dose of fear thrown in for good measure.

"This wasn't how you wanted things to work out?" I asked.

"No, m'lady. Our guild accepted the commission

to return her to the throne. It's obvious now that we have failed," he said. "When we return, we will be in disgrace."

"If I allow you to return. Maybe I should just feed you to the fishes. Can either of you swim?"

"Swim? N . . . no, m'lady."

"You two are such pains. But then so is she, and I'm not in the mood." I pulled out the Taser and jammed it against Sian's neck. The effect was quick and certain. She jerked like a marionette whose strings had been dropped, then crumpled to the ground. She lay there, eyes open and empty, her tongue hanging limply from her mouth.

"We'll just compost what's left of her," I said.

I let my words digest with them for several moments as their eyes darted between me and Sian's still form. Then I reached over and pulled their shirts open, just as Sian had told me to expect, there were two identical leather bags hanging around their necks. I yanked them free.

"I was going to kill you, and dump you over the bridge, but the river's too polluted as is," I said. "I have a better idea."

I gestured for Kent. He grabbed the shoulders of the smaller man and I grabbed his feet. We rolled him on top of the other one, face-to-face. I shoved one rune stone each between their lips.

"Don't swallow, fellows," I laughed. "You've got one chance, scum. I'd advise you to take it."

They understood what I was talking about, leaned forward, and touched the stones together. The air shivered, folded in on itself, and the two Head Hunters were gone.

"That's one way to make an exit," Kent said.

Sian moaned and began to blink her eyes. Kent scrambled to her side, checking her vitals. "Did it work?" she managed to ask.

"You betcha, sis," I said. "I have a feeling they're going to be required to think very fast to explain what happened. In fact I'm fairly sure they won't be able to admit a thing about what really happened. As far as your father is concerned, you are gone and will not be returning anytime soon."

"That's good, I just wish it didn't have to be this way. I love Daddy, but he can be hardheaded," she said. "Oh, but that thing you hit me with, sister mine, hurt like you wouldn't believe. Look, before we go much further, would somebody mind untying me. And I would appreciate a coat of some kind. It's cold out here."

Kent took a knife and cut the ropes around Sian's wrists, helping her stand up in the process. "We need to have a long talk, Kent, about your taste in women's clothes," she said. I didn't have to look over there to know he was putting on his totally innocent, "I don't know what you're talking about" face just then.

I had to say it had been an interesting weekend. I reached in my pocket and touched the rune stones. It occurred to me that smooth and flat as they were they would be perfect for skimming. I wondered how far I could throw them.

"No, maybe another time," I said to the wind.

"I don't know about you two, but I could do with some hot coffee," said Kent.

"What's coffee?" asked Sian.

A Tale of the Oroi
by Robert Sheckley

Robert Sheckley vaulted to the front ranks of science fiction writers in the 1950s with his prodigious output of
short, witty stories that explored the human condition in
a variety of earthly and unearthly settings. His best tales
have been collected in *Untouched by Human Hands*, *Pil-
grimage to Earth*, and the comprehensive *Collected Short
Stories of Robert Sheckley*. His novels include the futuris-
tic tales *The Status Civilization*, *Mindswap*, and *Immortality Delivered*, which was filmed as *Freejack*. He has also
written the crime novels *Calibre .50* and *Time Limit*. Elio
Petri's cult film *The Tenth Victim* is based on his story
"The Seventh Victim."

ALIX:
Like most fairies, I wasn't sure at birth if I
wanted to be basically bad or basically good. It was
all very new for me then and right from the start I
had many decisions to make. I hadn't even chosen
my sex, or my name. Nor did I yet have a reason
for living.

A reason for living is more important to a newborn
fairy than anything, even sex, which is pretty good
no matter which gender you choose to be, or at what
age you choose to start indulging in it.

I thought I had time to decide all that sort of thing
later. But the question of what I was here for—my
purpose—my reason for living—couldn't wait, since
it was what would guide, shape, and instruct my
actions from this moment onward.

Things were made more difficult for me because I was alone: My parents weren't present after I was born. Even in the long years afterward (and a fairy's years are very long), I never did see my father. As for my mother, all that remained of her, there in the cottage in Attica where I was born, was a fragrant memory of someone who went away shortly after giving birth to me.

Well, there it is, I was a fairy, born neutral, and trying to decide whether to dedicate myself to good or to evil. I also had to decide whether to be male or female. I knew I was growing up rapidly. But would it be fast enough for the invisible destiny that I already felt surrounding me?

There was a lot to think about, and a lot to do. I had to get fed, and soon. I had to get some clothes— it was getting chilly here with the fire dying down.

Under such circumstances, a human would have died. Fairy folk get along pretty well without parents. We grow up fast if we grow up at all. We cope.

I coped. Looking around, I saw an earthenware basin on a nearby table. I crawled over to inspect it. It was filled with goat's milk. I drank. Then I found a piece of cheese and ate that. Then a heel of bread.

Clothing came next. The goatskin I had been wrapped in was barely sufficient. I saw pieces of sheepskin, goatskin, cowhide, horsehide, on a little bench, and needles and thread were there, too. I crawled to the bench and sewed my own tunic.

Inevitably, while I was sewing, I was trying to think of why I was doing all this. Was I really in such a hurry to grow up? Or was all of this part of my destiny, too?

Life gives us little chance for quiet contemplation. I suddenly became aware that something or someone was moaning outside.

I left the cottage and walked in the direction of

the sound. I encountered my first elemental. It was huddled in the little garden. It was small, and pale, and almost transparent. It looked like a simplified human being.

"Mistress," it said, "I'm alone and I don't know how to find the others of my kind."

"Are you just born?" I asked.

"Yes. Born, pumped full of knowledge, and sent out into the world alone."

It was hard for me to sympathize. I was alone, too, and without my people, but was I feeling sorry for myself? I don't think so. Many of us fairy folk are solitaries. We shun humans and even other fairies. I'm that way, myself, except for Glaucus and Callicles, and of course Tim. But they don't come into the story until later.

I patted the elemental on his head and told him to look around, he'd be sure to find others of his kind soon. Then I looked up at the stars.

I saw a sparkling trail which cut across the sky, a trail of shining motes, which led off into the upper distance, marking where it had come from.

"What is that?" I asked the elemental.

"The stars," it said, looking up. "I can tell you a great deal about stars."

"I don't mean the stars, I meant the sparkling sort of trail in the sky."

"What you are looking at," the elemental said, "is the characteristic mark left by a time machine."

"A time machine?"

"A construction of the future. A mechanism that enables a human being to travel in time, either to a past age or a future one."

"How do you know this? Have you studied time machines?"

"Only in a general sense, in information I was given on Relating In Time."

"Where did that time trail come from?"

"From the future, as can be known by its reddish sheen."

"And if it were traveling in the opposite direction?"

"It would have a bluish-green tinge, of course."

I stared at the time trail with longing. I knew now that one end of it was in the future.

And the other end of it ended here, where Glaucus was.

Glaucus! Of course I didn't know his name then. But already I could sense his presence, his glamour.

"Good luck," I said to the elemental.

I had decided to be a girl. I would call myself Alix. And I would find Glaucus.

In a few minutes I sensed him, then saw him, up ahead of me, on the hillside, silhouetted against the sky. I moved to approach him.

*   *   *

Glaucus:

When I came to consciousness, the first thing I realized was that I didn't know who I was. That's not to say I didn't know anything. I knew I was out of doors, on a wooded hillside. I was wearing a leather tunic and a long gray wool cloak. I had on sandals, and there was a leather pouch slung around my neck with a leather strap. But as to who I was, or how I had come here, and why, I hadn't a clue.

It was a little frightening, but also strangely peaceful, just being a consciousness, with no ax to grind, with nothing I had to do. It was a relief just to live, not to have to live for something.

But I wondered about the pouch. It was heavy. I opened it, reached in, and, came out with a fistful of silver coins. I examined them. They were Greek drachmas.

* * *

I might have stood there mulling this for quite some time, but I became aware that there was a voice in my head, a voice demanding to be heard.

I listened to it.

The voice said, "Old pal, you're probably feeling completely weirded out right now, and you maybe don't know where you are or what you're doing there. Never mind, friend. This is your orientation lecture, and this is me, Billy Barnes, giving it. If the psychologists are right, you don't remember me, either. So to clue you, I'm your best friend as well as your brother-in-law. I've been married to your sister Claire for two years now. We're expecting our first-born within a few weeks.

"So there you are in ancient Greece! Wish we could have sent some more stuff with you, like a sleeping bag, and a Colt .45, but we had to be careful about anachronisms, leaving stuff that might change the course of history. Even the drachmas we made for you were a problem, though these will go to dust in a few hundred years.

"You're in the past, babe—in ancient Greece, about fifty years before the birth of Plato. The crazy time machine worked, and now you're there to pick up the manuscript of Homer's *Iliad*. Any local scriptorium ought to have it. Put it in your pouch, and you, the pouch, and its contents will be transported back to now.

"In the bottom of the pouch you will find, or have already found, a small bag of precious stones of the kind that were popular in Athens in the time we sent you to. You could buy a big farm with these, and still have plenty left over for Athenian nightlife, but you're not going to be there long enough for any of that. You'll just pick up the MS, (we've given you a fortune to pay for it), stuff it in your pouch, and in two weeks from today we'll bring you home. That ought to give you plenty of time for this. Just stay out of trouble.

"That's the main part of it—what you need to know—you're there to get the Homer and bring it back. It's probably written on papyrus. This talk-to-mind is a handy way of communicating, no? Better than leaving you a note. My voice was directly encoded into your brain. This message will only play once, but there's plenty of time to mention a few other things you need to watch out for—"

Here the voice ended. I waited, but it didn't start up again. I decided that science was marvelous, only it didn't seem to perform quite as anticipated.

Then, at the next moment, a person strolled into the scene. She was a small person, a girl, or a child just on the verge of womanhood. She had a lovely heart-shaped face. She was dressed in a tunic. She looked like a young Diana, or Artemis.

"Who are you?" the girl asked.

I came up with a name. "I am—Glaucus! I'm not from around here."

"Where are you front?"

"I come from the north," I said, annoyed that I had to explain myself so soon. "I am not Hellene. I come from the Celts."

Her Greek was pure and flowing. My own Greek, I knew, had a halting quality. Also, I didn't know all of the ways of saying things. I was sure what I was saying sounded uncouth.

"Where are you going?" she asked me.

"I need to go to Athens."

"You are still quite a distance away. This hillside is not the best way to Athens."

"How do I get to Athens?"

She pointed in a direction. "Go that way. It will

lead you to the village of Kyrellia. There they will put you on the road to Athens."

"Thank you."

She looked at me for a moment or two longer and said, "I am Alix. I will see you again." And then, abruptly, she turned and walked away.

I let out a slow breath. I literally hadn't known what was going to happen there. The girl was beautiful, but she seemed wild somehow, and strange. And very young.

Well, I thought, there was doubtless a lot more going on in ancient Greece than I ever knew or imagined. Time to get out of this particular bit of it.

Suddenly, I heard a voice not too far away, a man's voice shouting something. What in hell was going on? I began looking around for something to defend myself with. A cudgel, a tree limb. Although the hilltop had plenty of trees, I didn't find anything suitable.

"Hell!" I thought. "First time traveler to the past gets killed on a lonely hilltop in Attica."

Again the voice, speaking Greek: "Is anybody there? Can anyone help me?"

I knew I could stay perfectly still. Whoever it was was unlikely to find me on the dark hillside.

On the other hand, I could call out, accept the adventure. I knew I was going to have to meet people. Why not start now?

I summoned up my courage and called out, in Greek, "I'm here! Over here!"

I heard the sound of a body moving through the underbrush, branches snapping.

He called again, closer: "Where are you?"

"Over here," I called back, and set my feet firmly, prepared to defend myself.

The sounds resumed, and soon I could see a figure

silhouetted against the sky. The stranger came to a stop five feet from me. It was a young man.

"I am Callicles," he called out. "Who are you?"

"I am—Glaucus, a traveler from—far away. I have lost my way."

"Hail, Glaucus. Can you help me?"

"What is the trouble?"

"It's my wife. She's giving birth, up in the shelter. It's going badly. And the old woman from the village doesn't seem to know what to do. I thought I heard sounds, so I ran out here to find help."

One thing I knew was that I was no doctor. Still, I wanted to help.

"Show me," I said. "I am not a physician, but I'll do what I can."

The man moved closer to me. I felt strong fingers squeeze my shoulder. Callicles smelled of sweat and sheep.

"Thank you," Callicles said. "This way." He moved off into the darkness, and I followed.

In a few minutes I saw a glimmer of light. It came from a low hut made of branches and roughly plastered over with mud. I bent and followed Callicles inside.

Tward the back there had been a small fire, though now it was reduced to smoking twigs. I made out a rough bed on the ground in front of the fire, with a figure lying on it. Callicles knelt beside the figure, whispering to it. I waited, feeling awkward, wondering what I could do.

I was startled when Callicles let out a cry.

"What is it?"

"She's dead!"

I crept to the low bed and saw in the flickering firelight the slim figure of a woman, not much more than a girl. I bent over her, aware that my bare feet were suddenly wet, and a moment later picking up the scent of blood. I reached out and touched the girl's forehead. It was icy cold.

"Where's the old woman?" I asked.

"She must have gone back to the village when she couldn't stop the bleeding. I'll find her, I'll kill her!"

"No, Callicles," I said. "She must have been scared out of her wits. It was probably not her fault. Where's the baby?"

Callicles wiped his eyes and began to search.

They looked all over for the baby, but were unable to find it. Finally Callicles said, "Nona must have run away with it."

He bundled up his wife in her clothing lifted her to his shoulder and led the way out of the hut. I followed. I soon felt bare earth beneath my feet. We were on a path. It meandered down the hillside.

*   *   *

Alix:

I hovered nearby invisibly when Glaucus met Callicles. I saw the scene with the poor dead wife, though no one saw me.

I didn't accompany Glaucus and Callicles on their journey to the village. I was interested in where the baby had gone, and I knew that neither man would be of any help to me in finding it. The baby's scent was strong, however, and it was accompanied by a strong older scent that could only have been Nona.

I flittered up through the branching trees, my wings beating softly. They had sprung into existence as soon as I needed them, as proper fairy wings always do. I wondered what else I could do. I knew I would soon find out.

Above the treetops, still following the scents, I came to a mountain. At its top was a cave. I went in. It had all these weird triangular slabs of stone on the walls, and each stone was incised with letters, and some had cartouches, Egyptian work, I figured.

We fairies have an advantage in that we learn directly from our surroundings. I can't explain the process. Maybe I'll be able to when I'm older. A sort of mental osmosis, is the best I can do now. So I could more or less read the cartouches and the Greek writing. There was a lot of stuff about Gorgo. She's one of our Greek demons, but some people think that she came to us from the Egyptians.

Down on the floor, in a rough basket woven of twigs, was the baby.

There was a bad smell in the place, as of great beasts rutting. I didn't like it at all. Tall candles had been burning until recently in squat candelabra, but the flames were out now and the multicolored smoke rose straight up until it reached the ceiling, where it puddled in an unpleasant way.

The baby said, "You're one of the Oroi, aren't you?"

I was delighted to hear it. The name for my kind had been escaping me ever since birth—newborns sometimes have memory lapses, at least until they've learned a lot more than they started out with.

"Greetings, baby," I said. "I will call you Tim, if no one has given you a name before now."

"I accept it, at least temporarily," Tim said. "And to whom do I have the pleasure of speaking?"

"I'm Alix," I said. "One of the Oroi, as you surmised. I've come to take you away from all this."

"Awfully good of you," Tim said sweetly. "But I'm not sure I want to."

"Listen, kid," I said, "do you know where you are? In Gorgo's cave, that's where. There are some unsavory stories about that lady. You'd better get out while the getting's good."

"Gorgo? I thought her name was Nona."

"That is her name, but she was taken over by Gorgo, so that's who you'll be contending with."

"Interesting. She said she'd be right back with a bit of honeycomb for me, so you'd better get out before she returns."

I heard from far away the sound of something old and loud and clumsy dragging itself toward the cave. I decided to take Tim's advice. I needed to be a little older to stand up to Gorgo. Anyhow, it was kind of a standoff here. Tim was okay, and I wanted a look at that trail into the future that Glaucus had come here on, and after that I wanted to look in on Glaucus himself, see how the man of my destiny was doing.

"Well, I'll be on my way, then," I said. "Be sure to let me know if you want out of here. Just call. I'll hear you."

"Good-bye, Alix. And thanks. You're nice."

I got out of there. I flew above the mountaintop, and found the glittering path that I had spotted earlier.

The elemental had told me that this trail led into the future. I could also make out a network of finer, fainter lines which seemed to be time trails connected to the time trail. I stuck to the main trail that a time machine had laid down.

I came out in a dry, green-and-brown countryside with many small buildings dotted around. I had better give these buildings their proper names. They were laboratories, as I knew because I was taking in knowledge by mental osmosis. I was in California, there were laboratories, and in one of them was the time machine that had started all this.

I was standing in front of a small, red brick building. I followed it in invisibility mode, and found myself in a room with a long table. Half a dozen men and women were seated around the table, talking.

It didn't look terribly interesting. I decided to stay outside. I walked down one of the long corridors. It had windows which gave out onto a green space with trees. I saw someone go by outside, very quickly, more an afterimage than an image proper. It was somebody I recognized. But before I could consider the import of what I had just seen, I heard a voice behind me.

"Hello, Alix."

I gave a start and turned around. There was a fairy behind me. Practically in my face, as they say in this new age. He was about my age, and looked a lot like me.

"I suppose you'd like to know what's going on?" he said.

No time to be coy. "I would," I told him.

"Well, you and I are here in the opening years of the twenty-first century. Mankind has done great things with energy and related matters. Being human, they're making a mess of everything, but still going forward in their clumsy way."

I nodded. I couldn't have said it better myself.

"The people in this building have created a time machine. They sent back one of their number— Glaucus, I believe you know him as—to the past. He went to get a copy of the *Iliad* of Homer, who was a famous poet in ancient times. When they think Glaucus has been there long enough, they'll yank him back to the future, to here and now."

"Interesting," I said. "Will Glaucus signal when he wants to return?"

"There's no provision for that. The people here will just have to follow their best guess."

"Gotcha," I said. His words gave me an idea, but I wasn't going to discuss it with him, or even think about it until I was alone in a private place.

"What's your name?" I asked.

"You can call me Allan. I've had a quick look around. This place is fantastic, Alix. It's just what we fairies have been looking for."

"What makes this place so special?" I asked him.

"There are no spirits here," he said. "No talismans, no unclean things, no evil fairies, no forbidden areas where evil lurks. Those things were wiped out in the past, and haven't yet taken root again in a serious way. We fairies could live here without fear of supernatural retaliation by the other forces like ours."

"Until those forces got here," I said.

"Maybe we could prevent that."

"Do you really think so?"

Allan shrugged. "I don't know. But I'm sure that as soon as the fairies hear about this, they'll come flocking."

"It could be as you say. In any event, thanks for the information, Allan, and I'll be seeing you."

"Why are you rushing off so soon? Aren't you curious about who I am and how I fit into all this?"

"I've got an idea of who you are," I said. "I don't know that I much like it. See you."

And I flew into the air and rejoined the time trail.

I came upon them just as Glaucus and Callicles were making their way out of the woods, down the hill, and into the village. It was a collection of small crude buildings, some made of wood, most of stone. Callicles carried the body of his wife.

I decided to stay in invisibility mode, just to observe what was going on.

It was full night when they arrived. In the middle of the village was a small paved plaza. Callicles gently set down his wife's body, stood up and began crying and wailing in a loud voice. It took Glaucus a moment to make out what he was saying. Callicles was calling for his uncle, Iphicrates.

Torchlights sprang up in doorways. People came out. They ran to Callicles, who explained rapidly what had happened: Iona had given birth. Old Nona had been attending. The birth had been difficult. Callicles had run out to find help. Met this stranger, Glaucus, who came with him to assist. They could not find the baby. Nona was not there. He hasn't seen her. Had she returned to the village?

Hasty talk among the villagers. No, no one has seen Nona. Maybe the wolves got her when she ran away. Maybe a Spartan raider killed her.

A portly, middle-aged man came out, wrapped up in his cloak against the evening chill. Uncle Iphicrates! Callicles explained to him rapidly what had happened. Iphicrates wailed and drew his cloak over his head.

And soon there were new people to explain it all to. The wife's parents, a tall, thin, stern-faced man and his short, portly wife. The man was suspicious, his wife was soon hysterical. She clutched her dead daughter, wailing, and finally let a neighbor woman lead her away. The father wanted to know why Iona had gone to the mountain so late in her pregnancy. Had Callicles insisted that she come?

"No," Callicles protested. "I tried to stop her, to talk her out of it. But she insisted. She said she was not expecting for another two weeks. She insisted. I said no, but you know Iona always got her way in the end."

The father nodded reluctantly. He seemed to know what Callicles was talking about.

The discussion turned to Nona. Why had she disappeared? Afraid of a difficult birth?

An elderly woman had been listening. "No, Nona was highly skilled, and she was afraid of nothing. You remember the time . . ."

She seemed to be Nona's sister. She told a long

anecdote which Alix couldn't quite follow. But the point seemed to be that Nona had faced emergencies in the past, and had showed herself courageous. They'd probably find her dead in the morning with a Spartan spear through her! Unless, of course, the Eumenides had made an appearance. Or the Oroi . . .

At this point, Uncle Iphicrates cleared his throat and made a speech. "A terrible thing has happened," he said, "and so far there is no one to blame." He suggested that Iona's parents carry their daughter home, and that they all retire for the night. Callimachus, the headman, would be back in the morning. By daylight they'd search the hills for Nona.

That should have been the end of it. But Phineas, Iona's father, refused to take his daughter home. Everyone knew that a corpse in the house brought bad luck. His wife put in, "My daughter herself would never permit it."

It was decided that the girl's body would be taken to the House of the Dead. There her husband, Callicles, would stand guard over her all night. In the morning they'd sort this out.

"I'll stay with you," Glaucus said.

But Callicles wouldn't permit it. It was his duty alone. "You have done enough for me already, Glaucus. I won't let you risk the pollution. You will go with my uncle, Iphicrates, you will sleep in my bed. I will see you in the morning."

And so Glaucus went with Uncle Iphicrates to his house and spent a night in Callicles' room.

As for me, Alix, I was trying to make up my mind what to do next, when I heard a voice, the unmistakable voice of the baby I had named Tim. He was saying, "Alix, I'd like to leave Nona's house now, so could you please come and get me?"

I set off at once, mounting invisibly into the air.

*   *   *

Glaucus:

Despite the upsets of the day, I slept the dreamless sleep of the exhausted, that night in Uncle Iphicrates' house. I awoke disoriented when Callicles came for me.

"Wake up, Glaucus! Callimachus returned early this morning and he wants to see us both, at once!"

"And who is Callimachus?"

"The headman of our village! Come, we must go at once!"

But he gave me time for a quick wash, and a bowl of barley gruel and a half-cup of well-watered wine before we hurried out of the house and across the plaza to Callimachus' big stone house. There a servant told us we would have to wait our turn: a lot of village business had accumulated during Callimachus' absence, but he would handle everything in turn. We were welcome to wait out on the porch, with the other clients.

And so we lounged on Callimachus' shady, wide stone porch as the sun came up, taking the chill out of the air and finally bringing warmth, then heat.

I estimated that it was close to noon before Callimachus sent for us. A servant led us through the house to a shaded patio in the rear. Callimachus looked to be in his early forties, large and fit-looking, with a sparse beard. He wore a linen tunic, and had several scrolls near him on a small table.

Callimachus said he was going to look into Iona's death. He was not happy about me, Glaucus, for I seemed to have popped up conveniently out of nowhere. In these unsettled times, strangers needed to be accounted for. There were Spartan raiders in the area. Callimachus worried that I might be an ally of theirs, come through to check the defenses of the village.

I pleaded that I didn't know the Spartans, and had urgent business in Athens. Callimachus said in any event it would be impossible to go now because of the unresolved case of Iona, and the danger from the Spartans.

"I saw Iona's father earlier," Callimachus said, "and he is demanding Callicles' arrest on the grounds that he deliberately brought a pregnant woman into peril."

Callicles was outraged at this—he loved his wife, and could bring witnesses to prove that he vehemently and publicly tried to dissuade her from accompanying him.

"Then there should be no problem for you," Callimachus told him.

Callicles and I talked it over later and decided we'd better get away from the village, and go to Athens. Callimachus was no friend of Callicles, and accusations of witchcraft could be raised.

We set out at midday with other villagers looking for Nona. We gradually separated ourselves from them, and by midafternoon we were alone on the Attic plain, on our way to Athens.

We passed a nameless little village along the way. Here I was able to buy horses for Callicles and me. The horses weren't much good, but they were a lot better than walking. We camped out another night, and by midday the Acropolis of Athens was in sight.

*   *   *

Alix:
When I came upon them, they were at the top of a long rise. The road was lined with poplar trees. In

the distance, glistening in the sun, I could see the statues on the Acropolis.

"Hi," I said, becoming visible.

Glaucus made a sort of jump sideways, and almost fell off the road. He said, "Alix! Please don't come springing out at me that way. I'm not used to it and it startles the hell out of me."

"Sorry," I said, noticing how sweetly his dark hair curled on his neck, and how long and delicate his eyebrows were. I was realizing how attractive Glaucus was. But I knew also that I was growing up quickly, into young womanhood. It was my age and my time of life that was noticing him.

I hoped to be able to slow down my rate of maturation in the future, where he and I would make our home.

"Where have you been?" he asked me.

"I've been away doing things and finding out things," I told him. "Did you miss me?"

He looked at me. I felt momentarily shivery. "Alix, I believe you have grown since I saw you last."

"Maybe I'm just filling out a little," I replied.

"How on Earth do you do that?" He laughed. "Alix, you're pretty and full of fun, and I—I am quite taken with you."

He said this last in English, but I understood.

We were just entering Athens, and there was no telling what one of us might have said next if the night watchman hadn't butted in!

"Excuse me, sir," the man said. "What deme do you vote in? What district?"

"I don't vote here," Glaucus said. "I'm a stranger. I came here from the lands of the Celts."

"And I," Callicles said, "am from the village of Kyrellia."

"You are both foreigners," the man said. "You will have to come with me. The Council will need to talk to you before we give you the freedom of the city."

Several other men came up in support of the first. Glaucus and Callicles spent no time in arguing, but went along with them.

I had gone into invisibility mode as soon as the strangers appeared. I said to Glaucus, "Tell Callicles I'll get his baby and come back. I've named him Tim."

The Athenians looked around, startled, but I was nowhere to be seen. I was on my way.

Not long after that, I was back in Gorgo's cave. It looked pretty much the same, except for one thing— on a chair in one corner, someone had draped Nona's body. She looked like a sack of old clothing. Gorgo had eaten her soul, then cast her aside, after draining all her vitality. I thought it was a shabby way to treat someone who must have been a nice old lady, until her bad luck caught up with her.

Tim was sitting at a little table in a corner of the cave. He had grown older, was now more child than baby. He had a large picture book open in front of him. It was called WONDERS OF THE WORLD TO COME. Glancing at it I saw pictures of the *Titanic*, the Statue of Liberty, the Holland Tunnel, and the Bay Bridge.

"There's a lot of neat stuff in the future," Tim said.

"That was my impression," I said.

"Okay, you convinced me. Let's go to the future."

But there was no time for that. I could hear somebody stirring in the interior cave.

A moment later, Gorgo walked out.

What can I say about Gorgo? It's hard to say what she looked like because her body was constantly altering. While I watched, it changed from a large old woman to a sort of beast made up of different body parts. And these changed, too; her elephant's haunch turned into a goat's rear end, her hummingbird head developed a rhinoceros' snout.

"You're one of the Oroi," she said. "Get out of here. I don't want you. It's the kid I want."

"Why do you want him?"

"Maybe I'll use him to flavor a stew. Whatever it is, it's none of your business."

"I'm making it my business. I'm taking him away with me."

Her surfaces flowed and she changed into an enormous armored reptile. I suppose it was her fighting shape.

She waddled toward me, her movement ungainly, yet with a certain lethal grace to it. I dodged out of the way. Her tongue flicked out, longer than I would have believed possible, and wrapped around my waist. She began drawing me toward her gaping, fang-lined jaws.

At that moment, Allan appeared. He came out of the open air. One moment he was not here, the next instant he was.

"Desist, Gorgo!" he cried.

The reptile turned her eyes toward him. The tongue uncurled from around me.

Gorgo said, "And just who in hell are you?"

"The voice of your destiny, Gorgo," Allan said. "I am here to ask you to spare yourself defeat, humiliation, pain, and death. For it is written that this young fairy girl will defeat you in this fight; and so it is better for you to give up gracefully, now, while you have the chance."

"I don't know who you are," Gorgo said. "Though you look a lot like this young lady here. I think that you'd better get away from here as fast as you can, otherwise I'll give you what I'm about to give her."

"I hear wounded pride in your voice, Gorgo, but I do not hear good sense. The lady has you beaten already."

"How do you figure?"

"In the dark caverns of time, some things are shown clearly, others more obscurely. What is clear is the fact that will soon be known, that Alix leaves this noisome cave and goes again to the future. There she has a role to perform, and she will perform it. I have seen this, Gorgo! It is true!"

"And what about me?" Gorgo asked.

"If you continue this fight, you will die, and pass out of the knowledge of mankind. Your past will not be remembered, your future will not exist."

"But how could this skinny little thing defeat me?" Gorgo asked.

Allan shrugged. "I do not know. But you know what the humans say about life. They say: 'Shit happens.' There's a deep truth in that homely expression."

It seemed to me impossible that the great and terrible Gorgo could be won over by these arguments. But of course, she had already been won over, since the future existed and the time lines went in a certain way and no other. I had gone to the future, so I had not been killed in the past. I had a part to play in that future which required that I not be killed here in Gorgo's cave. Exactly how this was to be accomplished, I did not know. But it was as much a fact as anything could be, and with it was the incontrovertible fact that Tim had gone or was to go into the future with me.

Gorgo was an elemental figure without the reasoning powers of a fairy or a god. But even she knew when she was beaten, because even an elemental power knows better than to oppose the workings of Time, that force that drives even Nemesis to do what must be done so that everything will work out.

"I don't want the kid after all," Gorgo said, returning to a more-or-less human form. "As for your time story, I think I can see holes in your argument, but it doesn't behoove a being as fundamental as I am to engage in dispute with you. I'm going into my back room to take a little nap, and I expect all of you to be gone by the time I return."

And so it came to pass. Gorgo lumbered into her back room. I faced Allan.

"Why did you do this?" I asked him.

"Because it is fated that you and I shall do great things together, Alix. What these things are I cannot say, for time has not yet revealed them to me. But time casts a long shadow, and we see what we will become well before we become it."

"I want nothing to do with you," I said. "You serve the powers of Evil, that much I can tell."

"Somebody has to serve Evil," Allan said, "for anything to get done around here. I will see you later, Alix."

"Not if I can help it!"

"You can't!"

And a moment later, Allan was gone.

I got Tim out of there. It was time to see how Glaucus was doing. I mounted the invisible air, and in no time at all I was back at the spot in Athens where Glaucus and Callicles had been arrested. But, of course, they weren't there. The official and his men had probably taken them to a prison somewhere. But where? Was I going to lose my Glaucus in the old world without having a chance to live with him in the new?

I was standing there, shivering in the chill wind that was blowing through Athens, despite it being late spring.

I didn't know what to do. I stood there, and the fact is, I began crying. And then, through my tears, I saw a brightening in the air, as though a fire were illuminating it. The individual flames coiled around each other, and coalesced, and suddenly a being was there.

I fell to my knees, certain that it was a god. But the figure bent over and lifted me by my hands. I saw a beautiful woman, in appearance not a lot older than me. And there was something familiar about her. I knew that smile from somewhere . . .

"Mother!" I cried.

"I'm glad you know who I am," she said. "I've been meaning to look you up. You look quite distraught, my dear."

"I am!" I told her. "I met the love of my life, a young man named Glaucus, and now I can't find him, and we have to get a copy of Homer's poems and get to the future somehow, and I don't know how to do all that!"

"Don't panic, my dear, you've done splendidly so far. Now let Mommy help. Your Glaucus and his friend have been sent to Cape Sounion, to work in the silver mines there."

"His hands will get all twisted!" I cried. "That's terrible work!"

"He'll suffer worse than damage to his hands," Mother said. "Do you know the life expectancy in the mines? It's short, and brutal. And there's always the possibility of a mine collapsing."

"What can we do?" I asked. "Is there a god we can intercede with?"

"These Greek gods are unreliable. They're being superseded."

"What, then?"

"I'll go to Sounion," Mother said. "I will take Glaucus out of there—"

"Bring his friend, too, Mother," I said.

"Yes, I will bring Callicles, too. I quite fancy him already."

"And take them to the future?"

"I'm sorry, dear, I cannot do that."

"But I thought you said you had been there, you knew about it . . ."

"I have been there, dear," Mother said. "Thanks to your initiative. But I can't go again until I've gone there for the first time. The logic debt must be paid, you know. Here's what we'll do. You will go to a scriptorium and get a copy of the book Glaucus needs. Then you'll go into the future and arrange for his friends to set the time machine to bring us all back today."

"Actually, Mother, could we stay in this ancient world a little longer? I'd like Glaucus to see Delphi."

"I don't think it would be a good idea, dear," Mother said. "We need to hurry. There's already a stir in Fairyland. People have heard about the opening of a time trail to the future, and everyone wants to go there. The King of the Fairies and his knights are already looking for you. You wouldn't want all those fairies in your future, would you?"

"No, Mother. I've decided I'm a solitary fairy. Except for friends and family, of course."

"It runs in the family. So here's what we'll do. You will find the Homer, then go back to the future and tell Glaucus' friends to speed up the time of departure. Then come back here. We'll all go to the future together in the time machine."

"Do we have to do it in such a complicated way?" I asked.

It was here that Tim spoke up, with that horrible smug tone that bright young boys have.

"This is logically necessary, Alix, especially for you, since you have been to the future once but haven't yet justified it. Once you've traveled by time machine, all sorts of corollaries are possible to account for your having time traveled both before and after you actually do so."

I didn't quite understand what he was talking about, but Mother nodded, and I decided Mother knew best.

So, to work! I hurried into downtown Athens, found a scriptorium, stole a Homer, since Glaucus had all the money, went back to the future, and arrived at the meeting room where Glaucus' friends had been gathered the other time I was there. They were there still, or maybe they had gone home for dinner and a nap, then come back to the conference room again. Whatever.

They were thrilled by the Homer, of course.

I convinced them to set forward the time for bringing Glaucus back. They didn't want to do it. But they were intrigued to learn I was a fairy. I had to promise to let them study me when I was back. I didn't want to make that promise.

Then I heard a voice in my head. Allan's voice. He was saying, "Promise them anything. But when it comes the time to do it, I'll think of a way out."

"Allan!" I said. "What are you doing in my head?"

"Haven't you figured it out yet? I'm your evil side."

"I don't want an evil side!" I told him.

"Sometimes a bit of bad is needed to make good happen."

They were so delighted with the Homer, I probably didn't even have to agree to let them study me. Second sight is always clearer. But always a little too late to use.

I excused myself and went back to Athens, to the place Mother had said to meet her at. She was there with Glaucus and Callicles. They were all on the terrace of a café, eating sherberts.

"Alix!" Glaucus cried, jumping to his feet. "I'm so glad to see you! Can you tell me what's going on?"

"We're all going to the future. That is, if Callicles wants to come. too."

"I'd like to," Callicles said. "My life as an Athenian slave working in a silver mine doesn't look too good."

"We're ready," I told Mother. "The machine should kick in any time now."

We waited. Time passed and I ordered a bowl of sherbet.

After a while, Mother frowned ever so slightly. "My dear," she said to me, "are you sure you impressed on the future people the urgency of our situation?"

"I did, Mother," I said. "But I believe there are things they have to do first. It's techne, Mother."

"I never had much of a head for techne," Mother confessed.

"The sky is turning dark," Callicles said suddenly.

I glanced up. Though it was early afternoon, the sun was concealed behind thick purple-black clouds. A wind was rising through the agora, and we had to hold on to our sherbet cups to keep them from blowing away.

"Oh, dear," said Mother.

High in the darkening sky, I could see figures on white horses, carrying lances, and dressed in gleaming white armor. And behind them came another figure, larger than the others, dressed in polished black armor. I didn't need to be told that this was the King of Fairyland, arriving with all his host.

Everyone human had left the agora by now, and rain swept across the paving stones. The knight-errantry of Fairyland came closer, swooping low—

And then I felt a great force press against my body. "Join hands!" Mother said. We did. Me and Mother, Callicles, Tim, and my beloved Glaucus were lifted into the air, whirled around . . .

And we came out in California, the future, in a room filled with techne, where ten or so white-jacketed scientists were applauding.

*   *   *

So that's the story of how I, a fairy of the old world, found love and happiness with a human of the new world.

Our story continues, but the part I wanted to tell is over.

You'll have to imagine for yourself how the Fairy King and his knights found a bootleg way into our future, and the centuries of destruction that followed, and how Tim, grown to manhood, and aided by his father, Callicles, took up arms against them. But all of that is another story. This one ends here.

Summer

by Jack Dann

Jack Dann has written or edited over sixty books, including the international best-seller *The Memory Cathedral,* which is currently published in over ten languages and was #1 on The Age Best-Seller list. *The San Francisco Chronicle* called it "A grand accomplishment," *Kirkus Reviews* thought it was "An impressive accomplishment," and *True Review* said, "Read this important novel, be challenged by it; you literally haven't seen anything like it." His novel *The Silent* has been compared to Mark Twain's *Huckleberry Finn; Library Journal* chose it as one of their Hot Picks and wrote: "This is narrative storytelling at its best—so highly charged emotionally as to constitute a kind of poetry from hell. Most emphatically recommended." Dann's work has been compared to Jorge Luis Borges, Roald Dahl, Lewis Carroll, Castaneda, J. G. Ballard, Philip K. Dick, and Mark Twain. He is a recipient of the Nebula Award, the World Fantasy Award, the Australian Aurealis Award (twice), the Ditmar Award (twice) and the Premios Gilgames de Narrativa Fantastica award. He has also been honored by the Mark Twain Society (Esteemed Knight). His latest novel *Bad Medicine* (retitled *Counting Coup* in the U.S.) has been described by *The Courier Mail* as "perhaps the best road novel since the *Easy Rider* days." Jack Dann lives in Melbourne, Australia and "commutes" back and forth to Los Angeles and New York.

1.

THE sand is down there, down down down there, hard-packed and crusty under the snow and lay-

ers of translucent green ice; and somehow that gives
you comfort, albeit cold comfort to be sure. Even the
ironies, the metaphors and similes, freeze; the whole
fucking world is frozen. Everything is frozen, and
you—you came down here to Florida to get warm,
to get away from the snow and the forever grayness
of northern Michigan.

You'll think about Michigan later.

It's too dangerous to think about the past.

2.

But you can't help yourself, can you? Memory is
everything, and you stand and dream on the ice and
snow that is—or was—New Smyrna Beach, "THE
SAFEST BEACH IN THE WORLD," or so said the
sign. But that sign was there eons ago, millennia
ago.

Forty years ago. That's when it was, and it's all
frozen, all the seconds, minutes, and hours are now
unchangeable, impermeable. So you look out at the
gunmetal-gray purling sea, and you select a few perfect moments. Yes, life is a pack of cards. Now that's
a warm, palpable metaphor. Pick a card, Laura.
You've got a billion of 'em.

3.

You remember . . . you remember when the sun
was warm, when the sand would clot under your
bare feet, crusting between your toes. (Remember
when you could *breathe* . . . when you could walk
and not run out of breath?) The ocean would be a
warm roaring, as if you'd put a conch shell to your
ear, and your body was like new clothes. But you
were proud of that body, ordinary as it was.

There you are, melting back into the past, standing right here, right on this very spot, and you're practically naked. You've got small breasts, but they're good enough to fill out a bikini.

There's a couple sitting on a blanket a few feet away from you, and you can *feel* the man staring at you. You can feel that he wants to touch you.

How does that make you feel?

4.

You touch yourself, right here, right on this spot, right in public, although there is no public. There is no one here but you and the snow and ice and sea. The snow is beautiful. How many times have you told yourself that? How beautiful is a snowflake?

You've thickened in the hips and thinned in the lips. But it's more than that, isn't it? Everything has fallen. But you're there, like the sand under the ice. Your hair is gray. You gave up and stopped dyeing it. Your breasts are good, though. Small breasts don't sag so much. But when you look into the mirror, you're not the same person any more. Some rouged, prune-wrinkled, rather nice-looking old lady has grown over you, submerged you, subsumed you. She's pleasant enough looking, isn't she?

That's all you were ever going to be . . . you know that. You knew that.

You should have had more sex, but there was so much disease, wasn't there?

You should have stayed with Harold.

You shouldn't have gotten cancer.

(Ah, yes, why you? Why not him? *He* was the smoker.)

If you hadn't had cancer, you wouldn't have left Harold, you wouldn't have—

Don't think about that. Don't think about any of that. You've only lost the lower lobe of a lung. You've still got your breasts. They still look pretty.

(Stop coughing!)

But as you look out at the glacial blue divide of sea and sky, you imagine that you're looking into the mirror. You're deep inside that mirror.

The real you, the warm you, the beautiful you.

5.

You imagine that you can see the glint of one of the huge orbital mirrors in the sky, but you can't. You see a frozen, cloud-clogged sky that merges with the sea. Sea and sky united in . . . anger. Yes, that's it. Anger. The mirrors aren't working, of course, aren't warming the world enough, but they were a techno-logical feat. One of the last, hey?

You're late for school. You have an idea where to begin your lecture about Winter, which is a pleasant enough euphemism for Ice Age.

Eiszeit.

But German won't help you now. The world has become larger, rather than smaller. When were you last in Frankfurt? You laugh, for it was long before Winter.

You could open your lecture with the Little Winter that began in the fourteenth century and lasted—on and off—until the nineteenth century.

What caused that, class?

They won't know. But *you* know that Little Winter was caused (in part, not entirely—don't get carried away) by the felling of forests during the Middle Ages. Tell them that. Tell them that forests reflect between ten to twenty percent of the sunlight while snowfields reflect up to ninety percent. Explain albeido. (Ah, were it libido, but you couldn't explain that anymore, could you? Could you?)

Tell them that their ancestors helped make/made their very own Little Winter.

Did you make yours?

Did we make ours?

6.

You look up and see the smeary blotch in the cloud cover (the sun), and then you leave the ice floes of your sacred beach and march to school.

You're dressed like an Eskimo.

You're a twentieth century locomotive breathing steam. (Stop coughing!)

And you're still cold.

So much for modern technology.

7.

There are always enough students, and lecture hall #7 of the Chrysanthemum Heights School of Higher Education is packed with alert, motivated, bright, interesting students. The cream of the crop. (You can do better than that, Laura. You wanted to be a writer, remember? Choose a proper metaphor.)

You hate them. You love them. They are your life, or, rather, would be your life, if you had a life.

How many people are left in the world? you ask yourself. You should know the answer. You're an educator.

You've questioned the students about the migration plagues and their ramifications. Hands are still raised and waving, which makes you think of wheat fields. The cream of the crop (cream as metaphor being transformed into the plural) have a great need to respond, even if there is no question. You accommodate them with a question.

"Who was Genevieve Woillard?"

"She was a twentieth-century Belgian botanist who examined the pollen in peat in France and discovered that the pollen vanished," shouts a tall, skinny boy without waiting to be called on, without raising his hand. His head seems too large for his body. He'll grow into it. It isn't a bad-looking head. Thin features marred by pimples. He isn't wearing enough protection, even though it's cold enough to see your breath. Most of the other children are bundled up, as are you. Perhaps Mr. Clive Marsten—that's his name, you know all their names—is the New Man, the survivor who needs no clothes.

"Mr. Marsten, this class really isn't interested in the fractured response of a show-off. I might not be able to compel you to dress appropriately, but you *will* wait your turn."

"I humbly apologize, Ms. Fuchs."

There is always a whispered titter, as if you're a failure because your name sounds like the makings of sex, as if someone who's past it should give up the name and credentials.

"Apology accepted. Now perhaps someone else can enlighten us as to *why* Ms. Woillard is important and exactly what she was doing in the Alsace region of France?"

As if any of it is important.

There is a show of hands to choose from, and you listen as one Rita Byrne tries to answer the question. Sandy-haired Rita looks like you—like you used to look—doesn't she? No, she's prettier than you were. Maybe not. As smart, though. And a tomboy. Yes, that.

"112,000 years ago—during the last interglacial epoch—the climate changed from temperate to frigid within a twentv-vear span."

"And what," you ask, "does that tell us about our own Winter?"

"Well, isn't that obvious, Ms. Fuchs."

8.

You daydream, and the students try to answer your detailed questions; but you aren't there. You've left, and you daydream and dreamdream and like a ghost, you breathe and cough and whisper yourself through the storm-covered windows.

9.

Whisper yourself back home.

Oh, no, not your old home in Clarewood, Michigan, which you imagine is preserved without flaw or tear below the translucent blue-green depths of the glacier. Like Pompeii in amber.

No, no, no.

You can dream perfectly round and perfect dreams, but you know with the certainty of late maturity that your past—both geographically and reflectively—is tundra. Snowfields. Your stucco house (in Clarewood) on Saginaw Street (corner of Owosso and Blind River Drive, to be precise) is probably no more than a stone foundation.

If that.

No, you daydream—sweet sweetbreads of memory—of your present home right here in New Smyrna Beach, your dream home, your repro Conch house with gingerbread wooden grillwork, classic-cream double-decker verandas, shutters, a sloped blue-gray roof, and roof hatches (called scuttles). That's the daydream. That's the house of memory, but it's real. The roof has deteriorated and the verandas have become catchments for snow and ice, permanent snow and ice. The grillwork is long gone and the paint is scabbed, as if the house itself had acne like your preemptive student Mr. Clive Marsten.

The house is broken.

Snow-swept

Ice-capped.

Buried.

That's the reality.

But still, even now, in Winter Winter Winter (of course, you reflexively think winter *of your life,* but that's too obvious, isn't it?), you live there in the house that Harold built.

10.

Your honeymoon house.

Your classic-cream conch-shell honeymoon house.

Listen to the memories: summer, Florida summer, before Winter, when the sun on your arms smells like baked bread, when the beaches are tanned bikinied leggy bodies: television shots of adolescents laughing; volleyball; hot dog vendors; lifeguards (on elevated chairs) watching children wading into the safe shallow ocean; the ocean bubbling, like champagne; but that's such a lousy simile, and you know it.

You can hear the children from your bedroom in your new Conch house. You concentrate on every sound. Ah, memory, Laura, you can remember, *we* can remember: lying in bed all those summers ago (summer now just another metaphor for ice). Remember the pain, the numbing wheezing crawling pain? Remember lying there in your bed under the red linen sheets, lying in the selfsame bed you share(d) with Harold?

The chemotherapy induces constant nausea, infinities of nausea, and where are you, Harold, you sonovabitch bastard?

Bring me a Maxolon.

Rub my back.

Rub my shoulders.

Hariold, where are you . . . ?

11.

Oh, Harold had excuses, so many excuses, so many charming excuses. His father died, Harold had to be with him, too, you know; and he had to work. That's the best one, isn't it? He had to work to earn money. Who could argue with that? Certainly not his dear pals who loved him, his world of friends and supporters.

Everyone loved Harold.

You whisper (to him? To yourself?) "You could have been with me a little bit. You weren't working every night. You could have faced the truth, that I'm sick, that I might die." But he declaims (ah, what a word!) that he *is* there for you, that it's not his fault, that he has always been there for you, even as he leaves you, even as he hides away from you, from what you might become (from what you have become), and when you tell him to leave . . .

When you close up, shut up, lock up the pretty pale blue shutters that are your (you just can't resist another metaphor, can you?) eyes and ears and mouth (ears and mouths aren't blue!), Harold is honestly

Surprised.

12.

But not as surprised as you, Helen, lovely, blue-eyed, shutter-eyed, conch-shelled Helen; not half as surprised as you.

He left, as per your request/demand, disappeared into what became the cold Winter, and you missed him, loved him, wanted him back.

But you were . . . shuttered, weren't you, Laura. Frozen. "Incapable of any more humiliation." You weren't the same person that you were.

None of us is the same person that we were.

Don't try to diagram that sentence. Listen to me. I'm smarter than you, and I *know* you. And so you laugh, knowing that your narrator can't be your older self. Certainly not your younger, callow, gullible self.

"Who are you?" you ask. Talking to yourself.

Finally figuring it out.

Seeing yourself completely.

In and out of your history.

Such a small, such a profound epiphany.

13.

The bell rings, class is finished, the last class, and you wait while the cream of the crop pour through the high, metal double doors; and you mark their spot tests and leave them in a neat pile on the upper right-hand corner of your desk, which will be accessible to the students when they arrive tomorrow morning; and you attend a staff meeting, everyone keeping warm in the cold, yet heated conference room; and then you leave for the last time.

14.

You haven't even the slightest urge to return home, to take one last look. You go directly to the beach. It's low tide, and the beach is two hundred yards wide, as slick and smooth as a skating rink. But not for long.

Not for long.

You sit down on the ice floe—it takes time for the chill to reach into your thighs and buttocks and the balls of your feet—and dream.

Good-bye, Harold, you bastard. I'm sorry. You're sorry. Everyone's sorry. But I'm too young to waste my life. Too young too young too young, and as you chant your incantation to a Beach Boys' melody, you can feel the rising heat. The delicious smell of the sun and sea-salt humidity.

The ice is melting in the sun, and the ice turns to cool asphalt and then to yielding, smooth sand, scratchy and granular; and you pick up handfuls of it and throw it into the air. It tastes . . . warm, dry, like choking.

You stretch out, breathe deeply, and let the warmth in, even while you watch yourself simultaneously getting up and walking to the sea.

(Ah, the conundrum, which you is you? The narrator *you* or the you *you*? Let the narrator *you* be me.)

15.

Watch me, dear, sweet glacial Laura.

Queen mother of ice and dreams and broken conch.

Watch me slip out to the sea.

Digging in Gehenna
by David Gerrold

David Gerrold has written over forty science fiction novels, including *The Man Who Folded Himself*, *When Harlie Was One*, *The Voyage of the Star Wolf*, and four books in the epic *War Against the Chtorr* series. He has written nearly as many scripts for television series, including *Star Trek*, *Land of the Lost*, *Sliders*, *Babylon 5*, and *The Twilight Zone*. In 1995, he won both the Hugo and the Nebula Awards for his autobiographical story of his son's adoption, *The Martian Child*.

DADDY was arguing with Dr. Blom again, so Mom told me to stay away from the dig for a while, at least until tempers cooled off. That was the only thing likely to cool off anytime soon. Spring was rising, and so were the daytime temperatures. We would be heading back south to the more comfortable polar zones as soon as the last trucks were loaded and the skywhale arrived tomorrow morning. Twenty-four months would pass before the sand would be cool enough to stand on again, but nobody knew if we would be coming back.

"They're arguing about the *horn* again, aren't they?"

Mom nodded. "It's their favorite argument."

"Do you think Daddy's right? Or Dr. Blom?"

"Actually, I hope they're both wrong." Mom looked up from the fabber she was disassembling. "Pray that we never find out what the damn thing was really used for. If either one of them is proved right, they'll never be able to work together again."

"They'll just find something else to argue about."

"No, this is one of those arguments that people don't forget. If you're wrong, it's a career-killer. The only hope for resolution is for them to be equally embarrassed by the facts. And don't tell Daddy I said this. It would hurt his feelings enormously."

"I didn't think anyone could hurt Daddy's feelings."

"Only people he cares about." She closed the lid of the machine and handed me the used cartridges for the recycler. "Just because he doesn't show his feelings doesn't mean he doesn't have any."

There were over two hundred people on the dig. We weren't the only family here. There were twenty others who'd brought their children. We were a whole village. We had sixteen acre-tents and at least a hundred equipment and storage tents scattered around. Three of the acre-tents were habitats, with hanging rugs to give each family group some privacy.

We had offworlders here, too. The dig was big news all the way back to Earth; the first alien civilization ever discovered. And because the actual site was habitable only four out of twenty-eight months, this was a precious opportunity, especially for the PhD candidates, like Hank, the big goofy guy who called me "swee'pea" and "short stuff" and "Little Darlin'" until Mom gave him *the glare.* So of course, I wanted to see more of him.

Actually, she's my stepmom, and according to the rule books, I'm supposed to resent her, but mostly she and I are good friends. Probably because she's only twelve years older than me, so she feels more like a big sister than a stepmom, but I call her Mom anyway. I'm almost seventeen, old enough to get married; but Mom has this rule that nobody gets married until they finish college. She refused to marry Daddy for three years until she finished her doctorate.

Mom said that Hank was too old for me anyway. I respectfully did not point out that Hank was only five years older than me while Daddy was fifteen years her senior. I didn't need to start that fight. And besides, she was twenty-four when she married him.

Hank was one of the offworlders who had trouble adapting to Gehenna's seventy-two-hour day, but eventually he found his rhythm. The others settled in, too. Everyone does. Daddy says that twelve hours on and twelve hours off mimics Earth time almost perfectly—despite the fact that the sunlight doesn't match.

I'd been allowed to come on the dig because Mom and Dad were team leaders. There were another dozen college students who'd been brought along for grunt work and experience, so I was lumped in with them. We all had class in the morning, and chores in the afternoon. Then class in the evening and chores again in the early morning. Interspersed with sleep, of course.

I was part of the toddler-team; we took care of the little ones while the various moms went off to work. There were only five of them, but they were a handful. I don't think we ever had five dry diapers at a time. We solved the problem by putting one person on diaper-duty each shift.

There's this about changing diapers—it keeps you from biting your nails. My private goal was to potty train the little monsters as quickly as possible. We'd made real progress with the other four, but my little brother, Zakky, had so far resisted all inducements toward sanitary behavior. Despite that, I still thought he was cute. Mom said that my attitude would change as soon as Zakky learned how to say no. Once he learned how to argue, he'd be just like his daddy.

Daddy was famous for his arguments. Or maybe infamous. He wasn't loud or aggressive. I'd never even seen him raise his voice. He was painfully polite. He would make his points carefully, exquisitely, elegantly reasoned, making connections so obvious you could slap your forehead for not seeing them yourself. And when he was finished, he had assembled a framework of logic as marvelous as a Chinese tapestry—so beautiful and compelling and overwhelming in its construction you were left with no place to stand. You just wanted to find a great big club and whack him across the head with it for being so damnably, blandly, patiently, *right*. Again.

Daddy's brain never stopped working. The universe was a giant puzzle to him, and he felt it was his personal responsibility to fit the pieces together. When I was little, I was afraid of him; but now that I understood better, I admired him. I used to wonder why Mom had married him, but most times I envied her for the adventure.

But Daddy could get so preoccupied with solving the puzzles of the universe that sometimes he forgot everything else. Sometimes we had to drag him physically away from the dig just to get him to eat, and even then we could have put a slice of shale between two pieces of bread and he wouldn't have noticed, he'd be so busy talking about what he had found and what he had to do next, and what it might mean. Of course, that led to a lot of arguments with the other diggers, about what each new discovery *meant*. They were all on new ground here. Nobody knew for sure what any of it really was, so everything was still just opinion.

The one thing we knew about the tripods—that's what we called them—was that we didn't know anything about them at all. We had no idea how they had lived, what they ate, what they believed in, what kind of culture they had, or even how many sexes they had. Every new fragment suggested as many possibilities as it disproved.

Daddy wasn't the only one arguing, of course. Everyone argued with everyone. Mom said that was because -ology didn't mean "the study of" as much as it meant "the argument about." But Daddy *liked* to argue. He said that arguing was the highest exercise of intelligence at work, measuring, testing, and challenging ideas. He said that it was the passion of the argument that ultimately revealed the true self. Of course, Daddy would argue with the weather if he could. Failing that, he had argued for extending our stay on-site by an extra two weeks. He'd won half that argument. We were a week past our original departure date and already the temperatures were half-past unbearable.

But Daddy wasn't the only one who wanted to stay. Almost everybody on the team was so excited at what they were pulling out of the ground that nobody wanted to quit, even if it meant working in 110-degree weather. What if we were only half an hour away from finding the tripod Rosetta Stone? There might not be another expedition like this one in our lifetime. Gehenna's weather wasn't exactly friendly.

The tripod village had only been discovered six years ago, when one of the radar-mapping satellites found patterns underneath the sand. Detailed scanning showed eleven separate buildings embedded in the soft shale. The access team had trucked in huge sand-dredges and digging machines, and cut a ramp down to the target layers. Only then could the archaeology teams start working.

Once we'd finally gotten down to the roofs of the domes, and gotten inside a few, we began discovering the first artifacts of an entire civilization. Dr. Blom said this village was less than a hundred thousand years old. On a geological scale, we'd just missed them. Of course, having their star flare up might have had something to do with that, too.

Daddy's team had put a three-acre tent over the site. That got everybody out of the direct sun, and it brought the temperature down at least ten degrees; but mostly it kept the sand from covering the dig. The long nights brought hot roaring winds that could dry out your skin in an hour, leaving you itchy and cranky and desperate. Thirty-six hours later, when the sun crept over the sharp horizon again, there would be orange dust covering everything, sometimes as much as thirty centimeters. Everything had to be tented, or you might as well abandon it.

Mom's team kept busy cataloging the artifacts, scanning and deconstructing them, then test-fabbing duplicates and comparing them to the originals. When the dupe was accurate to the limits of the measuring equipment, Mom would finalize it, and make it available in the catalog. Then, anyone could log on and fab a copy.

Some of the artifacts were easy, because they were mostly complete. A knife. A basket. A bowl. A jar of dessicated grain. A stool. But some of the items were impossible to figure out. Not just because they were fragments, but because nobody had any idea what kind of people the tripods might have been. Like the hairbrush thing with two handles—what was that for? A toothbrush? A back scratcher? An envelope holder?

Even the word "people" was cause for argument.

Dr. Blom was an alienist. She said that alien meant *gaijin*. Different. Therefore, human paradigms couldn't apply. Just using the word "people" created an anthropomorphic mind-set.

So of course, Daddy took the anthropomorphic position—that life is messy everywhere, but it isn't infinite. The physics of the situation define what's possible. Life occurs as an expression of opportunity. And the same evolutionary imperatives are at work everywhere, regardless of the DNA coding; Gehenna had oxygen and water and a mobile temperate zone conducive to the carbon cycle, etc. etc. Therefore, knowing the circumstances of the environment, we know the limits of what kind of life is possible. Therefore, therefore . . . ad infinitum. Rumor had it that Dr. Blom had actually asked one of her assistants to fab a club . . .

Eventually, the whole camp was arguing the point—if the tripods were so alien as to be beyond our comprehension, and this dig represents an insoluble puzzle to humankind, then why are we even bothering to dig anything up and study it? Wasn't the whole point of any "-ology" to increase our understanding, not our befuddlement?

None of which solved the problem of the *thing*, which along the way had become the focus of the whole argument. Dr. Blom had found it in one of the broken domes. It was some kind of ceramic, so it was obviously manufactured for a purpose. But what purpose? She and Daddy had been arguing about it from the very first day.

Complicating the argument, the thing wasn't a complete thing. Mostly, it was a tray of fragments. Mom had spent a week, scanning them, manipulating the pieces around, extrapolating what the thing might have looked like when it was whole. That was a month's worth of squabble, right there—how did the fragments fit together?—with Daddy and Dr. Blom fussing over asymmetry, polarity, and even which end was up.

What they finally agreed to was that in size and shape, the thing could have been some kind of table vessel. Like a punch bowl or a centerpiece or a coffee-pot. One end of the thing was a bowl-shaped flare, like the horn of a trumpet; it narrowed into a hollow pedestal. The thing could have stood on the large end or the small, but it was obviously more stable resting on the large end.

Dr. Blom had initially suggested that it had a ceremonial function, like a wineglass or a chalice, except that the thing had three scooped-out openings in the sides of the flared end. The openings were supposed to be there; they were sculpted in. Daddy suggested that the sculpting suggested that another object was to be placed in the horn, perhaps a triangular bowl, or even a symbolic representation of the tripodal makers.

So then Dr. Blom decided that they were looking at it upside down. The horn-end was the bottom and the pedestal was a support for something else. Maybe it was a flower-holder, or a vase. Then she decided that it had a ceremonial function and was used for lustral rites. Some kind of purification ritual.

Whenever she said this, Daddy rolled his eyes in exasperation, and began muttering about Occam's chainsaw—whatever was the simplest, most obvious explanation, had to be the right one. Finally, in frustration, Mom fabbed a couple of dozen replicas of the thing and passed them out like party favors. Very quickly it became the symbol of everything we didn't know about the tripods. If it had been half a size larger, we could have worn it as a dunce cap.

If only there had been wall-markings in the domes or illustrations on the side of jars or something like that. But there weren't any. Apparently, the tripods didn't make images of themselves. And that was good for another whole area of argument—that maybe because of something about the way their eyes worked, or their brains, they didn't have visual symbology.

That could have been an even bigger disagreement than the argument about the *thing*, except by that time, we'd found the first skeletons and that's when the real excitement began. Everything before that was just a warmup.

Hank was on the exobiology team, so I heard about lots of stuff before it was presented, and some stuff that wasn't presented at all, because it was still only speculation. Most of the skeletons were complete and fairly well-preserved; carbon dating and iridium scanning showed that this village had died when the sun flared up.

Hank had a lot of ideas about that. His team had fabbed copies of three skeletons, two adults and a juvenile, and now they were working on the nature of the tripod musculature. As bad as the arguments were about *the thing*, the arguments about tripod biology were even worse.

First off, the tripod braincase was too small. It was a dorsal hump opposite what was assumed to be the rear leg. Channels in the bone suggested routes for optic nerves. Other structures might have been a nasal chamber, which would indicate an "anterior" as opposed to "posterior." But there was also the suggestion of some kind of a collagenous snout, like an elephant's trunk, only it seemed to serve as a mouth, not as a nose. But nobody wanted to say for certain, in case it turned out to be something else and then they'd be embarrassed for guessing wrong, so for the moment everything everybody said about the tripods was prefaced with "suggests," "could be," "possible," "might serve as," and even an occasional "probable." But the size of the braincase was clearly insufficient for sentience.

A full-grown tripod was only waist-high. Not much more than a meter tall. The exobiology team estimated that it would mass no more than 80 kilograms. So that would make it the size of a large dog, or a small ape; but the estimated size of the brain wasn't large enough even for that size creature. The exobiology team estimated that the tripods maybe had the intelligence of a cocker spaniel—just smart enough to pee outside. So that was another mystery.

And then there was the business of the fingers. They were short and stubby, more of a splayed paw than a hand, and not really suitable for grasping large or heavy objects. The simulations showed that if a tripod squatted on its hind leg, the two forward paws could be used to manipulate simple objects, but that was about the limit. The tripods would not have been very good typists. That is, if they had anything to type.

Dr. Blom said that intelligent creatures needed the ability to handle objects, not just as tools, but more importantly because the ability to understand an object was directly related to the ability to touch, feel, and manipulate it. "Fingers are the extension of the mind," she said.

Wisely, Daddy did not disagree with her on that one. Instead, he took a gentler tack, pointing out that dolphins and other cetaceans had demonstrated sophisticated language and intelligence skills without any grasping limbs at all; so clearly there was something else at work here. But dolphins and whales have very large brains, and tripods didn't—so that just brought us back to the problem of the too-small braincase.

But those were only sidebar discussions. The main event was much more serious.

Hank explained it to me, at dinner in the mess tent. Nowhere else in the universe—not in simulation, and not in the laboratory, and not on any other life-bearing planet, had nature produced a three-legged creature. The asymmetry of the species was unprecedented, and Hank said that it was going to cause a major upheaval in both biological and evolutionary thinking. There was no way it couldn't. This was the real issue: whatever the tripods had been, they were so far outside the realm of what we had previously known or believed to be possible, that they represented a massive breakdown in biological science. That's what was so exciting; this was a real opportunity for genius to prove itself by reinventing the paradigm.

After dinner, most folks gathered in the rec area for news and gossip and mail. Sometimes we'd see a movie, sometimes we'd have a dance or celebrate someone's birthday. Some of the folks played instruments, so we had a makeshift band. And the bar was open for two hours, if people wanted to have a drink.

But not everybody wanted to be sociable all the time. Some folks had to be alone for a while. They'd go outside and sit under the stars or maybe walk out to one of the boundary markers. It was hard to get lost in the desert. The camp gave off a bright glow, and if that weren't enough, the housekeeping team had installed three bright red lasers pointing up into the sky. They were visible for kilometers, so anyone who ventured too far out only needed to head for the light at the edge of the world. Folks who wanted a bit of solitude sometimes planned midnight picnics and hiked a few kilometers out to sleep on the warm sand. And no, sleeping wasn't all they did.

I wanted to go out on a midnight picnic with

Hank, but Mom wouldn't allow it; she wouldn't even let me appeal to Daddy, she said we didn't need that fight in the camp. So the most I could do with Hank was walk around the big tent once in a while, mostly when Mom wanted to be alone with Daddy. Some of the girls on the toddler-team went out for a midnight picnic once. I went with them, but all we did was giggle about the boys we liked and make lewd guesses of what we thought they looked like naked. Maybe that's fun when you're fifteen, but I was too old for that now. I wanted something more than embarrassed giggling.

And, there was that other thing, too. I didn't want to be the *last* one in the group. I didn't want to be the only one who didn't know what the others were giggling about. Though sometimes it seemed so silly I couldn't imagine any serious person wanting to do it at all, sometimes I couldn't think about anything else. I wondered if it was that way for anybody else. I wanted to ask Mom about it, but she was so busy she never had time; the one time I brought up the subject, she asked me to wait until we got back home, so she and I could spend some serious time talking about it. But when your insides are fizzing like a chocolate soda, there's no such thing as patience.

So that night, when Hank put his arm around my shoulder and pulled me close against him, he smelled so good, kissing him just felt like the right thing to do. The thing about kissing someone you like kissing— once you start, it's hard to stop. And I didn't want to stop, I just wanted to keep going. But then Zakky's diaper-monitor chimed and Hank pulled away gently and said, "Come'on, Swee'pea, I'll walk you home," as if that was all there was to it, and I wondered how he could be like that. Didn't he have any normal feelings?

And that's the other thing about changing diapers.

Mom says that they're punctuation marks in the paragraphs of life. Whatever thoughts you might have been working on, they end up in the diaper pail with all the rest of the crap. And that night, I understood exactly. Whatever fizzy feelings I might have had inside of me, they were all fizzed out by the time Zakky's messy bottom was clean again.

So when some of the team members said to me stuff like, "you can't understand how frustrating it is to be this close," I just smiled weakly and said, "Yeah, I guess so." They were the ones who didn't understand.

After a couple weeks of tinkering, Hank's team fabbed a walking tripod, just to see if they could build one that could walk, run, squat, or even mount another for mating; the only thing it couldn't do was lift a leg to pee on a lamppost.

The team went through several iterations until they hit the right combination of musculature and autonomic intelligence; then they fabbed a bunch more, for everyone else to play with, or experiment on. The 'bots weren't very big; the largest was the size of Zakky. Some of them had scales, some had fur, some had feathers, some had naked skin; and they were all different colors. At this point, the team was still guessing. It was kind of like having a pack of three-legged dogs from the rainbow planet running around the camp, but Hank said it was necessary for us to observe these things in action to get some sense of what the real tripods might have been like. I wasn't exactly sneaking out to see him behind Mom's back, but I did make sure that my regular chores took me through the bio-tent during his shifts. Mom certainly couldn't complain about me doing my regular duties. Of course, she didn't have to know why I had traded shifts with Marlena Rigby either.

Hank liked my visits. He gave me one of the robots, and even programmed it to follow Zakky around like a baby-monitor, so we would always know where he was. Zakky decided the tripod was a chicken and called it "Fuffy." I thought it looked more like a yellow cat with a limp.

When I said that, Hank admitted that getting the creature to walk right had been his biggest problem. He had started by studying the algorithms for three-legged industrial robots, but plastic autonomy is different than biological, and there are a lot of different ways a three-legged creature can walk. It can move one leg at a time, each one in turn, which means it sort of scuttles or zigzags or walks in circles. Or it can alternate moving its two front legs with its single rear leg in a crippled imitation of a four-legged creature. That was faster but it created musculature issues that weren't resolved in the actual skeletons.

Hank finally resolved it by not programming the tripod at all. Instead, he gave it a neural network and let it teach itself to walk. What it came up with was—well, it was just weird, but efficient. But it still looked like a yellow cat with a limp.

As a joke, Hank taught the tripod to squat on Zakky's potty chair. That made me laugh, and for a moment I thought Zakky might take the hint, but the devil-baby was actively disinterested. Instead, he put a plastic bucket on his head and banged it with a spoon, and laughed delightedly at being inside the noise.

On the last full day before the skywhale arrived, I was helping Mom disassemble the last three fabbers. We wrapped all the pieces in plastic and packed them in stiff boxes. Nobody knew if the Institute would authorize a second expedition. There was a lot of disappointment that we hadn't found more— no books or wall carvings or statues—so the folks who passed out the money had lost some of their enthusiasm. Despite their effusive praise at a job well done, despite their protestations of support, it was no secret that this expedition was considered only a partial success, which is a polite way of saying "an ambitious failure."

Some of the more aggressive members of Daddy's team were arguing for mothballing the entire site as a way of forcing the issue. With all of the equipment still in place, the Institute would have a financial investment in returning; but Daddy shook his head. If a return were guaranteed, then storing the hardware on-site made financial sense; but if the Institute decided not to fund a return, they would write off the machinery, and then it wouldn't be available for any other enterprise anywhere else, and that would hurt everybody. Daddy was right, of course.

Some of the folks were eager to head back home—like Hank; he said he had enough material to fund a dozen years of study, and he could hardly wait to get the skeletons back to the lab and begin microscanning and DNA-reconstruction; it was his hunch that the DNA sequences were too short for a creature this size.

But most folks were sad that the adventure was ending so abruptly, and without a real resolution. That was how I felt. Hank was going back to wherever, and I'd probably never see him again. So, I'd sort of made up my mind that I was ready to sneak away from tonight's party with him for an hour or two.

We finished packing the last fabber, and then the toolkits, and we were done. Mom sat down on a bench and sighed. "This was fun."

"Are you going to miss it?"

"Not at all," she said. "Once we get back home, I'll have so much work to do just sorting everything out, I won't have time to miss anything." And then her hand flew up to her mouth. "Oh, sweetheart, I'm sorry. I promised you that we would find some time together, just for us."

"It's all right, Mom—"

"No, it isn't all right. There are things you need to talk about."

I shrugged, embarrassed. "I'm okay now."

"Mm." She didn't look convinced. "All right, let me give you the speech anyway. I know you already know this, but I have to say it anyway, because if I don't say it, you'll think that I don't know it. Come here, sit down next to me."

She put her arm around my shoulder, pulled me close, and lowered her voice almost conspiratorially. "Look, Hank is a real nice boy—" she began.

"He's a *man*, Mom."

"He's a big boy on a big adventure," she corrected. "He won't be a man until he starts thinking like one. And you won't be a woman until you stop thinking like a teenager."

"What is that supposed to mean?"

"What it means is that sometimes, it isn't about *now*. It isn't always about what you want, what you think you need, what you think you have to have. Sometimes, it's about who you're going to be when it all works out, and your responsibility to that moment outweighs whatever you think you want now."

I didn't say anything to that. I could already see where she was headed.

"Sweetheart, here's the question I want you to ask yourself. What kind of a person do you want to be? Whenever you have a big choice in front of you, that's what you have to ask yourself? Is this the kind of thing that the person I want to be would do? What kind of memory will this be? A good one or an embarrassing one or a terrible regret?"

I stared at my knees. Whenever I sat, they looked

bony. Knees were such ugly parts of the body. Knees and elbows. Why couldn't somebody design joints that didn't make you look like a chicken? Like the tripods. They had nice joints. They could swivel better than human joints—

"Are you listening to me?"

"Yes, Mom."

"What did I just say?"

"You said that I shouldn't do things that I'll regret."

"What I said was that life is about building a collection of good memories. As you go through life, you need to choose what kinds of memories you want to collect. Because your memories determine who you are."

"Oh."

"All right," she said, patting me on the shoulder in a gesture that was as much resignation as it was completion. "I can see that there are some mistakes you're going to have to make for yourself. Maybe that's the only way you ever really learn where anything is—by tripping over it in the dark." She sighed. "Go ahead. Go get cleaned up for the party."

There wasn't much left to do. Most of the camp had already been packed up and loaded onto the trucks. So folks just stood around waiting, listening to the tent poles groaning in the wind. Overhead the lights swung back and forth on their wires. We waited in an uneven island of brightness. Only the generator, the mess tent, the hospitality tent, and the shower tents were left. Almost everything else had disappeared, or was in the process of disappearing under a fresh layer of sand and dust.

Zakky was asleep in the hospitality tent. His diaper was clean, so I decided not to wake him, Marlena would handle it. She was on diaper-duty tonight. I headed back out to the party.

The mess team had prepared a grand smorgasbord; we had to finish the last of the perishables, so it looked like more food in one place than I'd ever seen in my entire life. The bar was open, too. It seemed like an invitation to pig out and drink yourself silly. After all, you'd have twelve hours on the skywhale to sleep it off. But the disciplines of the past four months were too ingrained. The party was more subdued than usual. People were tired and a lot of folks seemed depressed as well.

The band played everybody's favorite songs, and all of the team leaders made speeches about how hard their folks had worked and how grateful they were and what a successful expedition this had been. And everybody made jokes about the thing and the tripods and offered bawdy speculations about where the thing might really fit and how the tripods made baby tripods, and so on. But it felt forced. I guessed the simmering resentments were still simmering.

I found Hank near the bar, chatting with the other offworlders, and a couple of the interns. He saw me coming and excused himself. He took me by the hand and led me out of the tent, out of the island of light, out toward the soft red sand.

"There's something—" I started.

"—I have to tell you," he finished.

"You first."

"No, you."

We played a couple of rounds of that for a bit, laughing at our mutual silliness, until finally, I just blurted it out: "I really like you, Hank" and he said: "I'm engaged to a girl back home" at the same time.

And then I choked on my tongue and said, "What?" and he started to repeat it, and I cut him off. "I heard you the first time." And meanwhile, my heart was in free fall, while my brain was saying, "Thank Ghu, you didn't give say anything stupid—"

and my fingers wanted to reach into his chest and shred his heart for not telling me this before.

He held me by the shoulders and made what he must have thought were compassionate noises: "—I just wanted to tell you that you're really sweet, and I'm sure you're going to find the right guy, and I hope you'll have a happy life because you deserve it—oh, look, here comes the skywhale!"

I turned to look, not because I didn't want to see it, but because I didn't want Hank to see the tears running down my cheeks. The big ship came majestically over the ridge, all her lights blazing, a vast platform in the sky. She floated toward us, passing directly over the camp, while everyone came pouring out of the mess tent, cheering and waving. The skywhale dropped anchor half a klick past the camp and began pulling herself down, like a grand gleaming dream come to rest.

The camp speakers came alive with fanfare and trumpets and everyone shouted themselves silly, hugging and kissing each other in celebration. It looked like the party was finally starting; but actually it was ending. This was just the final beat. We had ninety minutes to load and be away, if we wanted to beat the heat of the morning. There wasn't a lot of slippage on that; most of the tents and air-cooling gear had already been collapsed and packed. If we didn't get out on time, we could be in serious trouble.

I threaded my way around the edges of the crowd, looking for Mom. I wanted to tell her that I was going to grab Zakky and his diaper bag, my duffel, too, and just go on aboard, and curl up in a bunk somewhere. And not have to talk to anybody. There wasn't anything I wanted down here anymore. But Hank came following behind me and grabbed my arm. "Hey, Swee'pea, are you all right?"

"I'm fine, thank you! And I'm not your Swee'pea. You already have a Swee'pea." I pulled free and stormed away, not really caring which direction I headed in, so I ended up smack in the middle of the party, and that meant that I had to hug everyone good-bye, even though I'd be seeing most of them on the skywhale, and back home too.

—Until I bumped into Marlena Rigby. "What are you doing here?"

"What do you mean?" she asked, bewildered.

"Who's taking care of Zakky?"

"You're supposed to—he's your brother."

"We traded shifts, remember?"

"No, we didn't—I told you I wasn't going to miss the party."

"Oh, good grief. You are such a stupid airhead! We made this deal a week ago. Oh, never mind—" I headed off to the hospitality tent.

Zakky was gone.

Okay, Mom had come and gotten him.

Except the diaper bag was still there.

Mom wouldn't have collected the baby without gathering his things. I unclipped my phone from my belt. "Mom?"

I waited while it rang on the other end. After a moment, "Yes, sweetheart?" Her voice sounded funny—like she'd been interrupted in the middle of a mouthful.

"Where are you?"

"I'm with Daddy, down by the dig. We're . . . um, saying good-bye. What do you need?"

"Is Zakky with you?"

"Isn't he with you?"

"He's not in the crib."

"When did you see him last—"

"I checked on him thirty minutes ago. I thought Marlena was watching him. We had a deal. But she went to the party anyway." I was already outside, circling the hospitality tent. "He couldn't have gone far—"

She made an exasperated noise. The sound was muffled for a moment, while she explained the situation to Daddy. Then she came back. "We're on our way. You start looking."

Everybody I passed, I grabbed them, "Have you seen Zakky? He's missing—" Nobody had seen him. And nobody had time to help me search either. They were all hurrying to gather their things and board the dirigible. In frustration, I just stopped where I was and started screaming. "My little brother is missing! He's somewhere out there! Doesn't anybody care?"

The problem was, the skywhale had to leave whether everybody was aboard or not. She wasn't rigged to withstand the heat of the day. And most of the camp had been dismantled and was already on its way south on the trucks, so there weren't the resources on the ground to support more than a few people anyway.

Thirty seconds of screaming was more than enough. It wasn't going to produce any useful result and Daddy always said, "Save your upset for afterward. Do what's in front of you, first."

But the screaming did make people aware there was a problem. By the time I finished circling the camp, calling for Zakky everywhere, Dr. Blom was already organizing a real search. She came barreling through like a tank, snapping out orders and mobilizing her dig team like a general at war.

She had a phone in each hand, one for incoming, one for outgoing. "No, you're not getting on the whale," she barked at one of them. "We're not going home until we find that child. We'll ride back in the trucks if we have to." I was beginning to understand why Daddy had invited her along. She was good at organization. And no one argued with Dr. Blom. Except Daddy, of course.

She marched into the mess tent and started drawing on one of the plastic tablecloths, quickly dividing the camp and its environs into sectors, assigning teams of three to each sector. "Take flashlights, water, blankets, a first-aid kit, and at least one phone for each person. And a working GPS, dammit!" To the other phone: "Well, unpack the flying remotes, then! I don't care. We've still got twenty hours before infrared is useless."

Dr. Blom didn't stop talking until Mom and Dad came rushing into the mess tent. She looked up only long enough to say, "I need another thirty people to cover the south and west. Pull as many members of your team off the dirigible as you can."

Daddy opened his mouth to say something, then realized how absolutely stupid it was to object. He unclipped his phone and started talking into it. Mom did the same. In less than a minute, the skywhale started disgorging people, running for the mess tent. Other people began pulling crates off the trucks, cracking them, and pulling out equipment. I'd never seen so many people move so fast. It was all I could do to keep out of the way. I felt useless and stupid. But it wasn't my fault, was it? I mean, stupid Marlena was the one who screwed up, not me—

Daddy came striding over; his face was red with fury. "Go get your stuff and get aboard the whale. Now." I'd never seen him so angry.

"But I have to stay and help with the search."

"No, you will not. You've done enough already."

"Daddy—"

"We'll talk about this later. If there is a later. Right now, the only thing I want you to do is get onboard and keep out of the way—"

I didn't wait to hear the rest. I sobbed and ran. All the way to the gangplank and up into the whale, where I threw myself into the first empty seat I could find. Everything was all screwed up. I wanted to die. And I was so angry, I wanted to scream. If only—

Except there wasn't any "if only." There was only me. Stupidly chasing Hank. Stupidly not checking Zakky. Stupidly acting like a stupid little spoiled brat.

Suddenly, I stopped and sat up. Wait a minute. I bounced out of my seat and went looking for Hank. He was on the upper deck, already sacked out in a bunk. I shook him awake, hard. "Come on, I need your help."

"Huh, what—?" He rubbed his eyes. "Look, if you're going to yell at me some more, can't it wait until tomorrow?"

"Zakky's missing. You can track him."

"Huh? What?"

"Would you two take that somewhere else? People are trying to sleep here."

I said something very impolite. But I pulled Hank out of his bunk. I grabbed his clipboard and dragged him out. "The tripod you gave me for Zakky. You can track it!"

"Well, yeah," He said, still rubbing his eyes. "Only all the equipment is packed up."

"Well, unpack it, then!"

"The truck has already left," he said. "We sent it off an hour ago."

"Can we call it back?"

"No, wait—" He closed his eyes for a moment, thinking. He looked like he had gone back to sleep. "Yeah, that'll work." We headed down to the communications room of the whale. It was his turn to drag me. The communications officer looked annoyed at the interruption. I knew her from back home. The kids called her Ironballs, but her real name was Lila Brock. She was a wiry little woman with a hard expression and her hair tied back in a bun.

I didn't understand half of what Hank said to her; most of it was in another language, techno-babble; but even before he finished, she was already turning to her displays and typing in codes. The screens started to fill with overlaid patterns and colors. She frowned. "Wait a minute, let me see what I can read from the satellites." More typing. More colors, more patterns. "Okay, I've got probables." She tapped the big display. "Here, here, and here—"

Hank copied the feed to his clipboard and overlaid it on a map of the camp. "Okay, that first one is the truck," said Hank, eliminating the one that was moving too fast. "And this one is the lounge of the whale—"

"And the last one is in the center of the dig," I said. I recognized the spider-shaped pattern of the excavation. "Come on!" I was already out the door.

"Call the camp! Tell them!" Hank shouted back to Brock, and followed me down the gangplank at a run. The whale was closer to the dig than the mess tent, but there were rolling dunes in the way—it's not easy to run in sand of any kind. Hank made me slow down, lest I exhaust myself. He kept referring to the updated scans on his clipboard, steering us toward the west end of the dig, where the first big ramp had been carved into the shale. "Down there," he pointed.

I was already calling, "Zakky! Zakky! Where are you?" Off to the left, I could see the first few searchers rolling out of the camp on sand-scooters, and then a sledge carrying Mom and Dad. But we were already heading down the ramp. They were still a few minutes away.

At first it was too dark to see anything, but then the whole night lit up—as if a great white star had been switched on above us. It was startling. At first I didn't understand; we'd already packed most of our fly-beams; but Hank said curtly, "Satellite. False-white laser. Good idea. Somebody was thinking."

It wasn't quite as bright as daylight; in fact, it wasn't even twilight; but it was a hundred times better than the silky darkness. At the bottom of the ramp, there wasn't much to see. The important stuff had been covered with plastic sheets. Most of the open domes had been sealed. All except one.

Hank and I climbed down into it, peering into the different chambers. One still had an inflatable bed in it. The blankets were rumpled. Okay, that explained that. Zakky hadn't been down this way. But Hank wouldn't let me go into any of the tunnels. "We have to wait for the others. They'll have lights."

I called into each of the passages, "Zakky, want a cookie? Zakky?" We both listened, but there was no reply. "Zakky? Come on, sweety. It's cookie-time." Nothing. "That doesn't mean anything," I said. "Zakky has selective hearing. If he doesn't want to hear . . ."

Hank put his hand on my shoulder. "We'll find him. The tripod is down that one."

And then Dr. Blom arrived, scrambling down the steps into the dome, followed by Dad and then Mom and three of the folks from the closest search teams. Suddenly, there were lights flashing everywhere. I grabbed one and headed into the passage Hank had pointed out. "Zakky!"

The passage led into the next dome over. Zakky was sitting on the floor playing with three discarded replicas of the famous unknown *thing*. One of the replicas had been shoved point-first into the sand, and Zakky's toy tripod was squatting up and down on it. Its three legs fit perfectly into the openings in the sides of the bowl. "Go potty, Fuffy," Zakky said insistently. "Go potty. Do faw momma."

Daddy and Hank came scrambling into the dome after me. Then Mom and Dr. Blom. I pointed my light at the tripod and everybody just stared for a moment.

I couldn't help it. I started laughing. It was too silly. Then Hank started chortling. And then Mom. And Dr. Blom. And finally, Daddy.

"Well, I guess that answers that," said Dr. Blom. To her phone, she said, "We've got him."

Daddy shook his head. "How are we going to write this up?"

"With a straight face," said Mom, scooping up Zakky. He cooed at her; she cooed back at him, then turned to Daddy and Dr. Blom. "It's not everybody who discovers an alien potty chair. You realize, of course, that a potty chair will get you a lot more headlines than a lustral chalice."

"Yes, there is that," Dr. Blom agreed.

I cleared my throat. "It's not a potty chair."

"But of course it is," said Daddy. "Look at the way the tripod fits. Look at the way—" He stopped. "Why not?"

"There's a hole in the point. Whatever the tripod poops into the bowl is supposed to come out the bottom."

"Well, yes—" said Dr. Blom. "That makes it easier to bury the waste in the sand. It's a portable toilet."

"Yes, it's a toilet," I agreed. "But it's not a potty chair. It's a kitty box. Sort of."

They all looked at me. "Huh—?"

I poked Hank. "Tell them."

"Tell them what?"

"What you haven't told anyone else yet—that the tripods didn't build these domes."

Everybody looked at him. *Oh, really?* Hank looked embarrassed. "Um, I didn't want to say anything yet. Because I wanted to be sure. I wanted to run more tests at the University. But, well, yes. Their brains were too small, and their DNA sequences are too short. Too well-ordered. These things weren't sentient. And in fact, it's my guess that they weren't even natural. I think they were genetically designed by the beings who really built these domes. These things . . . well, they're just the equivalent of farm animals. Like pigs or chickens."

Daddy nodded, considering it. "It almost makes sense. This wasn't a village. It was a farm, and these are a bunch of kennels or coops and storage sheds. The tripods would wander around the crops, eating bugs and insects and little crawling things, whatever. But the horns . . . ?"

Dr. Blom looked annoyed, that same look she always got when Daddy was right. Had she just spent four months excavating a chicken coop? But to her credit, she tried on the idea to see if it fit. "We know that chickens can be designer-trained. We've done it ourselves. If you can train chickens to use a toilet, you don't have to shovel the poop. So why not put out the horns and let them fertilize the field for you."

Mom chimed in then. "Wait a minute. You're not going far enough. Remember that jar of seeds you found? It's part of the process. The farmer puts out horns and scatters seeds in the field. The chickens roam the field, eating the seeds. Some of the seeds get digested, but some don't; they pass right through the chickens. The chickens poop in the horns, and the seeds get planted in their own personal package of fertilizer. Then the farmer picks up the horns and moves them to the next part of the field and starts again the next day. He's planted his crop *and* fertilized it."

They all looked at each other, surprised. It fit. In a bizarre kind of way.

"That's the only explanation so far that fits all the available facts," Daddy said slowly.

Dr. Blom held up a hand. "Wait a minute. Not so fast. Answer one question. Why would any rational being deliberately design a *three*-legged chicken?"

"Isn't it obvious?" I said. They all turned to me, surprised that I even had an opinion. "A three-legged chicken gives you an extra drumstick." I took Zakky from Mom; his diaper was full. "Yick. Come on, baby. The skywhale is waiting."

Zolo and the Jelly Ship
by Nick DiChario

Nick DiChario's stories have appeared in dozens of
magazines and anthologies. He has been nominated for
the Hugo and World Fantasy Awards. In addition to his
job as the director of programming for one of the largest
nonprofit literary organizations in the United States—
Writers & Books in Rochester, NY—he has taught creative writing at universities, and he is the fiction editor
of *HazMat Review*, a literary magazine. One of Nick's
short stories can be found in *The Best Alternate History
Stories of the 20th Century.*

SO this was how it happened. This was how a man
and his jelly ship died in space. A dark, rolling,
translucent casket and a man's face as blank as stone.
Two organic engines, at one time vital and flirting
with the speed of light, now bobbing in a black pond
of death.

And yet . . . how beautiful . . . the man and his ship.

Poetic, almost, the way they floated.

No more speed or thrust, no more lines to draw
in space, but somehow not without purpose.

Meaningless yet hopeful?

An old man and his mate?

Till death do us part?

I brought my cruiser around to wet dock against
the man's jelly. I'd never been inside a jelly ship before. As far as I knew, no woman ever had. So little
was known about the jellies. I quickly ticked off what
I remembered:

✓Biological machines, the work of an alien civilization.

✓Soft, slick exoskeletons that protected an inner core of quantum engineering beyond human understanding.

✓The ships had been found stranded on Pluto; no one knew how many millennia they'd been there.

✓The jellies—the ones that were alive—allowed themselves to be piloted by men only. Only by men.

Had anyone ever seen a dead jelly before? I didn't know. I didn't think so. I forced a breach in the jelly with my emergency docking equipment. The ship pulled apart easily, a willing cadaver.

Was that a breath of dead air I felt enter my ship through the aperture? Or was it an invitation? Was it curiosity that killed the cat, or was it the object of the cat's curiosity? What difference did it make? I knew I must go.

I set my cruiser on standby and stepped slowly toward the alien ship. I told myself that I was doing it for the man. I would take his body back to Way Station One for a proper burial in space. It was the decent thing to do, after all. But there was more to it than that. I had come from a long line of proud female individualists, self-sufficient women living important lives. My mother was a linguist working on deciphering alien hieroglyphs, and my grandmother was a quantum physics professor studying the jellies. One of the women in my family—a great-great-great grandmother I think, Zolo, the woman I'd been named after—had been among the original settlers to colonize the Moon. If I could be the first woman to go where no other woman had gone before, into the belly of a jelly, regardless of what I did for rest of my life, I would make my own mark in history, just as the other women in my family had made theirs.

I touched the moonstone gem that hung around my neck. The necklace had been passed down to me through the female ranks of my family, from the original Zolo who had pioneered the Moon. My mother had given it to me when I'd earned my merchant's license and bought my cruiser. "You not only have her name," Mother said. "You have her spirit." Touching it always gave me a sense of power and purpose. It gave me the internal strength that only personal history could allow. My sum total was more than my parts. I could do anything.

I stepped inside the man's jelly ship.

What was that strange sensation? What was that hot-cold breath on my skin? The darkness inside the jelly surrounded me like a hard muscle. I felt something misty tickle my eyes. An ethereal presence swam through my body and mind, something that belonged to me in a way that a prayer belongs only to its originator and the god in which she believes— an exchange of trust and vulnerability. How could that be? This ship did not belong to me. This ship was dead, wasn't it?

I approached the man. He lay cold and still on the floor. Lifeless, but not cadaverous. He had died a very old man, yet he looked preserved, a doll, lovingly cared for by a collector of fine things.

I pulled him carefully across the floor, back to my cruiser. I should have closed the breach then and returned to Way Station One. That would have been the appropriate (and cautious) thing to do. I had a schedule to keep, after all. I was a businesswoman— and a good one. But I couldn't leave now. What would I say when people asked me about the jelly ship? "You're the first woman to enter a jelly," they'd say. "What was it like?" And all I would do is shrug. There was nothing of my experience worth repeating.

I returned to the man's jelly so quickly, I couldn't

decide whether I'd done it before or after I'd made up my mind. It was almost as if the ship was lonely and wanted my company. I felt strangely attached to it. Something guided me to the controls, and I instinctively punched in a series of commands that closed the breach between the two ships. How did I know to do that? It didn't matter. I was alone in the jelly.

With the breach closed, the mist became thicker, warmer, and filled my lungs. I felt the ship on my fingertips, as if it were hard clay, and I a sculptor shaping it to my mind's eye. The ship became more solid and real as I breathed it in. I felt suddenly strong yet contained, a beast inside a bottle, until the slick exoskeleton of the jelly ship began to feel like my own skin. My heartbeat felt like iron striking steel. A wave rose in my spine and crashed against my forebrain. Mortar hardened in my arteries. I could move a mountain with a twitch of my toe. I could wrestle a lion. I could drive a lance the length of my body into the earth with the power of my resolve.

The mist . . . the mist . . . the mist . . .

Warmed me, sated me, built me a body made of bulging sinew and hard water, earth and stars and fire and stone.

So this is what it's like to feel the strength of a man's body. This is what it's like to grow hair on your chest and live with the hunger to breed, to heave into things that are soft and succumbing, to understand the tragedy of quiet desperation and the burden of life and death.

So this is what it's like to be a man.

It was so different than a woman's internal experience—bigger, smaller, stronger, weaker, harder, softer, warmer, colder, different—just different—so very very different.

Sleep called to me with the voice of a god, and I could not deny it.

"I must remember everything," I whispered. Every thought. Every feeling. Every detail. There was no separating my dreams from the ship from the past from the future. There was only the jelly and the secrets of men it contained. Yes. Oh, yes. Now I would have much to tell of my experience.

But first . . . first . . . sleep.

When I awoke, I touched my penis, which felt, for the briefest of moments, completely alien to me. What a strange dream. I'd dreamed of a mother I did not know, of a grandmother I'd never met, of a young woman, completely unknown to me, as eager to live her life and make her mark as I was to roam the freedom of space with my jelly ship. Yet it seemed more than a dream, so much more real and powerful, for in the dream I had become this woman, hungered for the things she craved, breathed her air, and returned to myself only upon waking. It was such a disturbing and powerful dream that I could not shake it, so I ticked off what I knew to be true:

✓This is my jelly ship.

✓Together we are one.

✓I breathe for both of us, the jelly sustains me, and together, now and forever, the stars shall be our destination.

✓The jellies allowed themselves to be piloted by men only. Only by men.

I felt better already. I was of single mind now, and single purpose. I touched the moonstone gem that hung around my neck. I'd dreamed that the necklace had been passed down to me from a woman named Zolo, an original settler of the first Moon colony. Strange that I couldn't remember where I'd really gotten it. No matter. I had been to so many places, seen so many worlds, sometimes one forgets.

I sank my hands into the gelatinous controls of the ship, just as I had done for as long as I could remember, and I felt whole again. The jelly powered up, filled me with mist, and moments later, we shot out into space.

What an unusual dream I'd had, though, becoming a woman . . . how different . . . how very, very different . . . and real . . . so damned real . . .

But as my jelly ship flew out among the stars, my dream slipped away, wet like melted candy, warm like blood, dark like oil, so that only a stain of memory remained. A dark and disappearing stain.

No matter.

No matter.

The stars awaited me.

Love Story
by Frank M. Robinson

Frank M. Robinson has written fact and fiction since 1950, including science fiction, thrillers, and mysteries. His novels made into films include: *The Power* (MGM, 1969), *The Glass Inferno* (with Thomas N. Scortia; made into a film by Twentieth-Century Fox 1974), *The Gold Crew* (with Thomas N. Scortia, made into NBC movie-of-the-week as *The Fifth Missile*). Other books include *Pulp Culture* (with Lawrence Davidson), a coffee table book about the old pulps, and *Science Fiction of the 20th Century*, an illustrated history and Hugo Award winner for the year 2000. His latest thriller is *Waiting*. Frank was an editorial assistant at *Playboy*, where he conducted extensive interviews with Robert A. Heinlein and Arthur C. Clarke (in dialogue with Alan Watts).

I DISLIKED him before I ever met him—and I thought he was ugly before I actually saw him.

The marriage was a product of science, as well as politics. It was the first time we had encountered members of another species and we were shocked to discover that they had a civilization as mature as our own. They were scientifically advanced and had created outstanding works of art and literature, music and sculpture. They had few military installations compared to my home world, but in so many other ways, we were mirror images.

The most significant and upsetting way was that physically we very closely resembled each other. Our planets were so much alike perhaps it shouldn't have surprised us that we looked alike as well. Nature is economical and single-minded; what worked well on one planet could be expected to work just as well on another if the conditions were similar.

We weren't identical, of course but our scientists assured us that the few differences weren't that important.

None of that worried me at first. I was a highly specialized cultural engineer and looked upon the aliens as a curiosity. I was assigned to study and analyze them, but there would be little direct contact—that would be the work of underlings, those with strong stomachs who were tempted by high pay.

So much for the science. The politics were immensely more complicated and I quickly found out that I was directly involved. My superior was hardly tactful in letting me know. He was an older man, soon to retire, a thin, balding, sour individual for whom tact had never been a strong suit. The people who worked for him were mere chess pieces, to be moved about at whim. It mattered little to him that I might be shocked or repelled by his suggestions, which weren't suggestions at all but commands.

Our "embassy" was on a palatial estate across the river from the alien world's major city. We were on a small lake, surrounded by grassy hills and lush thickets of trees through which we could see the city's towers of steel and concrete. So much like home, I thought.

"It's a very pleasant world," my superior said in a brittle voice. "You'll learn to like it here. Your children should like it as well."

He had made no attempt to prepare me, to make it easy for me.

I stared at him. "I don't understand."

"We need a goodwill ambassador." His smile was cynical. "You'll be presented as one of our species who fell in love with their world, was enamored of its people enough to marry one of them and to raise her family here. The people will love you, of course, and in turn love us. Any friction between our species and theirs will become minimal."

I was surprised he was so transparent. "That's hardly what you intend, is it?"

He shrugged. "Sooner or later war will result from any such encounter as this. The majority party in the Congress is a war party, as you well know. You'll become its spy—well loved and honored here, rewarded at home."

"There are others who could do it as well or better," I objected.

"You underestimate yourself, my dear. You look in a mirror and all you see is the cultural engineer. Believe me, there's much more to look at. Ask any of your suitors."

"I don't have all that many." He was flattering me and I resented it. "What if I don't want to be a spy or marry one of *them*?"

He was already bored by the conversation. "What you wish has little to do with it. But if you refuse, I can assure you that your life will become . . . intolerable."

"You mentioned children," I said.

"Two, perhaps three." A small silence. "It's up to you."

"I presume the little monsters will come to term in glass bottles," I said sarcastically.

He shifted in front of the window so he had a better view of the small lake outside. Rumors had it that he owned a similar estate on our world, but I had never been invited to see it. That kind of invitation was reserved for department heads.

"You'll have your children the normal way. The genetic engineers will make sure that you'll conceive."

I didn't give up. "I'll be a poor spy. From what I've seen, they're ugly. And from what I've heard, they smell bad. I doubt that I'll be able to hide my discomfort."

He turned to the door. "Your comfort or lack of it is no concern of mine. You can always stuff cotton up your nose."

"You have my consort already picked out, don't you?" My voice had turned to acid.

"The man volunteered." He waved his hand at the desk before the windows. "We have photographs of him. Both clothed and naked so there'll be no surprises. He's considered handsome." At the door, he paused and said, "I didn't say it was an easy assignment. It will probably require you to be a great actress. I hope you're up to it."

After he had left, I went to the desk and inspected the photographs. They showed exactly the sort of man their diplomatic corps would be expected to pick. Average height and average musculature for their species, a thin, intelligent face topped with thick russet-colored hair. Those pictures that showed him naked were of only casual interest. Organs of procreation are designed for their utility, not for their beauty. Certainly not on our world; even less on his.

Despite what my superior had said, I thought the man was truly ugly. His nose was too large, his eyes too small, his ears huge. And I suspected the rumors were right, that he would smell bad.

There was nobody to whom I could appeal, nobody who would consider my objections as anything more than a disappointed woman's whining. Like it or not, I was expected to live with this man in close proximity day and night.

Over time, he would become easy to hate.

Our first meeting was stiff and unpleasant. I'm afraid that I stared, surprised that he was taller than in his photographs and that he had added more muscle mass. His ears were smaller and I wondered if surgeons had reduced their size. I checked later and discovered the photographs were six months out of date, taken shortly after we had encountered them. They could project political situations into the future, I thought, and felt a faint chill.

We posed for the cameras, both of us forcing smiles. Then the reporters and cameramen left, as well as the diplomatic functionaries, and we were alone.

He inspected me for a long moment, already uneasy. "I'm glad to meet you."

"I doubt it," I said crisply. "We were assigned to do this; neither of us had a choice." My response was unexpected and he looked surprised. "I understand you're considered handsome as well as intelligent," I continued, "which suggests you were probably thinking of marriage and were forced to end an affair."

I was more perceptive than I'd thought. "You're right. I had no say in the matter. And since you didn't either, we'll have to make the best of it." The friendly facade faded and he became very professional, almost curt.

"We'll be expected to be seen together at various functions—parties, sporting events, celebrations of one kind or another. We'll have to learn to smile a lot. We'll be slightly distant at first, then within several weeks we'll stand closer together, probably hold hands. In a month we'll look at each other adoringly and a month after that, we'll announce the marriage. I believe the department has it set for June."

"You have a daily schedule?" I asked.

He nodded. "The department has been very specific. It was all negotiated beforehand with your people."

My superior had neglected to inform me about any

of this and I wondered if there was anything else he had failed to tell me.

"I understand. It's strictly business."

"Strictly," he said with an expression I couldn't quite interpret. I thought at first that he was trying to hide a flash of attraction to me, then dismissed it as ego on my part. I didn't learn until much later that he had tried to cover his pity for me. He was much more empathetic than I and accepted both my irritation at the role I was forced to play and my feelings of distaste for him.

It was a point I reluctantly gave him.

The first two weeks were a whirlwind of social activity; as a cultural engineer, I found it fascinating. The similarities between our species went far deeper than I had thought. They liked to gather in groups and drink alcohol and flirt and attend sporting events. Like our own, there was often more violence in the stands than on the playing fields. But, perhaps understandably, their sports were less bloody. Their children were much like ours. They found it far easier to laugh than did the adults and frequently burst into giggles in situations where I could see no humor at all.

And then there were those cultural differences I found so annoying. Their manners when eating were atrocious and it was difficult for me to hide my revulsion. Their social order was based as much on money as it was on lineage, which I found odd. But what impressed me was their tribal cohesiveness, their closeness as a group. When threatened, they were almost monolithic in their response.

I reported all of this faithfully to the war party in the Congress and their messages back became irritable and a little fearful. The alien technology was advanced and getting more so every day. If there was to be war, it could not be long delayed.

As for my husband-to-be and myself, we had become cultural darlings, with numerous adoring articles in their magazines and newspapers that I thought were ridiculous and contrived. If only they had known!

The wedding was telecast to millions on both our worlds and my face ached from so much smiling. When he kissed me at the end of the ceremony, I almost cried from the pain. I could see years of deception in a loveless marriage where I could not bear to be touched by a partner to whom I barely spoke.

The wedding night was a horror. We both knew it was being surreptitiously filmed to prove we were doing our patriotic duty. It was an invasion of personal privacy and the act itself was repulsive and difficult. Love without feeling or passion is not that much different from rape, at least for me. I knew instinctively that it was for him as well.

When we were finally through, he got out of bed and toweled off the sweat, then searched for the cameras and tore out their electrical cords.

"I'm sorry," he said. "For both of us."

I shrugged. "I hope we were convincing."

"It doesn't matter; they weren't interested in it as entertainment." He mixed himself a strong alcoholic drink and another for me. "You're taking drugs so you won't conceive, aren't you?" he asked suddenly.

I froze. I hadn't thought anybody knew. Certainly my own department didn't. If they found out, the punishment would be severe.

I hesitated, then decided it wasn't worth the lie. "How did you know?"

"Because if I were you, that's what I would do."

For a moment the identification between us hung like a bubble in the air, to vanish with his next sentence.

"We spies have to hang together," he said casually.

I pulled away from him and felt for the slender plastic knife beneath my pillow. It wasn't there.

He watched me, faintly amused. "I discovered it earlier."

"You're going to report me, aren't you?" To be discovered so easily meant that I would be recalled in disgrace.

He shook his head. "Of course not. My department always assumed you would be a spy—our worlds are too much alike. Too evenly matched. Each side constantly trying for an advantage."

"I gave myself away," I said bitterly.

He smiled.

"It takes one to know one, doesn't it?"

The faint feelings of friendship didn't last and we both withdrew with mutual feelings of suspicion. I was not really his wife, he was certainly not my lover, we were simply agents doing our duty. We became frosty toward one another, professional to a fault—still smiling for the cameras and frequently seen in public buying baby clothes for children that would never be. My hope was that my own department would decide that for whatever reason, I was barren. I would be recalled without prejudice, perhaps to the sorrow of my adopted world but to my personal delight.

We held our three-times-a-week ritual for the hidden cameras, each covering for the other when we failed to become aroused. It was professional courtesy, nothing more. But I felt increasingly lonely, longing for the touch of my own kind, desperate for affection. I watched couples around me and felt my envy growing. I could hardly make real love with a man I couldn't talk to, a man in whom I didn't dare confide, a man who was much more my job than any kind of companion, a man who repulsed me . . .

I wrote to my superior about my feelings, my loneliness, my increasing isolation. I expected nothing. Much to my surprise, I got everything I could have hoped for.

He was taller than my consort, even more heavily muscled, with black hair and eyes that were wary and appraising but which smiled a lot. I wondered just how deep the smiles went but that was a subversive thought and I found it easy to dismiss in the light of everything else. From his bearing and appearance I assumed he was military. He was classified as my "adviser" from the home world, and I knew that at least part of his duties were to keep an eye on me. I had given them no reason to doubt my loyalty, but paranoia thrives in a militaristic society.

He was valuable to me in a number of ways. He reminded me of home and could tell me the latest in news and gossip that I couldn't glean from the televised reports. He was somebody I could talk to, provided I kept philosophy to a minimum, and more importantly he was somebody I could touch, somebody I could feel, somebody who was skilled in making love and in whom I took great pleasure.

We were seldom seen together in public and then only on "official" occasions. It would have been disaster to be discovered alone in the bedroom. Whenever he spent the night, I made sure the cameras were disconnected.

The one person I couldn't hide it from was my alien husband. I wasn't sure what his reaction would be and it was an admitted danger. But our own relationship was a sham, a drama for the public; I could see no reason why he would object to my having a private life.

I was surprised that I found it so difficult to tell him. When I finally informed him what I intended to do, he shrugged as if it meant nothing to him.

"It's your life, but . . ." And then: "Forget it."

"Forget what?" I demanded.

He hesitated a long moment. "I don't like him."

"That hardly matters," I said.

"I don't trust him," he added. "They didn't send him here to keep you happy in bed. He has another purpose."

"And what would that be?"

Another pause. "I don't know. But I'll find out."

"It's not your business," I said primly. "I'll be discreet. It would be folly to endanger the mission."

"Don't fall in love with him," he warned.

I was annoyed. The conversation should have ended minutes ago.

"Why not?"

"I think it might be dangerous. For you."

I looked at him, thoughtful. "Why should you care?"

He shrugged, but didn't answer, and that was the end of it.

I continued to go to functions with my so-called husband, hanging on his arm and on his every word. There were times when, to endear myself to the public, I showed a more independent nature. My husband would duck and smile to avoid a playful slap and the crowd would go wild. I made small contributions and appeared at numerous charity benefits, endearing myself to the public even more. My consort always appeared with me and I knew we were one of the most popular couples on the planet. He didn't seem to mind that I was more the center of attention, though he now seemed slightly on edge in public. He was afraid of something but didn't offer to tell me and I didn't ask.

I was too much the cultural engineer to let the adulation of the crowds affect me, enjoyable though it was. I was there for a reason and never forgot it, dutifully informing my home planet of the political swings of opinion, those measures of which the public approved and those which they didn't. I saw little of military preparations or installations, but I kept my superior apprised of everything important that I read or heard.

I found very little enjoyment in life except, of course, when I was with my adviser. He seemed to grow more handsome by the day and more attentive, more eager for my private company. It was the ultimate flattery. For my part, I found myself making up excuses to see him, and delighting as always in his touch. I discovered fragrance and powder, both of which were known on my world but which I seldom used, and learned how to apply them artfully. A touch of powder, a wisp of a haunting fragrance.

My husband noticed but said nothing, though I sensed his disapproval growing. My nighttime performances with him began to dwindle in frequency and when we were together, it was even more perfunctory than usual. More and more, my evenings were reserved for my black-haired adviser. I had never been that popular on my home world, had never known such skill as he showed in making love.

And yet . . . and yet . . .

There was something missing. My adviser spent little time making friends with military chiefs, or going on tours of military installations. He was available to me any time I wanted and perhaps it was that which aroused my suspicions. In one sense my assignment involved the entire alien world. But it was becoming more and more obvious that his assignment involved only me.

I thought several times of telling my consort my suspicions, then dismissed them. In any event, he would not be interested in my suspicions. Our relationship was just an assignment to him—as it was to me. It might last a lifetime but was merely an assignment nonetheless.

It wasn't long before I deeply regretted my silence.

*   *   *

Things began to unravel on a warm and sunny day, one of the few days when I was accompanied by both my so-called husband and my adviser. This time when I saw them together, I had to blink. My adviser was outstandingly handsome but even when standing next to him, my husband didn't look . . . quite so ugly.

We were on a tour of a factory that made communication devices and for once I was deeply interested. They were small and you could carry one around your wrist and through it communicate with anybody in the world. It was of burnished gold with small jewels set around the rim. There was a subtle blinking to the jewels and you could lose yourself just gazing at them. My adviser picked one up and inspected it, then reluctantly put it back on the production line. "Remarkable," he murmured.

"I'm sure they would be glad to ship a dozen to your world," my consort said, watching him closely.

"No matter—toys." But he picked up another one and fingered it, trying it on his wrist.

"I could probably get you one for yourself," my consort said. He caught my eye and we both stared at my adviser. It was obvious he wanted it for himself, and he wanted it badly. After another few moments of admiring the bauble, he casually accepted the offer.

Later that day I found his cache of other "toys" in the basement of the estate where we were staying. There were hundreds of boxes, dozens of articles packaged in see-through plastic. Communicators, games, other electronic devices, articles of adornment . . .

I didn't hear him walk up behind me, I was too engrossed in his interesting choice of merchandise. There was little that was military about any of it; they were all personal items.

"I thought you would like them," he said. The smile on his face was meant to be disarming.

"You never told me."

"A cultural engineer should be interested in objects which affect the culture, shouldn't she?" He shrugged. "You should ship them home to your superior. I'm sure he would be grateful for them."

"Of course," I said. I didn't believe him and it turned out later I was right not to.

It didn't take him long to lull most of my suspicions. When he came to bed that night, he was lightly oiled and his skin shone in the soft illumination from the ceiling lights. He was affectionate almost to the extreme and I gradually relaxed, delighting in the strength of his arms, the feel of his chest as he breathed, the warmth of his private places.

"The male—your husband," he said. "Do you like him?"

It struck me as an odd question. "Our relationship is professional, part of the plan."

He turned into me and for a long time I didn't think at all.

"Our plan or theirs?" he suddenly murmured.

I felt myself grow cold. "I didn't know they had a plan," I murmured.

"Of course they do. Domination of both worlds."

And then his hands became busy and we did no talking for the next thirty minutes.

When we finally relaxed, my head cradled by his muscular arm, he said, "Would you be sorry if I left you?"

I froze.

"You're being recalled?"

He said nothing for a long moment and once again I began to relax.

"I would be sorry if you had to leave me," he said slowly.

The thought had never occurred to me. "*I'm* being recalled?" I said, bewildered. Why would he know and I wouldn't?

"In a manner of speaking." I leaned on an elbow to stare at him, but he suddenly pulled me down and rolled over on top of me. He wasn't gentle this time and I winced with pain.

"The Congress has decided that the war can wait no longer. It has to start within the next month."

His hands were caressing my throat. I was suddenly terrified.

"They never told me," I said.

He laughed quietly. "Of course not. You're to be the cause of it."

His hands tightened, and I knew my breath would soon be cut off completely.

"I don't understand . . ."

"The plan!" he exploded. "*Our* plan! No world can go to war without the backing of its people! War fever is hard to build—there has to be a reason and your murder will provide it."

"They'll hang you!" I cried. I fumbled beneath the pillow for the plastic knife, then remembered it had been taken away weeks before.

"Not me," he whispered. "Your husband. He'll get the blame. We've been building a case against him for weeks. On our home world, the people will be told the alien has murdered our most beloved citizen. The cry will be for vengeance, for war."

"The motive," I said, fighting for breath against his tightening fingers.

I sensed his shrug. "It doesn't matter—husbands kill their wives all the time. What's important is that he's one of the aliens."

I arched my back and tried to push away his hands, fighting as hard as I could. But I couldn't get a grip—there had been two reasons why he had oiled his body. My body started to jerk uncontrollably, it was impossible to breathe. The room looked splotchy; pools of blackness spread from the corners to the center, the light started to fade—

I never heard the doors burst open and was only dimly aware that the pressure on my neck had ceased. I heard thuds against flesh and when my sight returned, I saw my husband and my adviser grappling on the mattress. My adviser was the stronger and had wrapped his arms around my husband's waist, trying to squeeze the life out of him.

I scrambled to my feet and ran to the small closet, yanked open the door, and fumbled on the top shelf. I hadn't been so foolish as to have hidden only one knife. I turned to the bed where my adviser had his knee on my husband's back, an arm wrapped around his neck, ready to snap it back and break it. I threw myself on him, grabbed him by his black hair and stabbed the blade deep into his side. He screamed and when he turned toward me, I slit his throat.

I never thought a body could hold so much blood.

We sat there in silence on the bloodstained sheets. It seemed like there was blood everywhere. My consort was covered in it and barely recognizable.

"They'll find him," I said in a dull voice. "And there's the blood on the mattress and floor and the walls . . ."

"I'll make a call."

It took the masked cleaners perhaps an hour to remove the body, to take away the sheets and the mattress, and to scrub down the floors and the walls. They were silent and very efficient, never looking at us.

After they had left, I said, "This is where I fall into your arms for saving my life."

He smiled slightly. "Or where I fall into yours for saving mine. I think we're even."

"You knew all the time," I said.

He nodded. "I'm sorry I got here so late."

"I found his storeroom of toys. He discovered me and I think moved up his timetable."

"We knew about the trade goods. In one sense, you can't blame him. The toys, as you call them, were designed to catch the eye, to inspire greed. We're very good at that." He looked away. "He was going to send them home as gifts for his wife and, of course, for himself when he returned. Perhaps he considered them part of his . . . commission."

I couldn't bring myself to admit how foolish I had been. "What do we do with them?"

"Send them to your planet, as he wanted. To your superior. We'll change the address, enclose a bill of lading saying that more will follow as per his request. The goods and the bill will be intercepted, of course. He'll be accused of corruption and I suspect he'll disappear."

"I don't know if he deserves that," I said. I tried to recall a few times when he had treated me with kindness and respect. There weren't any.

He frowned. "The plan was his. He knew when he sent you that he was condemning you to die. And when you confessed your loneliness to him, he sent you an assassin."

"There'll be an investigation about my adviser," I said.

"Of course. We'll turn over our dossiers on him to your authorities. They'll show that he was involved in a smuggling operation, that he had petty criminals for friends. That type disappears all the time."

I recalled the masked workers and said, "You've been much more than just my consort."

He smiled slightly. "I play a lot of roles. One of them is bodyguard." The smile disappeared and he looked embarrassed. "I didn't . . . dislike the assignment."

I'd sworn that I wouldn't fall into his arms and now I did just that. We sat there for many minutes, consoling each other.

"There'll be war," I said.

He shook his head, dismissing the possibility. "I don't think so. Yours is a world of war, ours a world of commerce. Over time, it would be no contest. As it is, half your Congress has already been bribed—it would be very difficult to pass any kind of war resolution. And in another year, your people will become addicted to our products. To live without them will seem impossible. Our biggest weapon is trade—and as I said, we're really very good at it."

Nothing more happened that night. The next day, we were seen in public as usual. Over the next few weeks, word came back that my superior had been arrested and had subsequently vanished. I was interrogated about that and also about the disappearance of my adviser. I knew nothing about the former and regretted the latter. He had been a close friend, I said. He had always given me good advice. I expressed sorrow for his family.

I remember exactly when my attitude toward my consort changed. We had seen a very funny play and came back repeating lines from it and erupting in gales of laughter. We started a friendly tussle that turned serious and I found myself crying and then relaxing, suddenly very hungry for him.

I have nothing more to write about that. Lust can be described; love cannot.

Since then my husband—my real husband now—has acted as both a genuine adviser and a lover. We're no longer written about as extensively as we once were—there have been other alien marriages and it's ceased to be a novelty. Our worlds have been tied together with a hundred different trade pacts and war between us would be unthinkable, as well as impossible. My husband and I have become content, a happily married couple with two children. I hope for a third.

It's been ten years now, but there are times, regrettably, when I still think human beings are ugly and smell bad.

Except, of course, for one.

Translated from the vernacular Xerxian by Frieda Longworth, PhD Exobiology, Greater Harvard University, 2406 AD

Mom's Paradox
by Dean Wesley Smith

Dean Wesley Smith has sold over twenty novels and around one hundred short stories to various magazines and anthologies. He's been a finalist for the Hugo and Nebula Awards, and has won a World Fantasy Award and a Locus Award. He was the editor and publisher of Pulphouse Publishing, and edited the *Star Trek* anthology *Strange New Worlds II*.

I WOKE up as a woman.

Not that I hadn't been a woman before that morning, before feeling those cotton sheets, smelling the faint scent of John beside me, hearing him snore deeply, the vibration shaking the queen-sized bed like a distant earthquake. It seemed I had a memory of going to sleep as a woman, lying there spent, but not satisfied from the too-short lovemaking.

I grew up a woman. The memories of my childhood, the pains of dating, of a first marriage, of childbirth were all there.

Yet—

For the first time this morning I awoke as a woman, *feeling* like a woman, as the sun filled the drapes with orange light. What a strange thing, to be a woman, yet have the feeling of waking up as one only this morning.

I lay there, letting John's snoting fill the small bedroom as I tried to place where the strange newness was coming from.

My name was Angie Sheldon. The man shaking the bed beside me was my husband. We had two kids, both just entering high school, a nice house just outside of Denver in an upscale neighborhood, not too many bills, and a decent retirement and college account. I could honestly say I wasn't unhappy with my marriage or with John, just not always satisfied. Yet that lack of satisfaction had never been strong enough to force me to make any changes. I loved John and my kids, so the feeling wasn't coming from there.

Yet I felt wonderful, free, almost as if I were alive for the first time just now, this morning.

I focused on more details. I took my creative energy and drive out on my job with a law firm downtown. Both John and I were attorneys, and had met in law school. Now he worked for the District Attorney while I spent my time on business cases for the state's third largest business law firm.

That wasn't it. Nothing felt right or new about the job either. It was just the job I had been doing for years.

But still it was wonderful to wake up a woman.

I eased over onto my side so my back was to John and stared at the dresser with the pictures of our kids, Beth and Danny. I could see them clearly in the morning light. My parents were dead, John's parents still lived in California. Nothing there to cause this wonderful emotion of newness and happiness.

I couldn't remember the last time I had just stopped and looked at my life. It felt as if I was starting fresh this morning.

Why?

Because I am starting fresh this morning. Or actually I will be shortly.

The other woman's voice inside my head damned near sent me screaming from the bed. Yet somehow my muscles didn't jerk, I didn't even jump or move, as if I was pinned there, staring at the dresser. But inside my head I was screaming. I could feel my heart pounding, like someone trying to beat her way out of my chest.

Calm down. This is strange enough as it is. Don't make it worse.

I'm dreaming. That's it, I'm just dreaming. I had to be. I tried to calm myself with that thought.

No, you're not dreaming. And neither am I.

I'm going insane!

The panic was a giant ball in my throat. I willed myself to climb out of bed and run toward the bathroom, but my body stayed on its side beside my snoring husband. Nothing I could do seemed to make even my fingers twitch.

You're not insane and you can't move because I have control of your body. And to be honest with you, it feels damned strange. I can also hear everything you think, so calm down, would you?.

I'm dreaming. I have to be dreaming.

No, you're not.

I have to be, or I'm going insane. There are no other choices.

Oh, sure there are. A ton of them, just none that you've thought of. And if I don't get you moving soon, some of those choices won't happen.

The newness and good sensation started to drop away, leaving me empty. John had accused me of taking the joy out of just about any situation I got into, but inside I knew I wasn't joyless. I just had a hard time letting go.

No shit. I could give you a hundred examples on how I know that.

I'm going insane. All I wanted to do was scream.

Can't you just relax and go with it? This is strange enough for me without you making it even worse.

Now I knew I had flipped out. "Gone around the bend," as John would say. I was asking myself to relax. This was the strangest dream I had ever had.

I give up.

The good feeling I had when I woke up was now completely gone. Suddenly my body jerked into motion, climbing out of bed, shedding my cotton nightgown before I even got across the room. I just left it on the floor. I tried to stop, to pick up the nightgown, but my body was moving on its own. I wanted to scream for John to wake up and help me, but I couldn't.

Thank heavens for some things.

Only on special nights, with the kids gone, had I allowed myself to be nude like this, yet now I was walking out of the bedroom in the morning light, across the hall and into the bathroom. Luckily neither of the kids was awake yet.

Just settle back in there and relax. A little stop here to get rid of what is pressuring your bladder, then we get to the job at hand, so to speak.

The door is open!

As I said, settle down. What, hasn't anyone ever seen you pee?

No.

Oh, man, I just could never believe you were always this uptight, but the more times I do this, the more proof I get.

More times you do what? What is happening to me?

Nothing you're going to remember, so don't sweat it. In fact, I think I'm just going to shut this conversation off for a few minutes until I get you ready.

The blackness crept up from the corners of my mind like a curtain being drawn over everything. I fought it, but everything just got blacker. The last thought I had was that they were going to

find me, nude, on the bathroom floor. How embarrassing.

Oh, give it a rest.

I came back to awareness looking into John's face.
I was back in bed, the bedroom door was closed, and
the covers on the bed were pulled back and off.

*You're going to have to help with some of this. I don't
really have the stomach or the inclination to watch.*

"This is a nice surprise," John said, smiling up at
me. His hands were firmly on my hips.

At that point I realized that I was wearing my
special occasion black nightgown, the one that John
had bought for me just after our honeymoon. John
had lost his pajama bottoms, and I was sitting on
him as he moved under me.

And inside me!

Tell him you always liked mornings.

I wanted to scream, yet at the same time what John
was doing felt wonderful. The short lovemaking last
night had left me wanting and excited. At least the
door was closed and the children weren't up yet. But
I had no idea how I got into the black nightgown
and in this position.

*Don't question it. Just enjoy it, because I can't watch.
Sorry, too weird.*

I should stop. This isn't right. What is happening
to me? I must be going insane. Voices inside my head
telling me to seduce my husband. We have never
done anything like this before. Or in this position.

More information than I need.

John moved a little faster under me. "What got
into you this morning?" he asked, his voice husky
from the way we were moving together.

*Let me give you just a little more help, then I'm going
to shut myself out of this. I've had enough counseling as
it is.*

Suddenly the good feeling I had when I woke up rushed back through me, pushing all my doubts, my worries away like leaves in a strong wind.

I was a woman, making love to the man she had loved for years. It felt great.

No better than great, it felt wonderful.

Perfect. I'll be back when this is over.

I seemed to forget where I was and what I was doing.

I wanted to forget.

Everything I had focused on the intense sensations of John Inside me, the movement of our bodies, and the pleasure of letting go and just being a woman.

"Is it safe?" John asked, his voice low, his face beaming in the morning light.

I didn't answer him, and I didn't care that it wasn't. I just wanted to keep going, not let these feelings ever end.

The morning seemed to vanish as everything focused down to just John and me.

Then the release that had eluded me last night swept up over my body as I rode John, grinding down into him and forcing him to come with me.

A few moments, maybe minutes later I collapsed beside him, not even caring that I wasn't covered.

"Wow," John said between gasps.

"Yeah," I managed to reply.

In all the years of being with John it had never been like that. Passion, filled with love and caring and wonderful sensations. Right at that moment I loved being a woman. And I loved being with John.

He leaned over and kissed me, gently at first, then hard. After a few moments he pulled back and smiled. "I have no idea what caused that, but whatever it was, don't fight it."

"Okay," I said, remembering the voice I thought I had heard inside my head earlier. What had I been thinking? Maybe it all came from not being satisfied last night. Right now I felt so good I didn't care.

He kissed me again, then rolled away, and stood. He pulled the blankets back up over me, then grabbed his robe and headed for the bedroom door.

I let the morning light, the wonderful afterglow of the sex, and the warm blankets lull me almost back to sleep.

Looks like it was good for you.

I felt so good I didn't even care I was making up a voice in my head again.

Now that's the attitude, Mom. Relax. Learn how to roll with things.

Mom! Now the panic of hearing a voice swept up over me.

Yeah, Mom. Sorry for the slip. Thank heavens my job here is finished.

What's happening to me?

Like I said, nothing that you're going to remember. I just needed to make sure I was going to be born.

What? Now I was screaming, but again my body wouldn't move, and no sound came out. In the distance I could hear the shower running and John singing.

Calm down. About six time lines over, you and Dad did that morning tango you just finished with, and got me as a little accident. I went on to be one of the major inventors of mind-jumping through time, a cheap effective form of time travel.

Time travel? Mind-jumping? I had no idea where the voice was coming from.

Of course you wouldn't understand what I'm saying. You never did understand me, or how smart I was. It took me five years of counseling just to get over being an un-wanted child, something you never let me forget, I might add.

I could feel the anger boiling inside me, but I had no idea where it came from.

My anger. Sorry.

The feeling died away.

Anyway, since I was born in only one time line that we explored, I decided to do the opposite of the old grandfather paradox, you know the one about going back and killing your own grandfather so you can't exist, thus you could never go back and kill him.

I had no idea what the voice was saying. I was going insane. I had to be.

Figures you'd think that. Oh well, the short of it is I jumped back here, into your mind on this time line to make sure I am born. Otherwise you'd have gotten up a little while back, made breakfast, and been tense and angry all day for no reason anyone could figure out. And I would never happen in this time line, and time travel would not exist here either. Not that any of that matters to you, or that you will even remember.

I've gone insane. I need help. Maybe professional help.

No, I'm the one who is insane, for even trying to explain the reason of my existence to her mother. You'd think after all these years I'd know better.

A feeling of disgust and anger filled me.

Oh, sorry, my issues, not yours.

The emotions faded quickly, again replaced with the intense joy of just being alive and satisfied.

I'll leave you feeling happy about the sex and not re-membering anything about this conversation. That much I can do for Dad. See you in about nine months. Be nice to me, would you?

The morning sun bathed me and warmed the bed-room as I rolled over and stretched. There was a nagging feeling I had forgotten something, but what did it matter? I just wish we had tried this morning sex thing years ago.

I kicked the covers back and just lay there, exposed to the room, my black nightgown not even covering all of me. I wonder what had gotten into me this morning?

Besides John that is.

The thought had me laughing all the way to the bathroom.

CJ Cherryh
EXPLORER

"Serious space opera at its very best by one of the leading
SF writers in the field today." —*Publishers Weekly*

The *Foreigner* novels introduced readers to the
epic story of a lost human colony struggling to
survive on the hostile world of the alien atevi. In
this final installment to the second sequence of
the series, diplomat Bren Cameron, trapped in a
distant star system, faces a potentially bellicose
alien ship, and must try to prevent interspecies
war, when the secretive Pilot's Guild won't even
cooperate with their own ship.

*Be sure to read the first five books in this action-
packed series:*

FOREIGNER	*0-88677-637-6*
INVADER	*0-88677-687-2*
INHERITOR	*0-88677-728-3*
PRECURSOR	*0-88677-910-3*
DEFENDER	*0-7564-0020-1*

0-7564-0086-4
To Order Call: 1-800-788-6262